Jones Whitman, Time Traveler

Geared to the Past

Jones Whitman, Time Traveler

Geared to the Past

by

Dana Bennett

TandemWriters

Geared to the Past

Copyright © 2015 by Dana Bennett

Cover design by Clarissa Yeo
Logo design by Olivia E. Bennett
Edited by Daniel James Johns Kenyon & Blakely Bennett

ISBN: 978-0-69240-968-8 (Trade Paperback)
ISBN: 978-1-94309-204-8 (eBook)

This book is dedicated to family and friends who take the time to read and comment. I am delighted to write stories for your entertainment.

ACKNOWLEDGMENTS

Never is a book is written in a vacuum. Since many people have contributed to the finished product, it would be impossible to assign credit to all of you. A special thank goes to my beta readers and to family who support me selflessly.

Friday, 12 June 1884, 6:30 am

Po-chi-lam Temple

Foshan City, Guangdong, China

Jones had failed to take into account certain logistics, whereupon he found himself still embracing Darcy, with his feet in the reflection pool and she just outside.

"So much for not attracting attention." She stood frozen, eyes riveted on the approaching orange wave of bald-headed monks.

Jones stepped from the small pond, pants and shoes dripping water and bowed. Darcy clutched his hand as fear ramped up her heartbeat.

"They mean us no harm, I assure you." Jones once again bowed slightly. "I am in search of Master Wong Fei-hung."

The group of monks who had surrounded them, slowly parted to allow a figure, in an orange robe with a red cloth draped over one shoulder, to step forward.

"I have been waiting for you, Time Traveler."

Jones grinned. "How did you know?"

"You have found the yin to your yang."

"I have, Master. This is Darcy Champagne," he said proudly. Jones threw his arm over her shoulder and hugged her to him. "Darcy, this is the famous Master Wong Fei-hung."

"I'm delighted to meet you." Darcy extended her hand and bowed at the same time. "That was awkward," she mumbled.

"It is an honor to meet you." Master Fei-hung bowed. "You must be a special woman to have tamed his nature."

"Well, I kinda hope I haven't completely tamed him." She immediately felt her face flush. "What I mean to say—"

"She *is* my yin, and we have come to ask you to oversee a ceremony where we may make a declaration of our love and commitment to one another."

"That's what I meant to say," Darcy said, pointing at Jones and bending forward slightly.

"I would be honored." Master Fei-hung fingered the edge of the metal box. "This must be the time machine?"

Jones unloaded the Atomotron from his back and held it by the straps.

"It is, Master. I worked for seven long years to manifest my Hung Gar name. Preparing for the first human trial, I inadvertently tripped the lever and found myself in Darcy's backyard, in the year 2012."

The other monks began to disperse in all directions, leaving the three of them alone.

"Do you still believe that it was an accident?"

"Frankly, I am of the opinion that I know even less about destiny than before."

"Ah, then you have learned well."

"Am I to understand that you believe it was fate?"

"And you, do you believe it was your fate to meet Darcy Champagne?"

"It must be true. I have never encountered a person I love to the degree that I love Darcy." Jones squeezed her hand and touched her face.

"I'm just super glad he messed up and we ended up together," she said looking into his eyes. "Fate or not, I'd never want to turn back the hands of time and undo what's

4

been done." Darcy pushed her palm against his.

Jones scanned the courtyard. "It is remarkable that I was here merely a year ago, in time travel, and yet many years have passed."

Master Fei-hung took Jones by the shoulders. "You have matured, I can see." He paused. "Is it possible that all of time is but a shadow? There are many secrets you have yet to experience. I look forward to assisting you once again in your pursuit of answers to your curiosity."

A young man approached and whispered in the master's ear.

"For now, I will have you shown to your sleeping quarters. I must speak to the Manchurian military waiting at the gate. When I return, we should begin the preparations for your wedding."

Darcy and Jones were taken to separate quarters and provided with a morning meal. Jones stashed the time machine beneath his bunk, in case the military returned without warning. He removed his wet boots and placed them under the cot as well. They both anxiously awaited the next step in their journey that was to begin with their commitment ceremony and then, a world of new adventures.

✿✿✿✿✿

"Time Traveler, I must speak to you about your arrival this morning. Apparently, the gate was open long enough for someone on the street to see you appear out of thin air. The visit from the Manchurian military was to seek assurances that the old man in the street was mistaken. They seem intent on a logical explanation."

"Should we consider leaving, Master?"

"No, I have faith in the outcome. You will need to be outfitted so you can move about without notice."

A monk, carrying an orange robe, entered and bowed. He placed the familiar outfit on the bunk and retreated from the small room.

"I suspect the general will have men stationed on the buildings across the street to observe for a day or two. Trust among the Chinese has suffered greatly."

"Shall I also have Darcy dress in a robe?"

He stripped down to his boxers and slipped into the orange satin garment.

"Ling is with her now. They can work together to help her disappear among the others."

"If I may, Master?" Jones bowed, pointing to the door.

"Certainly, her quarters are next to Ling's. I will join you for the daily meal."

"With admiration." He then made his way around the courtyard, staying close to the wall.

"*Duìbùqǐ*? Excuse me? I cannot remember... how do I get to Ling Lee's quarters?" He could feel the adrenaline flow to his stomach as he approached the tiny living space in the west wing of the monastery. The shutters had been closed, and the voices inside were muffled. Jones rapped lightly on the door. "Darcy," he called in a hushed voice. "Darcy, are you in there?"

Ling opened the door. "She is getting dressed. Do not be surprised by her appearance."

"You did not... shave... no." He pushed his way into the room. "That would be unacceptable." He rushed past Ling and searched the area with his eyes.

"Do you want her to be safe?" Ling took his arm and guided him to a chair.

"Of course I do." Jones sat rubbing his chin. "And you are correct, and I am an imbecile. Yes, whatever it takes to keep us safe. After all, as I am a living testament, hair will grow back."

Darcy sashayed through a beaded curtain in a royal blue, embroidered *Qipao* tunic with white cuffs. Ling had coiffed her hair on top of her head with a thin braided rope. She had applied dark eyeliner that gave her eyes a slight downward slant.

"You are remarkable." He stood and walked toward Darcy. "Ling, you have performed well. I do not think she could be noticed as a foreigner from a distance."

"She had a lot to work with." Darcy laughed as she twirled around. "You've really done a great job. Oh, and thanks for the outfit. I don't think I'd be as comfortable in the tunic. Orange and me? Not a great match."

"You are most welcome. I am glad we are the same size." Ling accompanied them both to the door. "We should prepare for our meal. I will meet you in the eating hall."

"Thank you again, Ling. I am convinced your talent will deter any further investigations."

Jones pushed his hands into his sleeves and led Darcy along a path into the courtyard. They followed the wall that terminated at the reflection pond and sat down.

"When I was here last, this was my only method of observing the changes that were manifesting." He drew his finger through the water. "That is why it is so sacred to me and the others."

Darcy looked for one building to the next. "This temple is so cool, so pretty. The dragons on the roof are a nice touch. Kinda like... heeey, this isn't a theme park, right?" She turned to Jones, who simply stared at her. "Never mind," she said. "It's so weird to think about age and time travel. Like, how old are you really?"

"I am still twenty-eight years old because my time is local, but with time travel, it would seem it is not. Master Fei-hung appears no different to me, but I, on the other hand, am older to him."

Darcy reached for his arm. "Do you—?"

"Not now. Do not touch my arm," he mumbled. "We should not display any physical familiarity. I am not sure, but I think the man on top of the building across the street is Manchurian military. We do not want to bring his attention to us."

"Even with everyone else walkin' around?" Darcy folded her hands in her lap and sat up straight. "No problem."

"So, you were asking?"

"Do you realize that, from my point of view, you guys are all, how can I put this… dead? But here we sit, alive and well. Mind blowing, I tell ya."

"I, myself, am both amazed and amused by this time travel phenomenon. The math and science are accurate, but cannot be complete without acknowledgment of a mystical aspect. By that I mean, an event that we are yet to understand."

"Dude, sometimes this deep talk makes my head feel full. Like my brain is workin' overtime. Like… I now have empathy for Roark." Darcy pointed across the plaza. "Jones, what's with the cool little bridges?"

"They are a physical symbol of an intellectual concept. We are always crossing bridges in life; however, one cannot actually cross a bridge before they have arrived at the landing. These exist as a corporeal reminder."

"Cool. I get it." She sat thinking for moment. "The temple and grounds are *so* clean. That's what makes it feel like a theme park. Geeze, I could never let Master Fei-hung into my house. He would flip out."

Jones closed his eyes and leaned against the wall of the pond, immersing his mind in contemplation.

"All I know is, I can't begin to tell you how glad I am that you ended up in my backyard."

Jones opened one eye in Darcy's direction. "It is the most wonderful misadventure yet. I do love you like no other."

"And I love you." Darcy giggled. "We're about to get married."

"I am very happy indeed. I now believe in a love that transcends time and space."

"How incredibly romantic." She stopped to gaze into his eyes, started to raise her hand but quickly withdrew it.

"We should consider taking our place at the table. This is the only full meal of the day. What we will be served is a daily surprise. You should sit next to Ling, and I will sit across from you. Our decorum will aid the other monks."

"I see, so the boys don't like the idea of us getting married?"

"These men and women have chosen this life. I have my doubts as to whether they care one way or another. But I believe they would feel more comfortable with this arrangement." Jones rose and extended his hand to aid Darcy to her feet. "Would you care to join me for a meal?"

"Yep. I gotta tell you though, this whole situation is blowing my mind… uh, I mean it's a little crazy. Think about it. Here we are in 1884 China, at a temple surrounded by monks, and a master. And it *feels* like it's present time, which it is, *only* over one hundred years before. Man, I just got a chill."

"Your mind is expanding."

"I'm gettin' there." Darcy looked up. "What're those

guys doing?"

"They are returning from a trek through the city collecting alms, gifts, and food for the monastery. They are literally carrying our meal in those bowls."

"No way. That's so… bizarre."

Darcy stood silently as the single file of monks carried vessels to the dining hall kitchen, through a side entrance. She thought of the homeless back in the States and could not imagine people giving alms to them as they walked around town with bowls in their hands.

Taking a different route, Darcy and Jones entered through a wide doorway, followed a long hallway and joined the others at the table in the dining room. Though there were many monks in attendance, the only sound was the dulled setting of wooden bowls and utensils on the table. The hall smelled of steamed sweet rice and vegetables. Then silence permeated the hall, leaving Darcy feeling out of place. She fumbled her way between Ling and Bamboo into her seat at the long wooden table. Jones put his finger to his lips. She nodded.

Each monk took a turn at filling their bowls with the mixture of steamy rice and vegetables, and silently passed them down to the next person. When Master Fei-hung entered the room, all activity ceased. Every head turned to him, waiting for him to motion that they may resume. They then passed a larger bowl. Each individual took a small portion from their meal, touched it to their forehead and placed it as an offering.

The silence was almost too much for Darcy to bear. The sounds of everyone chewing their food began to grate on her. She could feel the urge to shout becoming ever stronger. Jones looked over and got her attention. He took a deep breath, and exhaled slowly. Darcy followed his example and smiled.

Two monks rose and began to retrieve everyone's bowls, scraping the leftovers into the provisions vessel. They then carried it into the courtyard where they scraped the leftovers onto the ground thus returning the remnants to the earth.

✿ ✿ ✿ ✿ ✿

"I thought I was going to lose my mind." Darcy walked alongside Jones.

"I must admit I had that very thought as well." Jones chuckled.

"You, too?"

"No, you."

"Ah, was it that obvious?" She shook her head.

"I assure you that, while I believed you would be able to handle the situation, I did have a moment of concern. However, I also want to assure you that, had you spoken, you would have become the object of great scrutiny from everyone at the table."

"Great. Yeah, well, that's what helped me keep my mouth shut. That, and you taking the deep breath. That really did help me calm down."

They walked casually out into the sunlight and took a seat on the steps of the inner sanctum.

When a young man passed nearby, Jones held up his hand. "*Nǐhǎo.*"

The young monk raised his hand to his chest and bowed slightly. He grinned at the two sitting side by side. "*Nǐhǎo. Xíngshì.*"

"What did you say?" Darcy continued to watch the gazelle-like young man amble away.

"It is a greeting in Mandarin. He bestowed a blessing on

11

us. While I was here previously they made efforts to speak English, not always very well, as I did not speak even a smidgen of Mandarin. So I set out to acquire enough words to assist them in feeling more comfortable with me."

"Well, obviously it worked, because he was grinnin' from ear to ear."

Master Fei-hung approached. "I have assigned several of my closest associates to arrange your ceremony for the day after tomorrow." He sat next to Darcy.

"Thank you so much." Darcy reached out and placed her hand on the master's forearm, then abruptly removed it as if she had touched a hot burner. "I meant no disrespect."

"None taken." He smiled warmly and gently patted her arm. "I find your energy to be delightful. I can see clearly why Time Traveler is taken with you."

"She is a most wonderful companion." Jones exchanged a loving look with Darcy and then returned his attention to Master Fei-hung. "I am delighted that you approve so strongly."

"I am looking forward to joining your *jing*. You will become a formidable river together."

Master Fei-hung rose, bowed and glided away.

"I'm flippin' out here. This is crazy exciting. I can't believe I still have to wait for two days, though. Me whining. Sexy huh?" she said and laughed. "I've got this urge to dance or... maybe I could go for a run?"

"I am certain that is an idea that would bring about the most unwanted attention." Jones shook his head and chuckled. "I cannot even fathom the response of the townspeople."

Darcy laughed. "Oh yeah, I guess I didn't think that through."

"What shall we do?"

"You wanna go back to my room and make out?"

"Why, of course I do. However, we are guests here. And the protocol would be that we refrain from physical contact until after the ceremony, which simply increases the pheromones leading to an ecstatic celebration."

"Ohhhh, you *are* just messing with my pheromones right now, aren't you." She grinned. "I'm thinking I may like you feeling a little deprived and depraved." She winked.

"You are truly amazing to me. You just happen to be a splendid mixture of naughty and nice."

"Well, spank you very much. And I think you're just a wee bit strait-laced, but after our night in Hiva Oa, I'm also thinking you've got a wild side to you that we can work on."

"Oh, you are, are you?" He smiled and lay back on the steps. "I feel certain that we will be experiencing a few wild nights together, starting the day after tomorrow."

"You're such a tease! 'Cause you *know* I hate waiting."

The same young monk who had passed earlier hurriedly approached, waving to them to follow. Jones and Darcy eyed each other nervously. The monk led them through the broad opening of the monastery entrance, past the dining hall to the innermost sanctum of the temple. He motioned for them to crouch behind a table covered with candles and incense, then immediately took his leave.

"What's going on?" Darcy could feel the tension in the air, making her stomach tighten with fear.

"I assure you, I am no more enlightened than you, but if we are instructed to take refuge then it could only mean the military has come again." Jones leaned in close to her face. "They took a great deal of interest when I was here last. There is... was a struggle between those who are pro-western and the traditionalists. Many feel foreigners are a threat to the old ways. And it became more and more intense. Even in 1891, when I was back in Boston, the regime change seemed inevitable, but I really did not know what the future held for China. "

"They went through a lot. As I said before, history really isn't my thing but I do know just about everything we own back at the house is made in China."

Jones looked directly at Darcy. "Am I to understand that America invaded China?"

"No, nothing like that. They've become a huge trade partner, though. Are we in danger?"

"Perhaps we should forgo the ceremony. Possibly, I should make my way back to my quarters and retrieve the Atomotron before it is too late."

. "So we *are* in danger," Darcy whispered hoarsely.

"These monks will not let anything happen to us. They are all trained to defend if necessary."

"I'm scared. Seriously, I don't want to be here anymore." Darcy could feel her body shaking.

A rustling sound caused them to squeeze together as tightly as they could. They could hear angry voices speaking in Mandarin and assumed the soldiers had insisted on searching the grounds and monastery. The voices made their way into the room. Just as quickly, they faded into the halls leaving only the sound of controlled breathing.

Jones could feel the sweat that had collected on his upper lip and wiped it on his sleeve. He realized that he had come very close to combat in that moment. He also understood that he was more than willing to die for the sake of Darcy.

The young monk returned to the inner sanctum and bid them to follow him out. They cautiously moved through the building until they meet up with Master Fei-hung.

"They are gone for now. I have assured them there is no way possible for people to appear out of thin air. I had to be careful so that they do not retaliate against the old man who reported seeing you this morning. Let us return to our business."

Saturday, 13 June 1884, 9:30 am

Po-chi-lam Temple, Foshan City

Guangdong, China

"**M**aster, I am very thankful you have allowed us to spend the night together." Jones assumed a Lotus posture across from Wong Fei-hung. "Although, I have full confidence in Ling to protect Darcy, I was convinced Darcy would have felt abandoned by me had I not inquired of you to have the privilege of giving her comfort overnight. I am truly grateful."

Master Fei-hung studied the lines of Jones' face. "You were willing to die for her in that moment and... to me there is no greater expression of love. In my heart, I could not allow the kind of suffering that would manifest if I had separated the two of you. Time Traveler, I was happy to oblige."

Jones got to his feet to take his leave.

"One more thing. If you choose to leave sooner than expected, know you have my blessings, my *Xingshi*."

"It means a great deal to me, but I will trust your judgment in these matters. That being said, I must also speak with Darcy. Should she choose to leave, I will honor her request."

"I understand."

Jones made his way to the western end of the monastery to Ling's quarters, where he reunited with Darcy.

"I need to know with no uncertainty what you prefer. We

16

can stay and marry tomorrow or we can travel back to Snohomish at any time of your liking."

"And I need to ask you if you're convinced that we aren't in any danger."

"I cannot be one hundred percent certain."

"I don't know then. I gotta tell you that I'm pretty scared. Maybe I don't understand Chinese, but my intuition tells me those soldiers weren't very happy when they entered the room looking for us."

"Yes, I have to agree. I am puzzled by their interest in us. Foreigners are always visiting China, for many different reasons. Perhaps it was the observance of our entry into the courtyard."

"But Master Fei-hung said it was an old man. Why would they give him any credence?"

"These are strained times in China. There are diverse opinions about which direction to take forward into the future."

"We could help out by jumping ahead… wait, what am I saying, I came from ahead. I can tell them that things are really rough but they do get better, well, sort of."

"I do not believe disseminating that kind of information, well… let me just say it would equate to you running through the streets of Foshan."

"Okay, I get it. This is totally…"

"Mind blowing? You are certainly correct on this matter. I think we need to keep a low profile while this night passes. Should we inquire as to the availability of Master Fei-hung and let him know we are staying? Only if… you are *sure*."

"Yeah, okay. I'm about as sure as I guess I'll ever be." Darcy reached out, took Jones's hand and squeezed it. "Dude, nothing better happen to us. We've traveled too far to have this end in some kind of scary way. Weird I was expecting, but not dangerous."

"I assure you I will do everything in my power to keep you safe. If necessary, we will travel out of here at a moment's notice. I will go to my room and get the Atomotron and we will keep it with us at all times for the remainder of our stay."

"You don't think you're leaving me here?" Darcy stood quickly. "Sorry, but you're seriously stuck to me, and me to you, for the next twenty-four hours, *comprende*?"

"I… It is 'I to you.'"

"Thanks. Good to know. Now, let's go get that puppy."

Darcy took his hand and practically sprinted out of her room situated next to Ling's residence.

Jones chuckled. "Yes, let us do exactly that," he said as she dragged him into the hall. He followed closely behind her in the direction of his quarters but stopped abruptly in the dim hallway. "I adore you and your approach to life." His expression beamed with love. "You are the most compelling human being I think I have ever met. I am truly glad you are on this journey with me."

Darcy pulled him to her, wrapped her arms around his neck and looked him straight in the eye. "You have becharmed me, my lover, and I'll always be yours across time and space."

Jones kissed her lightly on her lips. "As long as we are together it really does not matter to me what time it is. Did you actually use the word 'becharmed'?"

"Yes I did, because you're rubbing off on me. And quite frankly I could use a little more rubbing in the near future."

They both glanced around the other into the darkness of the hall to confirm an all-clear, then shared a deep, fervent kiss.

✿✿✿✿✿

Jones pushed through a large wooden door and greeted Master Fei-hung with a head bow. Darcy followed suit, carefully watching every move that Jones made. He took his place in front of the master, waiting patiently for acknowledgement.

Wong Fei-hung waved to her. "Darcy, come sit by me," his voice was gentle and warm with affection. "I am curious about the woman who won Time Traveler's heart. You must be very strong and trustworthy. Throughout history, these qualities have taken ordinary men to great heights. It may seem to be his-story, but in truth, women have always been an integral part of the movement forward by humankind."

Darcy floated across the room to take a seat next to Wong, while watching his mouth form the words that she had embraced as a woman in 2012. "So why has it taken so long for men to come to grips with what you're saying to me right now?"

"Because, as men, we live in fear. We are always on the hunt or the lookout for danger."

"That sort of explains bromance. They'd rather spend time together with other boys than intimate time with their partner. But I guess it all depends on how the time is spent, if ya know what I mean."

"Darcy?" Jones opened his eyes wide.

"Sorry. I'm not used to being so cautious," she said to the master.

"I understand. Think of it as tribal and while that may offend you to a degree, it is not without merit in the survival of one tribe over another."

"Maybe someday we won't need to be so aggressive about impressing our point of view on someone else."

"That, I am afraid, will take many lifetimes and circumstances that will push all human beings to join together for ultimate survival. You will know those secrets in your lifetime, because you have been given the opportunity to free yourself from the shackles of time."

Darcy leaned back on her hands. "I keep forgetting that. And, I can tell ya right now, a whole new way of looking at things is taking place in my brain. This feels so cool."

Master Fei-hung raised his hand and a cloister devotee emerged from the shadows.

"Bring Darcy a cloak."

Jones leaned in and whispered, "Do not try to explain." He placed his hand on her arm. "Accept the generosity of the master and refrain from the need to simplify your language constructs." He winked.

The monk brought over a cloak for Darcy. She accepted it and draped it over her shoulders.

"Thank you. How do you say thank you in Chinese?"

"Mandarin and it is *Xièxiè*! But, it is not necessary, because it is our bliss to serve. That, in and of itself, is our reward."

"Hmm… I think I remember a similar conversation with another wise person of culture."

"I assume this is commentary regarding my opening doors and pulling out chairs?"

"Yeah." Darcy chuckled. "I guess it can be hard to just change your ways." She tilted her head to one side and grinned.

"I am pleased with your choice, Time Traveler. Shall we discuss the ceremony for tomorrow?"

"I believe this is Darcy's venue. So I will yield to her wisdom on these matters."

"Nope, no way. I want you in on everything. I mean… do you even know what's about to happen?"

"Actually… no. Perhaps we should leave this to Master Fei-hung and Ling to coordinate."

"I am sure that Ling would be a clear asset to me in arrangements. Darcy, if you would be so kind as to send her to me when you return to your room." Master Fei-hung slid his hands into his sleeves.

As Darcy and Jones made their way across the courtyard, Jones became aware of two men in Manchurian military uniforms standing on top of a building next to the compound.

"I believe we are being shadowed. I can only assume that our entrance yesterday aroused the suspicions of the local government. I am a bit uncomfortable carrying the Atomotron in plain sight."

"But we can't go anywhere without it, so who cares? What're they going to think it is anyway?"

Jones walked closer to the wall, with Darcy following, and made his way to his room. "We cannot be far apart at any given time, in case they insist upon interviewing us."

"I'm scared, Jones. What would they do to us? We don't have any papers or passports."

"It will never come to that, I assure you."

"Let's go to bed. The sooner we get married the sooner we can go back to Snohomish."

"Send Ling back to speak to Master Fei-hung and I will toggle in the coordinates. We shall be ready to travel at a moment's notice. Take the shortcut through the dining hall and I will meet you halfway and escort you back here."

"Are you sure? What if…"

Jones took Darcy by the shoulders. "I am sure. I do not think anything will happen today."

Darcy pulled the *Qipao* in close and stepped into the hallway. She made her way through the corridors to an alley that led to the outdoor entrance of the dining hall. She skirted across the massive hall, towards Ling's room and knocked lightly. "Ling, it's Darcy!" She stepped back in anticipation.

"Darcy, come in, please. You seem shaken. Your mind is not focused, as it should be. What can I do to assure you?"

"Assure me of what?"

"That you have an enormous amount of power on your side. The interest that the local people have shown has caused the town officials to be wary of the monastery, but that is nothing out of the ordinary. Please take a seat and I will provide you with a drink to calm you."

"No way. Not right now. The master wants to see you right away to plan our ceremony for tomorrow. That is if I can manage to stay that long."

"I understand. I will return soon and we can prepare your attire."

"I'm supposed to meet Jones halfway and go back to his room."

"Fine then, I will stop by and see you both."

As Ling left the room, Darcy could hear a commotion in the courtyard of the temple. The Manchurian army had forced their way into the plaza and spread out, combing the monastery. She retreated to the back of the bedroom area and cowered in the corner beneath several blankets.

✿✿✿✿✿

"Halt! What is your name?" the soldier demanded.

"I am Ling Lee, student of Master Wong Fei-hung and these are my living quarters."

"Then you have no reason to object to us entering unless you have something or someone to hide." The stout commander swept past Ling with his massive arm and reached for the door.

"It is not necessary to treat me as your enemy." Ling bowed slightly and kept a close eye on the three soldiers surrounding her.

The commander paused. "That remains to be seen." He pushed open the door with such force that a cracking sound left it certain he had broken the hinges.

Ling stood quiet and calm, restraining her warrior self for the sake of Darcy. She followed the commander into the living area.

The officer shouted several orders in Mandarin as Darcy trembled in anticipation. She could hear the soldiers pillaging the rooms... getting closer. She felt suffocated and her heart pounded. Suddenly, fresh air engulfed her when the soldiers ripped away the blankets. In an instant terror and pain overwhelmed her.

"Arrest them both. And make sure this one is hand tied." He pointed at Ling. "She leaves me cautious."

Ling bowed her head and offered her wrists.

"Not in the front. Tie her hands behind her... and tightly. These monks are trained for battle and trust me you are not trained nearly as well."

Ling stared through slits at the commander, but smiled demurely when she caught his attention. The soldiers escorted Ling and Darcy towards the courtyard.

"What's going to happen to us?" Darcy heard the fear in her own voice and could feel her legs weaken from dread.

"Stay as calm as you possibly can." Ling walked with her head bowed.

As they approached the throng of soldiers and monks, Darcy scanned the crowd for any sign of Jones. He was nowhere. Master Fei-hung stood quietly before the people gathered waiting for the commander to approach.

The general marched defiantly up to Master Fei-hung's face. "You have made a huge mistake this time. I will be the beneficiary of your dull wit." His smile bared the gold tooth of a man who had caught his nemesis in a snare from which he would not be able to tear loose. "Do not arrest this monk. We have other plans for him in the near future."

"We have no quarrel with you or your army. We are peaceful warriors and only mean to assist those who are in need. We are but humble servants intent on providing for the spiritual welfare of others."

The commander leaned in close. "I would say, as of this moment *you* are the one in need."

He laughed loudly and waved his hand toward the massive open gate.

The regiment formed to escort Darcy and Ling out into the street. A crowd of townspeople had collected to witness the arrest.

"Jones," Darcy screamed. She felt the sure hands of the soldiers holding her upright. She struggled to break free in an attempt to run back into the courtyard, only to realize there was no escape. One soldier placed his hand on her head and forced her to look at the ground.

When Jones heard the cry for help he jumped to his feet and bolted for the library door. He grabbed the handle, but it would not open. He backed up and prepared to kick the door in, but found his body unable to move forward. When he turned to Chung, the Wise One, he saw that a great calm had come over him. "Am I to understand that you, through mystical force, have taken over my body?" Jones demanded.

"My orders are to keep you safe until Master Fei-hung

returns from the courtyard." Chung continued to stand, hands folded in front of him with his eyes closed.

Jones intended to sprint out the door and rescue Darcy. As he pivoted and lunged, it was as if an invisible wall stood between him and the door. He bounced backwards, falling at Chung's feet. "You have rendered me helpless. I may have lost my way. I am not thinking clearly. Please forgive me, but my wife-to-be and my truest love is in the hands of the enemy."

Jones rolled onto his back and sat up into the lotus position. He took a deep cleansing breath to quieten his mind. In a matter of moments, he could feel the strength of his ch'i returning him to a place of wholeness. Anger gave way to the sense of a clear and powerful direction. His body, mind and spirit melded into one invincible source.

✿✿✿✿✿

"Master, I understand you have a plan, but am I not to be privy? I am ashamed that I could not come forth to declare myself. Darcy surely must be feeling abandoned and I have great guilt concerning her predicament."

"Time Traveler, you will be of more importance to us as a free man than in shackles. I do have a plan but it will take tremendous effort to execute in a clandestine manner. When I reveal our warriors, you will understand the power of the universe. I will assemble a team tonight and we will discuss our strategy in my room."

"How many monks will be involved?"

"I will decide that before we discuss the rescue of Darcy and Ling. We have monks who are very familiar with the jail where they will be taken."

"My mind, body and spirit are razor sharp and ready for any circumstance we may encounter."

"Remember the sanctity of your chi. Allow yourself to fall back in time to a lesson you learned from Ling. Your sexual nature must not be allowed to interfere with the warrior's task at hand."

"Master Fei-hung, what I am experiencing is far beyond my sexual nature. I have fallen in love with Darcy and I am distraught that I did not follow my basic instincts and leave today."

"Then you should let this be a lesson to you. I am confident that all will turn out for the best."

Jones reached for the master's right hand and clutched it between his own. "I can only hope this means my vision of our future together will manifest as I see it. We will all be reunited even if only to say our farewells before we take our leave."

"Try to live each moment of time, allowing your future to unfold in front of you, not unlike water seeking its own level. Be prepared to respond to each new situation as it happens. Do not live in the future where infinite possibilities narrow to one path but perhaps not the path you find the most favorable."

"That is difficult for me, even knowing that not so long ago I had no true idea of how time travel would become a reality. Yet, I have a time machine that is of no use to me at this moment. I cannot return to the future nor can I return to my immediate past without Darcy. I have no idea what would become of her, or me, for that matter. I will not leave her here in China."

"Then we shall make plans for your return to the future. Both of you."

Saturday, 13 June 1884, 3:30 pm

Foshan District Detention Center

The loud shrill of Mandarin spoken by the soldiers, exacerbated the fear pounding in Darcy's heart. The unfamiliar faces and aromas made her sick to her stomach. She could feel the pressure on her throat, urging her retch. Tears tumbled from her eyes, down her face, as she trudged through the streets filled with gawkers, some of whom threw spoiled food at the procession in an attempt to soil her. She struggled woozily while Ling walked resolutely and steadily under the guard of four soldiers.

"Where are we going?" Darcy whispered through her tears, moving closer to Ling.

"To the main jail here in Foshan."

"Then what will they do?"

"They will never get the chance, Darcy. I am certain that a plan for our rescue is in the making even as we speak."

"Do you think they arrested Jones?"

"No. We happened to be in the wrong place at the wrong time. We will be rescued, but you must maintain an open mind and heart for what you are about to witness."

"What the...what does that even mean?" Darcy stumbled forward.

"Just remember we are far more powerful than you may be able to accept without very careful guidance. You are about to receive your food for thought for a lifetime in one meal."

Saturday, 13 June 1884, 6:30 pm

Po-chi-lam Temple

The bright sunshine had begun to wane and the town had grown quiet from the busy day, as families gathered to share their evening meal. Jones joined Master Fei-hung in his room where he found six monks sitting crossed legged in two rows. Lanterns filled the room with a warm and calming glow.

"*Xíngshì*. Blessings, Time Traveler." Master Fei-hung motioned for Jones to sit next to him. "I will introduce each member of the team. I also have decided to give you an explanation of the role assigned to each devotee and how they will execute their task."

"Yes, Master. I am intrigued to say the least."

Master Fei-hung rose to his feet and instructed the first row to stand, placing his hand on the shoulder of the first monk.

"This is Hong-li, Great Strength. He is a master of powerful physical feats."

After Hong-li sat, he moved to the second monk.

"Time Traveler, this is Zhu, Hung Gar name: Bamboo. She is small and versatile, with the appearance of a simple reed, and can bend against a raging wind and never break." She assumed her previous seated position. "There will be six warriors working together to rescue Ling and Darcy. This is Feng, Silent Wind. He is an invisible force. You can see his effects but cannot know from where he approaches. He can be unseeable one moment and in human form the next."

Silent Wind took his seat and smiled at Jones. The second row stood.

"Then there is Yun, also known as Cloud. He is quite capable of creating cover for a great escape. And often partner to Cloud, Xue, whose Hung Gar name is Snow."

Jones bowed to the group and turned to Master Fei-hung.

"Each Hung Gar name is given for a specific purpose. But how do they manifest these attributes, Master?"

"As with you, Time Traveler, each has earned his or her name. All have a quality that contributes to the longevity of the Buddha."

He stepped forward to the next person, who towered over the rest of the group.

"This is Gao, Hung Gar name: Tall Tree. It would seem obvious why."

"He is formidable, no doubt." Jones leaned back and rubbed his chin. "I have just now had a thought. There is one more warrior I would like to bring into our group, but I must take a moment to retrieve him from the future. His name is Roark Fogerty and he was my bodyguard, when I lived in Boston in 1891, and a close friend in 2012, which I find fascinating. I believe he would fight to the death for Darcy's sake." Jones returned his gaze towards the group and found them watching him with wide eyes. "Master Fei-hung named me Time Traveler. The Atomotron is the manifestation of his teachings." He stood to address the group. "I am here from the future."

Jones waited for a response but the silence gave him the impression they were not rattled in the least.

"When will you leave?"

"I will travel immediately and return five minutes after the time of departure."

"Very well then. We will be here meditating." Master Fei-hung sat in front of the team and closed his eyes.

In unison, the group sang the sacred Om.

Jones retrieved the Atomotron and his journal, locating the coordinates for Hiva Oa. He then toggled in not only the coordinates but also the time of arrival so that he would arrive a day after he and Darcy had departed. He strapped on the time machine, amassed his chi and switched the Atomotron on. The whirling gears built up to the perfect universal pitch. Jones felt his body begin to dematerialize. He closed his eyes and without fear surrendered himself to teleportation.

Saturday, 13 June 1884, 4:00 pm

Foshan District Detention Center

Darcy and Ling entered a room with a table, chair, and windows barred with thick bamboo. The gray of the walls matched Darcy's feelings to the core.

Ling struggled with her tied wrists, turned her back toward Darcy, and took her hand. "You must center yourself. Do not allow your mind to wander to the possibilities of harm. Direct your energy towards a positive outcome. Use your anger... but do not show it."

"I'm scared shi... to death." Darcy's eyes darted around the desolate room.

"I understand."

"Stop talking." The commander approached from behind. Darcy could feel his hot breath on the back of her neck. "You will have plenty of time to discuss your fates sitting in your cell. That is, if you can stand the crowded conditions and the stench." He made his way around the small table and took his seat. "So what shall I charge you with so that I can get revenge on Fei-hung? Any suggestions? No? I guess not. I will ponder this while I eat. You, on the other hand, will not eat. The most I am willing to offer is a cup of water."

"That is kind of you, commander," Ling said. "We are grateful for any hospitality you choose to offer."

Darcy's head swooned and she felt sure she would pass out, but was too afraid of what could happen if she did. She took a deep breath and attempted to conjure her ch'i, the way she had in Snohomish when practicing the Tao exercise. She

31

released the breath, focused her eyes on the officer in charge and felt a new sense of power. "I'm not thirsty at the moment, could you have it brought to my cell later?"

Ling bowed her head and Darcy could see her smile.

"This is precisely how I know you are a foreigner. You show nothing but disrespect for authority."

"You can go fu—"

Ling stepped partially between Darcy and the commander. "She is new to these circumstances," she threw in. "I will teach her what she needs to know about our culture. Please may we know where we will be—"

"I owe you nothing." He stalked around the table and stood squarely in front of them. "Your fate is in *my* hands. I will decide how and when you will find out about your destiny."

"My *destiny* was written long before we met. We shall see who is correct about how my life continues." Ling locked eyes with him briefly and then looked at the floor.

The commander leaned forward, no more than a few inches from Ling's face. "Yes we will. Untie her hands and take them to their cell."

Monday, 20 June 1892 9:00 am

Atuona, Hiva Oa Island, French Polynesia

As Jones materialized, he found himself surrounded by a pristine white sandy beach, great blue skies, and the emerald green waters of the Pacific Ocean. A warm ocean breeze gently caressed his face as he skittered over to the same tree as the night before. He stashed the Atomotron and marched in the direction of the village. As he approached, two villagers waved and pointed toward the bay. Jones nodded and sprinted toward where he assumed he would find Roark. As he slowed his pace, he could see a figure in the distance standing above the rest of the natives, who were fishing for the day's catch, with nets and lines, in the shallows of the bay. Roark cast a net widely with his massive reddened arms.

"Roark!" Jones jogged to his companion's side. "I have much to explain and I need your assistance if you so choose to undertake a task with me."

"Methinks ya sound troubled. What's 'at ya wearin'? Didya time machine break?" Roark continued to tug on the net.

"It is a tunic." Jones pulled on the top. "No. I have hidden the time machine in the same location as before. I have traveled back from China to ask if you could help me free Darcy. You see, the Manchurian army has arrested her. It is a very complicated situation. Master Fei-hung has gathered a team to rescue her and I am of the opinion that you may be able to offer a great deal of assistance in the matter."

Roark waved to an older man to take the frond rope and approached Jones onshore.

"I like Darcy." Roark stared into the distance and then took large strides toward the village. "Come with me and I be tellin' my women I be gone fer a piece."

"Explain as best you can that you will return later this afternoon. I will toggle in a time that will make sense to them."

" 'ey ain't sure what time is."

They traversed the beach, taking the first beaten path they came to while Jones explained to Roark the details of the visit to Foshan.

"Methinks you two will be married fer a long time." Roark halted. "She shouldn't be in jail. Jail's notta place fer Darcy." Roark turned back and strode even faster than before.

When they arrived at the village, Roark went about explaining to his hut mates that he would return when the sun was high in the sky.

"Time ta go. Ya go first and I'll follow."

They made their way to the beach and turned north to make the trek back to the Atomotron. As they passed the bluff where Gauguin often painted, they could see him sitting with his young wife on his lap, applying color to burlap while she cuddled up against his chest. If he did see the time travelers, he made no indication of interest.

"You understand the circumstances we are about to travel into?"

"Methinks I do. We do this fer Darcy. Dun't really need more of a reason, do I?"

"You are a remarkable friend... to us both. I will forever be in your debt."

"Then methinks I will buy your contract and tear it up,"

Roark said with a broad smile.

"Then I shall be forever grateful. Thank you, Roark."

Jones pulled the Atomotron from behind the palm tree, toggled in the coordinates, adjusted the straps to the maximum length, and held it up to Roark. He then slid it up as far as he could and allowed Roark to wrestle it into place.

"Now, my friend, I will proceed to turn on the time machine while you hold me close. We shall be in China 1884 in a matter of, well no time."

He turned the switch. In a few seconds, he felt the tingling, as his cells began to expand and the white noise in his ears reached a fevered pitch. They vanished and were on their way to Foshan, China, 1884.

Saturday, 13 June 1884, 6:35 pm

Po-ch'i-lam Temple

Master Fei-hung's room

Jones and Roark appeared in the exact spot from where Jones had departed, only five minutes before. The soothing sound of Om filled the room as the monks sat, eyes closed with straight backs and fingers forming a circle that rested on their knees. Each exhaled the Om, mirroring the rotation of the universe and inhaling in a round of continuous sound. Jones and Roark waited respectfully. Master Fei-hung spoke to the group who then became silent, opened their eyes, and smiled. Tall Tree immediately stood.

"He's a big fella." Roark had never been in the presence of another human being taller than himself. "What's ya name?" He looked at Jones, who in turn glanced at Master Fei-hung.

"This is Goa, also called Tall Tree," Jones answered.

" 'at's a good name fer ya." Roark stepped in closer and looked up. "Wouldn't want ta meet up with ya in a dark alley."

Tall Tree quietly smiled at his newfound friend. He then did something completely unexpected; he patted Roark on the head and grinned. The rest of the monks laughed and gathered in close around the new person.

Master Fei-hung looked over at Jones. "This is your companion from another time." He bowed from the waist toward Roark. "It is an honor to meet you."

"If ya the master Jones was talkin' about, I'm honored to meet ya." Roark awkwardly attempted a bow almost colliding with the master. "Eh, sorry." He recovered, stood straight up and glanced at Jones.

Jones slapped Roark on the back. "We shall work on bowing some other time. We have much to plan. Roark, these are the members of the rescue team. This is Silent Wind, Great Strength, Tall Tree, whom you have met, Cloud, Bamboo and Snow. Each will be assigned a different task as we move forward. And master, what role shall Roark and I play?"

"Roark will fit in seamlessly with the plan I have in mind. We will need his strength and your ability to strike invisibly with the shadowless kick if it should become necessary."

"Methinks that me boxin' can be a good thing fer gettin' Darcy home."

"Gather in a circle and we shall begin." Master Fei-hung took his position and the others took seats next to one another, shoulder to shoulder, to form a circle.

He unfurled a parchment and placed it in the middle of the group. He then took a small paintbrush, dipped it in an inkwell and began to draw out a rough schematic of Foshan.

"We are located here, Time Traveler." He dipped and drew a line through the streets, ending with a small circle. "This is the location of the detention center. Each of you will play a role. We will create a distraction one *li* away, allowing others to move freely for a short period of time."

Roark glanced around the circle at the monks who all leaned in attentively.

"Ying is not present as I have sent him to gather information of the activity and location of the guards. He will return with numbers in a matter of moments. We will then clarify how to proceed."

"Ying, Master?" Jones asked.

"Ying, whose Hung Gar name is Black Eagle, will fly above the jail to provide an accurate accounting of the challenges we must face."

Jones cocked his head to one side and scrunched his forehead. "How will he fly?"

"As you know from your own experience, each person who graduates from the Po-chi-lam Temple is endowed with a specific skill secreted from those on the outside, used only in the case of protecting the monastery or a person with whom we have great relations. You will have access, on this night, to revelations of ancient secrets. You must commit to absolute silence in the observations of what you will witness."

"I have made this commitment in the past and will never break that promise. I must admit that I did not have this particular knowledge when here last."

"We did not know if you would return and chose to keep our secret from you. We now know we can trust you without hesitation." Master Fei-hung turned to Roark. "And your companion? What does he say for himself?"

"Methinks I've seen more 'an any man should see already. I've not told a soul." Roark folded his hands on his lap. "I can be trusted with anythin' ya can trow at me."

"Although you have not graduated, you are a most trusted companion to Time Traveler. By association, you are welcome into this monastery anytime you should need refuge. I will give you an honorary name… *Zài shàngmiàn báishān xiǎofáng*."

The monks chuckled softly and nodded.

Roark continued to sit in silence, with his eyes glued to

the master.

"Master, what does this mean?" Jones looked back and forth from Roark to Fei-hung.

"This name means white mountain with fire on top."

Roark smiled approvingly and pushed lightly against Jones.

"I am indeed happy for you." Jones smiled broadly and turned back to the master. "However, I am still very curious about the method Ying utilizes to fly."

"Ying is a shape shifter. He can become any bird of prey, but is limited to that skill as is each of the others. They are specialized in the manifestation of their names."

"Am I to understand that Yun can become a cloud and Xue become snow? That is why you spoke of the two of them working in conjunction?"

"That is correct." Master Fei-hung scanned the group with great pride.

"Methinks 'is may hurt me head even more 'an time travel." Roark placed his hands around his head of red hair.

"And the others? How do they manifest?" Jones surveyed the monks.

"Feng, Silent Wind, approaches as an invisible entity. They will feel his presence but have no idea what they are experiencing until it is too late.

Goa, Tall Tree, can plant himself for the purpose of climbing a wall or to a cell window where another can then climb to break through the bamboo bars meant to hold in the prisoners."

"How does Bamboo fit into this scheme?" Jones stared at her.

She smiled at him and nodded.

The master explained, "You are the most vulnerable. You

and White Mountain will need a hiding place. That is where she comes in. She is able to manifest as a stand of bamboo to give you cover."

"I see. You have thought of everything as usual," Jones responded with more ease in his heart.

Saturday, 13 June 1884, 7:00 pm

Foshan District Detention Center

The crowded cell was almost too much for Darcy's mind to withstand. She paced back and forth in the small space like a caged tiger. Ling sat in a Lotus posture with her eyes closed while people milled about, bumping into one another. The smell of stale urine and sweat left Darcy feeling panicked. She raked her hand on the wall as she passed in an endless circle. The rest of the prisoners stopped moving to observe her anxious behavior. After a short moment, they once again began to mill about, biding their time.

Ling opened her eyes and caught Darcy by the hem of her *Qipao*. "Come sit with me." She patted the ground next her. "I will calm your spirit."

"I don't think I can sit down right now. Seriously, I feel like I'm having a nervous breakdown… like, I'm going to lose it. This place is a disgusting, filthy, mind blowing pile of—"

"Come sit here. Take my hand." Ling calmly reached for Darcy's hand and took it securely into her own.

Darcy melted, as if hypnotized, into a Lotus position next to Ling.

"Close your eyes." Ling placed her hand delicately on Darcy's eyelids.

After a few moments passed, Darcy whispered, "This is amazing. What have you done to me?"

"I am introducing my internal self to yours. As they become familiar and willing, they can join forces much like

41

streams forming a river. But we must maintain a state of calm to avoid confusion. We must act in tandem when the time comes."

"I hear what you're saying… the words I mean, but I have no idea what you're talking about. Act in tandem? That would mean I would have to know all the stuff you know."

"And you will."

"Like taking over my mind? Wait a second, this is getting a little too freaky for me."

"Only with your permission and then, your body will *know* what my body and mind can do. If you do not wish to have these skills available, I will honor your request sincerely with no judgment." Ling released her hand only to feel Darcy grab her wrist.

"Okay, I'm in. So, I just have to center myself and you become a body snatcher?"

"I am sure that has some meaning to you, but I do not understand."

"I'm just being me. Forget it. The more I try to explain the worse it would get."

"Darcy, close your eyes and relax. Open yourself to experiencing that which you have yet to experience. Breathe in slowly. You will begin to feel the sensation of heat and your mind will seem as if it is dreaming but you will not be dreaming. The images you will see in your mind and the sensations you will feel are actually my thoughts. I will not harm you and when I leave, you will return to being yourself but you and I will know each other deeply."

"So your eyes are open now? Because I can see a group of people standing bent over close to your face."

"Keep your eyes closed and continue to tell me what you see." Ling stood and walked to the cell door and returned.

"Tell me."

"I walked over to the door and looked into the hallway, I mean, you walked…"

"Precisely, but you observed. We can also use this technique to assist you in defending yourself. This allows me to be in two places at one time and use your body."

"So will I remember the techniques when you leave me?"

"Some but your performance can only reach high standards with many long days cf practice."

Darcy felt compelled to rise to her feet. "Excuse me." She bowed to a short man who nodded with a toothless grin. Darcy stepped back against the wall to steady herself when lightning speed took over her hands and arms. "What the…"

She could see her body moving; she could even feel strength and agility come over her, but it was not her at all. Ling sat quietly on the floor while Darcy performed a kata that she, until then, had no idea existed.

"This is… so….cool," Darcy uttered as she formed the snake pose.

The others in the cell moved to the sidelines dumbfounded.

"I want to… learn to… do this," she said in a strained voice. Darcy spun on the ball of her foot, throwing a roundhouse kick in the direction of the older toothless man who threw his arms up in front of his face.

He then laughed heartily and mocked her with a slow kick of his own.

She assumed the grasshopper stance and flowed effortlessly into the leopard position.

A guard made his way to the barred door and peered in. "*Shénme zài zhèlǐ* ? What goes on in there?"

The crowd quickly filled in the space around Darcy and

began to shuffle about.

Darcy rushed to sit next to Ling. "How do you do that?" She clapped her hands lightly. "I feel like an excited little girl. I never thought about taking martial arts before, but I'm thinking it's about time."

"What I performed through you takes many years of rigorous practice. Master Fei-hung has pushed me more than most because I am a woman and the expectation of failure by most men is very high."

"Sounds familiar." Darcy's eyes widened. "Oh no, I have to pee."

"What is this?"

"I have to pee, urinate." Darcy resorted to using hand gestures. "You know, pessssshhh."

Ling chuckled.

"There is a trough against the wall in the back."

"OMG, there is *no way* that I'm gonna... I'll hold it." Darcy craned her neck to take a quick look at the folks lined up. "Yeah, I'm pretty sure I'll bust before I go back there."

"It is not healthy to control elimination."

"Why are we even talking about this? I'll hold it as long as I can."

"There is a way. I can merge with you and walk you over."

"Whaaat? No way, I mean I like you and everything, but you are *not* going to pee for me."

The guard came to the door and opened it. Two soldiers entered and took three men from the cell, slamming the door shut after them.

"What's going to happen to them?" Darcy moved a little closer to Ling.

"I am not acquainted with these men so I have no idea

what their fate may be."

"Do you know what our fate will be?" Darcy rocked back and forth as a way of distracting her mind from her predicament. "I've decided. I'm goin' over."

"Shall I accompany you?" Ling said, standing up.

"Wow is this where it all started? In my time, in the future, it's a thing for women to accompany other women to the bathroom." Darcy rose to her feet. "Difference? We've got privacy stalls and flushing toilets."

The two meandered to the back. Ling kept watch as Darcy followed the example of the others who were already underway. She shyly removed her panties, balanced against the wall, adjusted the *Qipao* in such a way as to cover the greatest area of her body and tried to relax.

"It's not working. Excuse me but could you look in another direction?"

The older woman squatting next to her stared blankly at Darcy's mouth.

"I think I'm too tense. And it doesn't help to have folks lookin' right at me." Darcy extended her hand for assistance from Ling to pull away from the wall, but as soon as their hands touched Darcy could feel the relief begin. "Dang, how'd you do that?"

Saturday, 13 June 1884, 7:30 pm

Master Fei-hung's room

A high-pitched screech sounded from outside the shuttered window of Master Fei-hung's warmly lit sleeping quarters. Moments later a second sharp scream left no doubt that Ying had returned. Bamboo and Cloud immediately rose and held open a robe while Great Strength lifted the heavy wooden cross-brace, and threw open the shutters. Everyone stood, staring out the open window into the dusky evening sky.

What followed left Jones and Roark wide-eyed with awe.

A large eagle flew into the room through the open window, talons extended, as if to attack. Instead, it flapped its wings and morphed into an older monk. He broke into a warm grin as he took two steps forward into an awaiting robe. He wrapped his body in the orange garment and bowed.

Bamboo and Cloud returned a bow to Black Eagle and stepped away. Once again, everyone formed a circle, with the exception of Roark who was drumming his fingers on the floor.

"Methinks 'at was a miracle. I dun't know how 'at's done, but methinks I want ta learn so I can change inta a cat."

"Why pray tell would you choose to be a cat?"

"Cause 'ey sleep all the time. 'At's somethin' me likes just about more 'an anythin'."

"I see." Jones felt the pressing stares from the others and returned his attention to the discussion.

Master Fei-hung motioned for Eagle to begin.

He pulled the brush from the ink well and drew a rough sketch of the jail and yard where the military slept.

"There are twenty soldiers sleeping here and four guards that keep watch over these two cells where Ling and her companion are being kept. The commander does not live on the premises, but a few dwellings down the street."

"And what is their condition at this time?" Master Fei-hung asked.

"Were you able to see Darcy and Ling? What was your approximate distance?" Jones asked.

"Perhaps you are unfamiliar with an eagle's ability to see a great deal from great distances. I can report that they appear to be fine."

Bamboo pulled her praying hands to her chest. "Ling will take great strides to protect Darcy. She has expressed a true caring for her. I am sure she has already begun to teach Darcy her way."

Jones held his hands out in front of him. "What is Ling's way? I was unaware that she is also a master of a powerful attribution."

"She has become superior at mind/body transfer."

"I see… well, actually I do not, but another time then."

Master Fei-hung again pointed at the sketch. "We shall move forward with this plan. We Chinese are a superstitious lot and frighten easily by things that seem out of place. Therefore, I want you, Silent Wind, to make your way to the camp of the off duty soldiers, once they have begun to sleep. I want you to switch their helmets and weapons from one to the other. Exchange as many as you can before we arrive."

"Yes, Master."

"We shall go to the detention center in a certain order. The goal is to have Darcy and Ling freed and back here by early morning. Do not engage any soldier in combat unless you must defend yourself. We must be clever... and in being clever, we will execute the plan in such a way that the commander cannot lay blame at our feet."

"Who will follow Silent Wind? And what roles will Roark and I play?"

"He will be followed by Cloud and Snow who will create a great distraction. Time Traveler, White Mountain, Tall Tree and Bamboo will go as a group. When Yun forms a cloud over the area, the guards will think it is a fog; however, Cloud will thicken the fog until only voices can be heard. Should it become necessary, Xue will make snow. This will capture their imaginations. They will become frightened to see snow in the summer, creating a further confusion. As they rise in disarray, they will discover they have the incorrect gear. Chaos will ensue.

"Time Traveler, your group will make their way to this location here." Master Fei-hung used the pointy wooden end of the paintbrush to point to the outside of the cell. Tall Tree will lift White Mountain to the height of the window to pull out the bars. Bamboo will accompany you in case you are in need of protection."

Bamboo smiled at Jones. He could see her youth in her bright eyes, but reminded himself of advice once given to him concerning Ling. 'A purring cub will someday become a tiger.' Jones smiled and bowed his head to her.

"I have every confidence we shall be successful. Just take a gander at this formidable group of warriors." Jones leaned forward and slapped a few monks on their knees. "Master, I have only heard what others will do. What do you expect of me?"

"You are a great martial artist and if need be, you will

engage the enemy with great skill. However, the most important role you will play is to greet Darcy upon her escape. She will be elated and relieved to be back where she belongs, unharmed. We must not fail her or Ling."

"This is indeed clever. How can I ever repay your kindness?"

Master Fei-hung addressed the entire group. "Again, know that this is our bliss. This is what we do for pleasure." Master Fei-hung radiated a smile that lit up the room. "It is time to dress as town folk and ready ourselves."

"Ya, methinks 'is could be a lotta fun." Roark pounded his large fist into his palm a couple of times and chuckled. The group did not return his smile that time.

"Violence is not the answer. Even when defending oneself, you must maintain a pure heart so that if you are able, you can disarm your opponent with as little damage as possible."

"Methinks I've a lot ta learn." Roark leaned back on his hands.

Saturday, 13 June 1884, 7:00 pm

Foshan District holding cell

The guards shoved a meal of sticky rice and a few vegetables through an opening of the door. Although they were encouraged to eat by the others, Darcy and Ling declined the offering and returned to their seats.

"I am not even hungry. That looks disgusting."

"Understand that you are a fortunate one. After several days, this food takes on a different appearance. It is a reflection of your desire to live. You are not at risk... at least at this moment."

"Hey what does that mean? 'At least at this moment.' I'm gonna ask you a question and you don't have to answer, but are you merging with anyone back at the monastery?"

"No. The distance is too great for my skill, but when they approach, I will be able to see what the others see. Tall Tree will be the easiest to merge with because he is innocent in his approach to life. So when he gets close enough I can begin to see through his eyes."

"How do you know he'll be along?" Darcy lay back to stretch and felt Ling's sure hand stopping her without even looking in her direction. "Eh yeah for sure... don't want to lie back on that I guess. Thanks. Do I seem like a dork to you? I mean like you guys are all so in touch with your inner selves and got super powers and shi... stuff. I feel like a simpleton."

"You are a free and open human being. We like your energy. It is pure and unadulterated."

"Oh for sure, you're not gonna find an adult in here right

50

at the moment. I'm just kiddin'. There's definitely an adult in here somewhere."

"This is why we want an extended relationship with you. Not to change you. That would be a mistake, but to give your character direction. Never would we want to change Darcy Champagne, the soon to be Darcy Whitman."

"OMG." Darcy leaned back against the wall and looked up. "I am about to become… hey maybe he should become Jones Champagne. Nah, never mind, that sounds way too metro."

Saturday, 13 June 1884, 9:45 pm

Streets of Foshan City, Guangdong Province

"Let us set our plan in motion." Master Fei-hung pointed to Silent Wind. "Remember to be cautious so as not to awaken them too early. You must exchange as much equipment as you can."

Silent Wind sat in a Lotus position and took three deep breaths. Jones and Roark watched carefully as he rose to his feet, eyes still closed and walked out the door.

"Methinks 'e could be hittin' a wall or somethin'."

"I am sure he has other methods for detecting his whereabouts." Jones jumped to his feet and ran to the window, only to see the massive wooden door slowly swing open, but no monk to be seen.

"He has begun." Master Fei-hung placed his hands together, in front of his chest, and began a round of Om. After several cycles, Tall Tree ended the chant with a deep bass vibrato that slowly trailed off to silence.

"Cloud and Snow, make your way to the area using the back alleys and find cover to wait for Silent Wind to complete his task before you manifest your part of the plan."

"When will our team leave? I am without a doubt becoming more anxious to be underway, as time seems to have slowed to a crawl, which is of course, impossible because time remains at a constant or so one would think."

"It is time for you to conjure your chi, Time Traveler. You must make the shift for the sake of Darcy and your group. It is time to become a warrior with singularity of purpose."

Jones understood even before the master had finished. He took a deep cleansing breath, closed his eyes, delicately placed his encircled fingers on his knees and quieted his mind. His energy began to organize itself around the challenge that lay before him. He could foresee the obstacles that lay ahead in his mind and raced through the possible solutions. Learning in this manner allowed him to practice in the virtual world of his imagination.

Jones, Roark, Bamboo, and Tall Tree stood together in a tight circle, heads bowed.

The master's voice broke the silence. "It is time for us to leave."

"Us? Master, are you saying that you will be attending the rescue?"

"From afar. I want to watch over all of you who are my students and my children. I will intervene if the plan should fail in some way or if any one of you falls into danger."

"I am most impressed and glad you will be participating." Jones started forward to share a hug, pulled up short and bowed instead.

✿✿✿✿✿

Silent Wind hurriedly snaked through the streets of Foshan towards the jail. He continued through the closed market to the steps of the Foshan District Detention Center. As assigned, he then walked among the off duty soldiers who had crowded around large fire pits for an evening of carousing. One by one, the soldiers dismissed themselves and wandered off to a makeshift latrine to relieve themselves. After that, they crawled off to their mats, laid their weapons and helmets on the ground within arm's reach, and prepared to sleep it off. As the night wore on, snoring covered all other sounds. Silent Wind took the opportunity to switch both

53

headgear and swords from one mat to another so most of the infantry would awaken to helmets that did not fit and unfamiliar weapons. He took one last look around the campground, materialized, and strolled away.

Just as he reached the back corner of the market, he saw Cloud and Snow approaching.

"It is done." Silent Wind smiled. "If they should awaken there will be more fighting amongst themselves than with us."

"I look forward to observing that event. I am about to cloud their minds. Snow, you should remain with Silent Wind for a short time. You may not need to use your skill after all is said and done."

"But I like snow. I wish it would snow year round. It was my favorite way to spend time with my family and friends as a child."

Cloud placed his hand on her shoulder and grinned. "Perhaps we should make it snow a little, just for your amusement."

"Let me know when…"

"Someone is coming. You two walk casually across the market square." Silent Wind became invisible, snuck up next to Bamboo who was coming down the street, and whispered, "Bamboo, you were making more noise than you should at this time of night."

She bowed her head and said, "White Mountain and Tall Tree are like little boys. It is difficult to keep them quiet."

"Methinks we talk too much maybe."

"Speak with softer voices," Bamboo said quietly.

Tall Tree spoke in his bass voice, "I'm sorry." but no matter how much he tried to whisper, it still came out as a low growl.

They joined the others in the alley next to the detention center.

"Cloud, it is time." Silent Wind patted him on the back.

Cloud stepped forward into the dim light that emanated from the center's window and held out his arms. He closed his eyes and began to spin. Jones, Roark, Bamboo and Silent Wind watched as he spun faster and faster, until he suddenly became a swirl of cloud. The cloud spread, flowing down the alley and across the campground in an ever-increasing density. The haze became so thick that they could feel moisture against their skin.

"Perhaps we should find our way to the cell wall before it's too late to see." Jones listened for a response.

"Silent Wind can lead us. We are not far away at all," Bamboo whispered.

Using the side of the building as a guide, they ran their hands along the rough stone until they saw a faint light coming from a window high above.

"The window is situated at twice the height of Tall Tree and then some. Perhaps Roark could stand on his shoulders," Jones whispered.

"Methinks I might be too heavy for Tree to pick up."

"Perhaps the other way around then," Jones said.

"White Mountain should sit on my shoulders. Then I will extend myself to the window to allow him to grasp the bars and pull them from the wall. Great Strength and I have performed this once before."

"But how will Ling and Darcy get to the raised window to escape? And what do you mean by extending yourself?" Jones added.

"Gao, is also known as Tall Tree for a reason." Silent Wind chuckled. "When he stands still, he can root himself in the ground and grow as tall as this building and more."

"It may seem obvious but why then is it that he is unable to remove the bars?"

"Because he becomes the tree and no longer has use of his arms. He has limbs but not the right kind." Silent Wind moved forward fluidly. A barely visible ghostly apparition replaced his physical body.

The crew heard voices coming and fell into silence as the soldiers passed within arm's reach. They hugged the wall and held their breath while the voices disappeared into the fog.

"Perhaps we should take this opportunity to make an attempt while the guards make their rounds." Jones reached out to touch Roark. "Tall Tree, kneel down, and Roark get on his shoulders in a seated position."

"On my left shoulder. You should not straddle my neck as it will grow quite rapidly." When Tall Tree stood, he locked his legs and, with a slight rumble, began to change. Although it was dark and foggy, the others could see Roark now in the light of the cell window.

Another set of guards came around the corner of the building and one bumped into the tree.

"What is this? I don't remember this tree. I must be losing my mind."

"It's the mist. Very strange things happen in the fog at night. It is difficult to stay sane when you cannot see what you are familiar with."

"Come on, or we will be in trouble for being late."

The last sound of armor clinking abated into the fog.

"What if me make too much noise?" Roark whispered.

"That being the case we will have to resort to an alternative plan." Jones stood at the bottom of the tree, resting his hand on the trunk. "It is almost impossible to see you."

Silent Wind stepped close to Jones. "We do not have unlimited time to use our attributes, so we must hurry."

"What does that mean?" Jones asked.

"The fog will be lifting soon so we must take advantage of this now."

"Roark, make an attempt to pull the bars out," Jones called up in a whisper, watching intently as Roark seized the two bars of the window and pulled. He strained but to no avail.

"You must gather your chi," Jones said to Roark. Looking toward Silent Wind, he said, "I am not sure that he can conjure the strength."

Roark grabbed the bars once again and yanked. "Methinks I need to get mad," he growled, snapping the bars in two.

Everyone in the cell fell quiet.

Roark stuck his head inside and looked for Darcy.

When she saw him, she flinched, and broke into a huge smile. "Roark? Where the hell did you come from?" She danced around, then stopped. "Where is Jones?"

" 'e's waitin' fer ya ta come out and go back with him. 'e's right below me."

Ling stood by Darcy's side. "This is where my skills will save us both, but we must be very cautious. Should we make too much noise, we will be overrun by guards."

"Methinks it's too high fer me ta reach ya," Roark said in a hushed voice.

"Not to worry. Darcy will come to you first. Be ready to grab her arms when she reaches you."

Roark nodded.

"Roark. Do you see them?" Jones asked.

He looked down and nodded. "Methinks they have a plan."

"What can I do?" Jones called out softly.

"Tis gonna happen soon now." Roark took off his shirt, quickly folded it over the short pieces of broken bamboo sticking out of the wall, and laid his upper body just inside the window.

Ling sat and quieted her mind.

Darcy suddenly felt the urge to back up to the door of the cell. She then turned and, without hesitation, sprinted straight up the wall into Roark's massive strong arms.

"Me gotcha. Careful when I pull ya through."

"Holy crap, that was… Roark." She hugged him tight.

"Sit here fer a bit on 'is branch and I'll catch your friend." He once again stuck his upper body inside.

Ling bowed gracefully to the others who all stood by watching, walked casually to the cell door, and heard a guard coming. She waved Roark back out of the window and gestured for everyone to sit. The group followed her lead just as the guard stuck his face up to the bars of the cell door. Everyone sat as still as they could as he slowly looked around the cell.

"Why are you so quiet?"

Suddenly, a voice called from down the hall and he walked away.

Ling merged with Roark to let him know all was clear. Roark appeared in the window in that same moment. She stood and quickly climbed the wall, in the same manner as Darcy, and into the arms of Roark.

"Methinks you need to eat more. Ya seem a bit light." He pulled her through the window and onto the tree limb.

"How are we gonna get down from here?" Darcy peered toward the ground. "Jones?" Her eyes began well. "How do we get down?"

The tree lurched downward.

Darcy felt as if she was on an elevator, descending several floors of a building. "What the hell?"

As they approached the ground, they could hear soldiers talking as they came around the corner. Tall Tree had resumed his human form and flattened himself against the wall with the others. The fog, although still dense, had begun to lift, exposing their feet. The two men carried on a conversation while walking arm's length from the group. No one moved. Once the guards had disappeared, the group left the alley and entered a side street.

"It will be safer if we split up," Silent Wind suggested. He turned to find Jones and Darcy holding each other tight, and rocking back and forth. "We must keep moving."

"Yes, we have the rest of our lives to share affections. With whom shall we return to the monastery?"

"You, Darcy and Snow will go with Bamboo. White Mountain, Ling, and I will wait for Cloud."

"But I wanted to make snow, at least a bit of snow."

Silent Wind chuckled. "Then you will stay with me, and White Mountain can go with Bamboo."

"Me likes 'at better. Now we have Darcy I can spend time with her and Jones, just like the good ole days."

"I believe that is an excellent idea. Not another moment of hesitation, shall we?" Jones motioned to Bamboo.

Bamboo started out in the lead followed by the others.

Darcy stopped for a moment and looked back. A light silent snow had started to fall. She had to pinch her arm to make sure she was not dreaming.

"I had no idea." She looked at Jones who was also staring at the drifting white powder, only a short distance away. She grabbed his hand. "Let's get outta here."

They caught up with Bamboo and Roark who had taken a side street closer to the woods. As they arrived at a trailhead, they could hear the soldiers had indeed awakened and were marred in confusion. Off in the distance, Bamboo could hear the jailers screaming about an escape.

"We must hurry," she said as she picked up her pace.

Soldiers ran across the road as Bamboo started down the trail. The last infantryman caught sight of the foursome and pointed in their direction.

"Quickly... we must find a clearing." Bamboo ran as fast as she could.

"I can't keep up." Darcy was breathing heavily.

"Darcy, you must listen to me. We are in grave danger should you not push beyond what you think you are capable. Find your chi and make a heroic effort for both of us."

Darcy stopped short, with her hands on her knees, panting like a wild animal.

Bamboo looked back to see both Roark and Darcy struggling to recover from the sprint.

The soldiers were now on the trail within earshot.

Bamboo quickly gathered the three in one place. "Step off the path here and stand very still."

She then squatted and stuck her fingers in the ground. As she disappeared, a stand of bamboo cane grew tall around them. They stood in awe as thick vegetation concealed them completely.

"Oh jeeze. Jones, take my hand please," Darcy cried.

Jones wrapped his arm around her shoulders and pulled her in close.

Darcy then felt the weight of Roark joining them in a group hug.

"They are very close," Jones whispered. "I am convinced

we are safe."

"Methinks 'ere's no way we can be seen." Roark stood up straight and cocked his ear in the direction of the men slashing through the brush, their charged up angry voices getting closer every moment. They arrived in front of the bamboo stand and stopped.

"Listen carefully," said the patrol leader.

A deafening silence followed, broken by the remote voices in the distance toward Foshan.

"You two walk the perimeter of the bamboo and see if they are hiding on the other side. The rest of you start up the trail slowly and let me know if you see any broken branches." He handed his lantern to the first soldier who passed. "I will join you either way in a few moments."

He then reached out with both hands and attempted to separate the tall reeds in front of him. The two who had been walking along the perimeter joined him.

"No movement, captain. It does not seem they stopped here."

"This stand is so thick I can barely push the bamboo aside," the captain said.

One of the soldiers drew his sword and took a great swing at the base of the stand dropping a clump of reeds.

"Don't waste our time. If you must cut through, how could they possibly have made their way into the center? Put your sword away. Let us continue."

The men started up the trail once again leaving the three holding their breath and clinging to one another.

When it was apparent the soldiers did not intend to return, the stand began to shrink until Bamboo was once again squatting on the ground.

Darcy grabbed her robe and placed it across her back,

while Roark turned away and Jones stepped forward to assist. "Bamboo, your leg is bleeding." Darcy quickly knelt beside her to examine the wound.

"This is most unfortunate." Jones pulled the robe aside and examined the lesion. "I fear this needs medical attention right away. Will you be able to walk?"

"Methinks that cut is deep." Roark reached down and gathered Bamboo in his arms. "Tell me how to go."

Bamboo pointed in the direction back toward Foshan.

"Methinks we 'ave too many waitin' there."

She laid her head against Roark's chest. "We must go this way for a short distance and take another trail. Trust me; this is the right thing to do."

Roark led the way out with Darcy and Jones constantly checking the rear. Within a matter of moments, they came to an underused trail that Bamboo indicated would be their next direction. As they turned onto the path, they saw Master Fei-hung, twenty feet away, standing with his arms outstretched. Roark stumbled through the underbrush and handed Bamboo over. He watched as the master closed his eyes and began to glow deep purple. Darcy approached slowly, as did Jones, to discover the wound had stopped bleeding.

Roark grinned and shook his head. "Not sure I'll eva be the same again."

✿✿✿✿✿

Master Fei-hung lowered Bamboo to the ground. "The others are being pursued by the soldiers. We should hurry to their aid."

"Why do they not use their powers to distract the army?" Jones asked.

"Once used, they must recharge by sleeping. We are vulnerable under these conditions."

"It's my fault," Darcy said.

"There is no blame, only circumstance," Master Fei-hung said.

"Should Bamboo return to the monastery?" Jones asked.

"That decision is up to Bamboo," Master Fei-hung said, placing a hand on her shoulder.

"The bleeding has ceased and I cannot leave the others behind. I will be fine."

Jones squatted and pointed to the cut. "Admirable, but the cut is still open. Are you certain it won't... never mind, I am convinced that should it begin to bleed again the master will take care of it."

"I will lead." Master Fei-hung closed his eyes for a moment. "They are hiding across from the center just inside one of the canopies in the market place." He started back down the trail to the main path that led back to Foshan.

They scurried close to the buildings, hesitating occasionally to check the surrounding area before moving forward again. Within minutes, they joined Cloud, Ling, Snow, Silent Wind and Tall Tree, who were hiding in the darkness of a lowered cloth awning. They could hear the clatter of metal and leather suited soldiers close by, running through the streets.

"Do not leave any stone unturned," the commander called out. "I want these lawbreakers arrested and placed back in the prison before the sun rises."

Master Fei-hung stood quietly conjuring his chi and the others followed suit.

"Methinks there's too many," Roark whispered.

"We will engage only if we are caught, otherwise we shall attempt to escape without engaging in combat," Master Fei-hung said.

Silent Wind peered from under the canopy to discover the streets were indeed deserted. He motioned for the others to follow. Tall Tree and White Mountain lifted the edge of the canopy for the others to escape into an adjacent alley.

"Darcy, take my hand." Ling closed her eyes and Darcy felt a surge of confidence. "We will meet this challenge together. If confronted, I want you to position yourself back to back with me. Do you understand?"

"And I will remain at your side no matter what should happen." Jones gave her a brief hug. "We are going to be fine."

"I've never been so scared in my life." Darcy's eyes were wild with apprehension.

Ling turned to her and looked her in the eyes. "Conjure your chi and allow me to transfer. If you should come under attack, remain calm and I will protect you. Remember that fear is your greatest enemy. These are indeed frightening circumstances, but we have the universe on our side."

"Damn it." Anxiety surged through her stomach. "I'm gonna try my hardest but I can't promise that I can keep it together."

"Darcy, I understand how this situation must feel to you; however, you must allow Ling to sponsor your reactions. She is a formidable defensive fighter. It would take an army to lay a single blow to Ling. Roark will take up position on your other side."

"Methinks 'at you will not need more 'an us three."

"Okay, I'm feeling a little calmer but I really would like to sneak on outta here and just go back to the monastery and then home."

"And so we shall. I will take your advice this time." Jones caressed her shoulder. "I am truly sorry you are in this situation and I will do everything in my power to see you safely back to Snohomish."

Three soldiers started up the alley, stopping short when they saw the group. They looked at one another and then charged. Silent Wind, Cloud, and Snow dropped into the five elements stance simultaneously. The soldiers drew their weapons and ran full speed toward the waiting monks. In one movement, the monks leapt into the air with perfect synchronicity and rolled forward over the top of the three infantrymen, landing in a snake posture. The soldiers stopped, turned and prepared to attack again. Roark and Tall Tree both growled at their rear. One soldier yelped and ran off leaving two behind. Roark pounded his fist into his hand. The loud smacking sound caused the two remaining soldiers to collide as they attempted to flee, knocking each other to the ground. Tall Tree grabbed one and Roark the other.

"Master, what shall we do with these two?" Tall Tree asked in his raspy bass voice.

Master Fei-hung approached. "Go in peace. Save yourselves. This is done."

The two men ran off toward the compound.

"Others will come quickly. We must take this opportunity to return to the trail. We can hide in the woods if necessary."

Cloud struck out at a fast pace followed by the others in single file.

No sooner had they made straight for the trailhead than they encountered a group of Manchurian infantry.

Master Fei-hung asserted himself to the front of the team. "Remember, defense only. Wear them down."

"Oh crap. This is not gonna be easy." Darcy grabbed Ling and Jones by the arm and pulled them close.

Ling reached and pushed Jones's arm away. "Let me

have her. I cannot transfer if you are holding onto her arm."

Jones broke away. "I will be right here."

Roark took up his position on the other side and stood as tall as he could. He ruffled his red curls and made a grunting noise.

Several soldiers also stood up straight, heads cocked to one side. As the infantry once again prepared to charge, the monks slowly and deliberately formed a line with the master at the center. Darcy pushed herself up against Ling's back and held her breath. Just as the attack was about to commence the monks began to chant Om, causing confusion among the ranks of the military.

The soldiers held off for a moment, regrouped, and then their leader called out to charge. The battle began and chaos reigned. They fanned out and managed to surround the monks.

Using ancient martial arts techniques, the monks separated the soldiers from their weapons.

Darcy could feel Ling's expectancy and gave in to the transfer. She found herself moving from snake position, to stork, to tiger, while Jones performed the shadowless kick to deflect spear after spear.

It took less than four minutes to disarm the entire group of enemy soldiers who were exhausted but unharmed. Roark and Tall Tree once again used the power of their size and voices to scatter what was left of the military. Only Ling suffered a small cut on her arm.

"Are you okay?" Darcy took Ling's arm into her hands.

"It is a small cut. I am fine," Ling said. "Thank you for your concern."

"Okay, that was pretty cool... but now I feel like I'm going to pass out." Darcy leaned into Jones, who picked her up and started out with the rest.

Snow took the lead and Bamboo brought up the rear. They travelled the eight *li* back to Po-chi-lam Temple where many of the devotees greeted them at the gate and rescued them by creating invisibility through sameness. The team quickly disrobed from their town folk disguises and donned their robes.

Master Fei-hung led the others into the gym. "We must remove any suspicions. I am sure the commander will not wait until morning to push through the gates. We must move around with as little provocation as possible. Ling, you must leave immediately for *Nanhua Si* Temple, in the *Qujiang* District. I will send Hong-li, Great Strength, with you as your traveling companion. I have sent Ying to announce your arrival. You must dress as peasants. Change quickly and see me before you leave."

Ling and Great Strength left for the cloakroom to recover ordinary clothing hidden for just such occasions. They quickly changed, pulled on their conical hats and returned to Master Fei-hung.

"You are one of my favorite children and a very special devotee. This poultice will heal your wound. A close friend of mine will assist you in *Nanhua Si*." Master Fei-hung sighed. "I will see you in six months' time. If the way is clear, I will bring you home. If not, we shall have tea together and talk of old times." Wong Fei-hung bowed low.

Ling ran forward and wrapped her arms around the master. "I will wait impatiently until we are reunited." She wiped a tear from her cheek. She then approached Darcy and Jones. "I am grateful to have met you, Darcy. Jones, you are a brother to me. I shall remember you always. I am saddened that I cannot be here for your wedding." She bowed

"Hey, if you can hug the master, then shoot, why can't you hug me?" Darcy took Ling by her arm and pulled her into an embrace.

Jones waited and then spoke, "You are my favorite and only sister. If I can, on my next occasion to travel to Boston… may I take a message to your brother?"

"Yes please, tell Ma Chun that I miss him and I love him dearly." She spoke softly. "Explain that I have gone into hiding for now."

"I shall." He held her tightly. "You must be off then. Take remarkable care of yourself and Hong-li. Even strong men need taking care of on occasion."

"*Nihao!*" she called out as the two of them left by a hidden opening in the back wall.

✿✿✿✿✿

"I'm sad. I'm torn up over all of this. How can I have this experience and then just walk away?" Darcy asked.

"Am I to understand you are not ready to return to Snohomish?"

"I'm just saying… I don't know what I'm just sayin'. This experience, even if it scared me to death, and even knowing it may not be over just yet, I'd feel strange showing up in Snoho after this. Never mind, this is just me babbling on."

Jones opened his arms and she came to him. They stood rocking back and forth while the others talked about the night's activities. "I get the distinct impression you may want to stay a bit longer."

"Well, methinks I should learn Hung Gar." Darcy said, casting a glance at Roark, who was standing alongside Tall Tree in the courtyard. "That's the best I got."

Jones chuckled. "Ah, yes, Roark. I need to return him to

Hiva Oa. That means for a few minutes you will here on your own. How do you feel about that?"

"I can hang with Snow and Bamboo. Geeze those two are, wow... what can I say?" Darcy sat down on the steps leading to the inner sanctum. "I don't want to become a monk but, man, to have those kinds of abilities."

"Your ability would be different I am sure of it." Jones took a seat next to her. "Am I hearing you correctly? You are giving credence to the idea of training?"

She nodded her head. "It would take months, huh. *But* if we go back at the same time we left no one would be the wiser, right?"

"How would you explain the haircut?"

Several monks stopped in front of Darcy and Jones and bowed. "*Zhù fú.*"

"*Zhù fú,*" Darcy said, smiling broadly.

"We need to make a decision. If we are to stay, we must both shave our heads immediately and don robes. It would be of the utmost importance that we follow every advice afforded us. I am sure Master Fei-hung will welcome you with great interest."

"Shave my head. Hmm, I would look like Ling and Snow... and Bamboo and the other women. Dude, now that's what I call a sistahood."

"We shall approach Master Fei-hung after I return from Hiva Oa. I will collect Roark for a good-bye."

"Okay, I'll be right here."

"I am inclined to encourage a close proximity to both Bamboo and Snow while I'm gone. Should a circumstance arise that they are needed."

"I hear ya. I'll stay close to them."

Jones retrieved Roark after he said his goodbyes to the

rest of the team. Tall Tree once again patted Roark on the head, eliciting a blush and a warm smile. They shook hands and then hugged.

Roark stepped over next to Darcy. "Me can't wait ta see ya as a married woman all thick with child."

"Hey, easy there buddy. I got some travelin' to do before settling down with a child." Darcy embraced Roark. "I'm gonna miss you. I love you for coming to rescue me. I'll always remember our crazy night in Foshan." She broke the embrace. "By the way, tell Gauguin I said hi."

Jones had retrieved the Atomotron and his journal from his room. He toggled in the coordinates and the time for Hiva Oa and assisted Roark into the straps.

Sunday, 20 June 1892 2:00 pm
Atuona, Hiva Oa Island, French
Polynesia

The serenity of Hiva Oa was a sharp contrast with the Po-Chi-Lam Temple. The two materialized on the beach edge as a slight breeze blew Roark's curls back over his forehead. The crisp clean air, the emerald green waters, and the lush mountains wooed the hardiest souls to try to relax and succumb to the life of an islander.

"Roark, my friend and companion, you have given me a greater appreciation of what true love can be among friends. You have risked your life for a part of my own that is irreplaceable. Darcy is my true love and I can never thank you enough for what you have accomplished on my behalf." Jones stepped back and forth in the sand.

"Dun't believe 'is'll be the last time we see each other. Methinks a hug is good and fer sure 'at we'll get together soon."

"I do not see any good reason not to get together in the future. For now my dear friend, I must bid you farewell. I am anxious to get back to Darcy."

After they embraced, Roark backed up and like other occasions he witnessed his best friend disappear right before his eyes on his way back to China, in the year of 1884.

❀❀❀❀❀

As Jones reappeared, he became aware of Darcy sitting a few feet away on the steps to the temple. She jumped to her feet and ran into his arms.

"Was Roark sad? How's Gauguin doing?" She bobbed alongside Jones. "Is he still living with three girls? Did anyone ask about me?"

"Where to begin. Roark may have indeed been sad. I know I was; however, he is not the type of man who displays his emotions. Gauguin was nowhere to be seen. I am sure the six hours he was here, at least in their minds, would not be a sufficient amount of time to establish new relationships. And I did not see anyone else from the village but had I, I am sure they would have inquired as to your whereabouts."

"You're pretty good. Let's go inside. I feel like I'm constantly being stalked from the tops of buildings."

As Jones and Darcy took the steps up to the inner sanctum, they heard a commotion from behind. Jones did not bother to look back because he recognized the sounds from before. Silent Wind ran next to them, along with Snow and gestured for them to follow. The foursome took a new route this time down several steps into a cellar where Silent Wind and Snow pushed aside shelving, exposing what appeared to be a crack in the back wall. However, when Silent Wind stepped on a stone in the floor, previously hidden by the shelving, the crack widened. Snow clutched the edge and pulled, but failed to budge the enormous door. Jones hurriedly joined her and between the two, they managed to free the opening.

"Quickly hide in here. You will be safe. We will return, as soon as possible, to retrieve you." Snow placed her hand on Darcy's back to usher her forward.

"Can we have a lantern or something?"

"No. The soldiers would smell the oil burning and become suspicious. There are only two air holes, so rest, meditate, and we will return soon."

"In the complete dark? I don't even wanna know what kind of bugs might be in there." Darcy peered around the edge of the stone wall opening into the dark empty space.

"When you close your eyes, are you not in complete darkness?" Jones asked.

"Well, yeah, I guess so, but I'm rarely in a cave at the time, dude." Darcy took a few steps forward, turned around, and quick stepped out into the light again. "You go first and I'm right behind you."

Snow and Silent Wind began pushing the massive stone, assisting Darcy in making her decision. She and Jones stumbled forward into the emptiness and waited. Darcy heard her own labored breathing.

"How long do you think we'll have to wait?" Darcy raised her hand to where she thought Jones's face would be and touched him lightly.

"I should think as long as it takes for the commander to satisfy himself that we have fled the monastery. I can assure you there will be drawings of us posted all over southern China."

"Well, I hope they draw my good side." Darcy scooted closer to Jones. "You wanna make out?"

After a long silence, Jones put his arm around her and said quietly, "Certainly, why not, we have time."

They broke off their kissing when they heard muffled sounds coming through the wall, like objects thrown with great force against the opening.

Darcy scrunched under Jones's arm and pulled her legs in tight. "Jones," she whispered. "I love you and I always will, no matter what happens."

"And I you. Suffice it to say these monks will do

everything in their power to make sure no one is harmed and that they harm no one… except as a last resort."

✿ ✿ ✿ ✿ ✿

"This should take a couple of days to clean up." The commander grinned, then waved his men to the gate to return to Foshan. "And you had better hope and *pray,"* he said sarcastically, "If ever I find out you lied to me, I will cut off your head myself."

He pushed past Master Fei-hung who stood calm and silent with Bamboo, Silent Wind, and Tall Tree by his side.

In the midst of the chaos, the monks had gone about their business as if nothing frightful had taken place. As the soldiers exited the destroyed rooms, devotees immediately began to clean and straighten up the mess.

"We must be vigilant. He only needs a slight provocation to attack the temple. For now, he has convinced himself that Time Traveler and Darcy have fled with Ling. They will be looking for three. Go and bring Darcy and Time Traveler to me."

From inside the cave Jones and Darcy heard sounds, then the wall moved and slowly opened. The light seemed especially bright after sitting in complete darkness. The cellar room appeared untouched.

"I am curious to know what the multiple thuds were against the wall." Jones stood, with his hands on his hips and chin raised.

Silent Wind put the palm of his hand out in front of him. "Some of what you heard was the sound of wooden boxes filled with tools, being thrown against the wall to break them. Their anger is for show, mostly, but it intimidates the town's people. For us it creates tasks that we do not normally attend to, so it makes life more interesting."

"You guys are strange. I mean... I like you 'cause you're so cool, but you say some of the weirdest stuff."

"How so?" Silent Wind asked.

"You were practically invaded this morning and you liked that it broke up your daily routine. I just think that's funny."

"Master Fei-hung would like for you to come see him now," Snow said.

"That doesn't sound good." Darcy looked at Jones.

"Did the master express his concern to you?"

Snow stopped and turned back to Jones. "He will tell you everything when the two, eh three of you are together."

"Okay, now I'm a little concerned again. Silent Wind didn't smile. Snow has barely looked at me. What's goin' on?"

"I assure you..."

"No... I don't mean that I expect you to know. It's a rhetorical question."

"I believe it is safe to say that was not a rhetorical question."

"Ouch. Spank you very much." Darcy quickened her pace to keep up with Jones.

"Rhetorical means to speak using language to effectively please or persuade another. Your question was 'What's goin' on?' I hardly think that qualifies."

"Damn, ouch again. What's goin' on here? Are you okay?"

Jones halted. "I am tired and suddenly discombobulated... I am feeling very human right at the moment."

"Welcome friend." Darcy reached out to shake his hand.

"Welcome to my world."

They approached Master Fei-hung who seemed unusually quiet. "I am saddened to report that a traveling monk has approached the gate with news that a peasant man and woman trying to pass themselves off as monks collecting alms have been beheaded on the highway to *Nanhua Si* Temple, in the *Qujiang* District. I fear it may have been Hong-li and Ling. I will dispatch others to confirm."

"Master, are you not able to see what has happened?"

"I am only able to see a certain distance. Beyond that I am as ordinary as the rest of you."

"This can't be happening," Darcy said. Her stomach knotted and churned. "I don't like how I'm feeling right now. I feel responsible for all this."

"This would be a good time for the two of you to join forces in meditation. You may both reside in Time Traveler's room."

Jones and Darcy clasped hands and set off for his quarters. Jones threw open the door and walked straight to the cot, shoving the Atomotron out of sight. "I, too, am saddened to hear this news." He turned to see Darcy with her head in her hands, crying. He sat next to her and pulled her in close. "This must be very difficult for you to comprehend. Life in these times is precarious at best. When Master Fei-hung refers to being vigilant, he understands that life can seem tenuous to many and should never be taken for granted."

"I've got to be honest. My life back in Snoho is so fantastic by comparison. I didn't realize just how much I took it for granted until now."

"When we return, you will have changed a great deal. People will notice that you are somehow different. You will seem calmer and more powerful, but they will not understand why."

"I really do miss home. I may have changed my mind about staying."

"That is your prerogative. I will support whatever decision you make." He took her by the hand and led her over to the cot. "Can we lie here together? I would very much like to simply hold you in my arms."

She stared into his silvery blue eyes. "I think that would be very nice. Why can't we go back to Snoho and come back before Ling's death and change everything around?"

"It has not been established that Ling and Hong-li are dead. If indeed they are, I am not sure they can be saved. That bridge is down the road and we will cross it together at the appropriate time."

They dozed off in each other's arms.

A light knock on the door startled them.

"Yes, come in." Jones rose to his feet, followed by Darcy.

Master Fei-hung entered the room. "Have you made a decision concerning your stay with us?"

"I'm not sure. I was planning to stay until I heard about Ling and Hong-li, but now I feel we should think about getting back home. I don't want to be the cause of more tragedy."

"I understand." Master Fei-hung bowed. "Snow and Bamboo have requested to speak to you privately, if you feel comfortable. This is not of my doing. They approached me before I came here."

"Eh, well, I guess." Darcy reached for Jones's hand.

"What harm could it do to speak to them? Perhaps their want has nothing to do with you staying or leaving."

Darcy directed her attention to the master. "When do they want to meet?"

"Soon. When the decision is made, I will have the barbers

shave your hair from your head so that you may blend in among the others."

"So this does have to do with me staying." Darcy stood and paced around the room full circuit. "All right. Let's get this over with. I have one question though. Master, if I change my mind at a later time, can I take Jones and go?"

"You are always free to travel," he said, taking her hand. "Perhaps we should have a quiet ceremony this evening to declare your *jing* official. That would allow the two of you to remain in the same quarters."

"Are you bribing me?" Darcy smiled and bowed to Master Fei-hung. "Where will I find them?"

"You should remain here. I will send them to you." Fei-hung returned the gesture and left the room.

"Jones, tell me honestly what you think." She sat on the cot next to him.

"I think sleeping with you whether here or in Snohomish is a great honor." Jones smiled.

"No, I get that." She laughed and pushed him. "What I want to know is whether or not I should shave my head and train with the master."

"I can contribute little to your decision, but can express that I too felt ambiguous when I first arrived. My life has been remarkably different than it might have been I should think and this is directly attributable to my stay here in Foshan. I do not believe I could have accomplished as much on my own and most importantly, we never would have met."

"So, wait a second. Does this mean that I get a Hung Gar name to bring to life? Whoa, that would be freakin' awesome. Plus, I would get my black belt? Geeze Louise, what kinda girl would I be in the end? Okay, I'm talkin' myself into this, but what about the hair?"

"Perhaps you can start letting it grow in before we return."

"Sure, and I can tell people I got it cut to do something really different. I was tired of the same ole thing."

"That sounds more than reasonable. Which establishment did you use, because someone is sure to ask."

"Good thinking. Let's see. Clearview, I got it cut at the place in Clearview."

Jones rose and peered down the hallway, where he found Snow and Bamboo only a few feet away, coming towards him. "*Nihao*. I am about to make myself scarce while the three of you talk over the ramifications of Darcy's decision."

The two female monks smiled and bowed. They glided past Jones into the room and closed the door behind them.

"Yes," Jones said to the closed door. "I shall be out here if you need me." He leaned against the wall and stroked his chin.

"So, guys, what do you want to talk about?" Darcy sat on the floor, joined by Snow and Bamboo.

Bamboo spoke first. "Master Fei-hung has related that you have an interest in becoming a student of Hung Gar. We are here to evaluate your motives."

"The training is rigorous and even more so for women. The master will have high expectations of your commitment. He believes that women should have an equal place among the men." Snow closed her eyes. "He is a kind and gentle soul, but a taskmaster when it comes to training." She opened her eyes and looked straight at Darcy with a penetrating stare.

"Are you reading my mind? Is that also one of your attributes as you call it?"

Snow maintained her gaze. "I am looking to see your

reaction to the information that I am sharing. You seem calm."

"I'm surprisingly calm, given what's in front of me. I want to understand what you know. *And* I want to know what my attribute might be. Does he know ahead of time?"

"Your attribute is something that comes naturally to you. It is in your nature now, but less manifested than it could be," Bamboo said.

"Hell, I have no idea." Darcy leaned back on her hands. "Do you?"

"We do not. You will begin to understand as you train. The master will know when you know. It is at that time you will begin to practice how to best bring out your attribute and use its full potential."

"But only if I stay. I'm not usually this flustered, but this is a big decision for me. I'm still not sure how we'll work out going back. How would I explain?"

"This present life is but once to live. It is most important to live it in peace and harmony. You will learn to center yourself so that peace and harmony involves all who you meet."

"Yeah." Darcy paused in thought. "Will I change so much that my friends won't recognize me?"

"You will be a different but a better version of yourself. You will live without fear," Snow said. "It would be appropriate for you to meditate on your answer."

"When you have made your decision, let us know. We will be at your service to assist you in any way we can," Bamboo said.

"So, did I pass the interview?" Darcy asked.

Snow smiled at Bamboo. "Ling recommended you for training should you want to join us. Bamboo and I find you fascinating and want to learn from you as well."

The two rose and bowed. "*Nihao.*"

Jones stood as they walked past. "*Nihao. Zhù fú.*"

✿✿✿✿✿

As Jones closed the door to their quarters, there came a light knock.

"Geeze, Grand Central Station," Darcy groaned.

"Enter," Jones said.

Master Fei-hung pushed the door open and joined them. In his hands were two rolls of parchment that he laid on the cot. "These are the ceremonial commitments I planned to use this evening. If you choose to use these you will need to study several passages."

"We want to honor you, Master. If these are of your choosing, then we will abide."

"Darcy?" Master Fei-hung said. "Are you also in accordance with Jones on this matter?"

"Actually...eh, well, eh...what... how would you feel if we wrote our own vows. That's what everyone is doing in the future."

Jones spun around. "As long as you are not offended, Master."

"I am in agreement with Darcy. Since you come from different centuries and different cultures, I believe flexibility is key to the success of your marriage. I have no claim on the rites of how two people wish to demonstrate their love for one another. It is done. The ceremony will take place in front of the altar in the inner sanctum at sunset."

"Seriously? We've got a lot of work to do." Darcy started pacing back and forth. "What will I wear? Jones, I can't wear this. As great as it is, I wore it while in jail."

Master Fei-hung smiled. "Snow and Bamboo will assist

you with preparations. This is your night and they want to make you feel beautiful. Trust them."

"And myself? I only have jeans and a regular shirt," he said to Darcy.

"I'm sure that Master Fei-hung can come up with something. Right?" Darcy said.

"I believe Time Traveler will be very handsome in the traditional wedding attire of the Chinese groom. You have one hour and then we must get started. A fire is warming your water for your bath."

"A bath? That's awesome. I need a bath in the worst way."

Jones glanced at the master. "Just go along with what she says. I find it most interesting but confusing sometimes."

Fei-hung smiled. "I understand a great deal more than you might think. I will send Snow for you shortly, Darcy."

✿✿✿✿✿

Snow stuck her head just inside the room. "Your bath is waiting."

Darcy kissed Jones, walked to the door and stopped abruptly. "Don't forget to work on your vows, buddy. I'm already working on mine." She leaned against the doorjamb.

"I believe my vows were written long before we met. It is because we are sharing this moment that they will flow forth from the millenniums where they laid dormant until now."

"Wow, nicely put, sir. See you soon. I love you." She disappeared into the hallway.

Three monks stood waiting, just outside, to escort Jones to his bath.

"The ceremony is underway." Master Fei-hung bowed low and left.

Darcy and the other two stepped into the bathing room, lit

by a plethora of candles, where a small wooden tub filled with steaming water waited. The warm and relaxing atmosphere filled her with calm. To her surprise, Snow began to lift the *Qipao* over Darcy's head.

"That's okay I can get it," Darcy waited for a moment. "I got this. I've been bathing myself since I was a kid."

Neither woman moved.

"Okay what's goin' on here."

"We are your servants for the ceremony. You must not lift even a finger in preparation for your wedding night."

"You guys aren't planning on coming along all night, I hope."

They smiled.

Bamboo stepped forward and once again took the hem of the *Qipao*. She lifted the garment slowly and gently over Darcy's head. Darcy covered her body as best she could.

"Have you never been naked in front of other women?" Snow asked.

"No. I don't think so. I can't remember ever being completely naked in front of a woman."

"You are most beautiful and should never be ashamed." Snow tested the water. "Is this the right temperature for you?"

Darcy short stepped her way to the tub keeping her arm over her breasts and her hand covering her privates. "OMG. That's perfect." She suddenly realized she had let her arm fall from her breasts. "Sorry. Okay, so I'm a little shy. Can you turn around while I get in the tub? Just in case I fall over or something."

Snow and Bamboo snickered but did as requested.

Darcy lowered herself into the small wooden tub, immersing herself in the warmth. "Oh, this feels so good."

Snow picked up a cloth and walked to the tub.

"Oh no. I definitely can do *that* myself." Darcy scrunched down in the water.

"Very well." Snow handed her the washcloth and poured a small vial of oil into the tub.

"Can you guys wait outside for a few minutes? I'll call you when I'm done."

"We cannot leave you, but we will meditate while you bathe," Snow said.

The two women assumed the Lotus posture, and closed their eyes.

"So, I guess singing would be totally out of the question." Darcy looked in their direction but there was no response.

After bathing, Darcy rose from the tub and stepped onto the tile floor. She retrieved a neatly folded robe from the shelf and pulled it on herself. "Okay, you can open your eyes now."

Snow smiled broadly and Bamboo laughed.

"That is a man's robe. Look how big it is. You will not wear that for the wedding anyway." Bamboo jumped to her feet. "Come, let me show you your wedding gown." She took Darcy by the hand.

Snow and Bamboo opened a wooden closet, and there before them hung a white floor-length *Qipao* embodied with colorful cranes. On a cloth lay long dangling gold earrings, a gold necklace and shoes that looked like ballerina slippers. Draped over the neck of the *Qipao* were white leggings that rose to mid-thigh.

"Wow, so beautiful." Darcy's eyes were wide with joy but then her expression changed. "I can't. I just caught a glimpse of Ling in my mind." She slumped back against the edge of tub.

"You must know that Ling would have wanted it this

way." Snow lifted the gown from the closet. "Ling had a very special affection for you after your time together in the detention center."

"But how would you know that?"

"When you went with Bamboo and Ling went with our group, she talked about you with all of us. She felt sure you would benefit from living here for an extended period of time to discover your attribute. We feel the same."

"But this is about the wedding. I don't feel right celebrating a wedding after such horrible news."

Bamboo sat next to Darcy. "Ling held much affection for Time Traveler. They had a past together, a rich and loving past. He was her other brother, she, his only sister. This is the honorable thing to do. You must celebrate with Ling's smile in your mind."

Darcy sat quietly for a moment, mulling over her words. "Then tonight has to be celebrated for Ling. I need to get my sh— stuff together and do this." Darcy undid the robe. It was the first time ever she had stood naked in front of other women.

Jones had finished his bath and begun the process of dressing for the wedding. Doa, Hung Gar name Cobbler, along with Dun also known as Shield, and Shui, meaning Water, assisted him. Master Fei-hung had assigned them as his valets. Cobbler removed a waist-length bright red *Qipao* with gold trim from a hand-carved, dark wooden box and laid it out on a table next to the tub. He then laid out the matching red hat also trimmed in gold, black knee length pants, gold satin leggings that bound his calves, and black slippers with black leather crisscrossed straps.

"What a remarkable outfit." Jones smiled and held the

Qipao up to admire the embroidered handy work. He turned it around and found a large image of a tiger sewn into the back of the garment.

"Thank you. It will be remarkable if it should fit me well."

"This belongs to Master Wong Fei-hung. He wore this when he married his first wife."

"First wife? How is it that he is no longer married?"

"She crossed over when she was young. The disease was too great to arrest. He would be honored for you to wear this at your wedding."

"And so I shall."

Jones stood with his arms out. Shield and Water raised the garment and eased it over Jones's head and muscular body. Jones placed his hand on Shield's shoulder and stepped into the black pants stretching them tight around his well-defined thighs. Water then cinched the pants at the waist. They wrapped the gold satin leggings tightly around his large calves up to his knee. Jones lifted one foot and then the other as Cobbler slipped on the wedding shoes. Shield tucked the last of the golden legging into itself, followed by the black leather crisscross strap.

"Surely these do not belong to Master Fei-hung." Jones held in the *Qipao* to get a better look at his feet.

"No. Those belong to me." Cobbler smiled. "I am in charge of making footwear for new monks who join us and repairing shoes that have worn out."

"The fit is excellent. You are a remarkable smith."

Cobbler smiled broadly. "It is an honor to provide footwear to my fellow monks. I can cut a pair just by observing the foot. I no longer need to measure."

"It is obvious to me that you very much enjoy your task."

Shield placed the hat on Jones's head. The three monks chortled when they saw the hat was too large.

"Perhaps we can pin it in the back," Water said. "Fold over at the edge here on this seam." He took the rim of the hat, made a vertical fold and used a clip to hold it in place. "There, that is better."

Jones turned about.

"Master Fei-hung will be very pleased. Your appearance is very much Chinese."

Shield put his hands together, in front of him, as though to pray and bowed, followed by Water and Cobbler.

"Gentlemen, you have made me a very happy man."

The sanctum had been transformed into a wedding hall and although the guests were not biological family, they were nonetheless the witnesses to the commitment that Darcy and Jones were about to make. In an impressive display of color, hundreds of prayer flags hung from the ceiling. Each monk sat next to candleholder with a lit candle, which would burn during the ceremony. A temporary altar sat in front of the shrine, covered with incense and candles.

Water approached Jones. "Master Fei-hung will act as Darcy's father. We must escort you to the altar in a few moments."

"I am both excited and nervous. I did not think I could ever experience this depth of affection for another. She is my life and will soon be my wife."

Shield stopped him short and looked him up and down. "You are very handsome. You will do well this night. Find your chi that you may merge with Darcy's. This experience is far more sensual than anything you have yet to experience."

Jones bowed.

The four took to the hallways and the side entrance of the sanctorum.

The monks moved fluidly as they escorted Jones through the catacombs to the entrance of the inner sanctum.

"This seems out of a fairytale." Jones turned full circle to admire the grandeur.

They reached the altar where more than one hundred monks sat quietly in perfectly aligned columns; a sea of orange illuminated by small candles. Their calm demeanor and shadowy faces, etched with joy, made his eyes well up. He had been among these brothers and sisters only a year ago in their time, but seemed a lifetime ago to him.

Sword raised his hands and pulled them into his chest. The devotees began to chant the Om, the voluminous sound filling the hall and raising the hair on the back of Jones's neck. The energy washed over him and he could hardly contain himself.

Slowly a wave of quiet ensued and all eyes turned to the left. Darcy, on the arm of Wong Fei-hung, promenaded forward in her white *Qipao*, translucent veil and leggings, more beautiful now than Jones had ever seen her. Master Fei-hung proudly escorted her to the altar. He invited Jones to stand next to her, while he took his place. Master Fei-hung lit several sticks of sandalwood incense and placed them in a holder. He rang a small bell to signal the commencing of the vows.

Master Fei-hung bowed. "*Zhù fú.*"

"*Zhù fú.*" The crowd responded.

Jones and Darcy walked slowly to the front and turned to face one another.

"At the request of Time Traveler we are privileged to witness a love that transcends both time and space. And even as our brother and sister are from the future we welcome them to our present. At the request of Darcy, they will each share their personal vows as they do in the future world. We are here to bless this *jing* and send them off into their future together with strength and a life free of fear. *Zhù fú*."

Master Fei-hung assumed the Lotus posture with the rest and waited quietly.

"You go first," Darcy whispered with her head bowed.

Jones chuckled and began, "This is a part of you I want to treasure for all eternity. Your openness and childlike approach to life are most inspiring. Your fierce honesty and loyalty are truly trustworthy and I am confident these characteristics will bolster our most unparalleled adventures, and most importantly our marriage. I do love you with all my heart and soul. You have brought a joy to my life that if not for you, I would not have otherwise known. Darcy Champagne from Snohomish, Washington, 2012, will you be my wife in accordance to universal laws of attraction, across space and time, for as long as we both shall live?"

"Wow, yes, yes!" Darcy said as she lifted her veil exposing the absolute joy radiating through her smile and eyes. "I'm vibrating, like ten times more than when we... sorry, ha, a little nervous here." She glanced in the direction of Master Fei-hung, then Bamboo and Snow all who smiled back at her. Bamboo waved with the back of her hand.

Darcy continued, "Time Traveler, you've become my best friend. From the moment you landed in my backyard, I knew there was something oddly attractive about you. It was when you pulled off the goggles and I looked into your silvery blue eyes that I instantly knew we were going to marry. I would have waited until the end of the universe to be right here and now. I love you with every cell in my body. I cannot wait to share our wedding bed tonight." She turned to Master Fei-hung. "Is that okay to say?"

He smiled and nodded.

"Anyway, Jones Whitman, aka Time Traveler, will you do me the honor of becoming my lawfully wedded husband according to the laws of time travel, because you have traveled over time and space to be here right now. And really, if you think about it, where else can you be? Sooo having said that, will you marry me?"

"Without any hesitation whatsoever. May I kiss the bride?"

"Can we do that?" Darcy asked.

Fei-hung nodded.

The two embraced in a kiss that left them swirling in a timeless space. Everything disappeared apart from the kiss that sparked a raging desire between them. They broke free from their embrace to find a horde of smiling monks surrounding them, offering congratulations and small gifts of incense, cloth, Buddha statuettes, oils and tea.

"Thank you all so much for being here and for your loyal friendship. Without it this couldn't have taken place." Darcy stepped out into the front and turned to bow. "*Zhù fú.*"

The festival continued for two more hours and included a special meal, music, and a closing Om meditation. As the monks cleared the area, Jones and Darcy prepared to take their leave.

"Master Fei-hung, this has meant the world to me. Thank you so much for sitting in as my father. He would have been so proud." Darcy started to bow but instead hugged the neck of Master Fei-hung.

"Thank you, Master. You have assisted me in becoming a whole man, uniting two streams… yin and yang. I hold you in the highest esteem. If I may?" Jones approached for a hug and, to his surprise, Master Fei-hung smiled and accepted.

Jones took Darcy by the hand and led her back to *their* room, all the while chattering about what a wonderful experience they had had.

"It's weird, ya know. No family, but I got to admit this was way beyond what I expected. Master Fei-hung is a powerful man to command such an undertaking and have it done so quickly."

"He is apparently a professor of the proverb 'many hands make light work'. It was truly amazing to see so many assembled in one place."

"Where do they all go during the day?"

"They are out and about, engaging in many tasks. Not to mention how similar in appearance they are, so perhaps you *see* less of them." Jones halted pulling Darcy back. "We are here. Shall I carry you over the threshold?"

"If ya think you can handle my *Qipao*."

"I think I have made that clear in the past."

"Look at you gettin' all double entendre on me." She giggled as he picked her up into his arms and lightly kicked open the door. "What the heck is this?" Darcy jumped out of Jones's arms.

"It would seem that Master Fei-hung has thought of everything."

"This is like twice the size of the cot." She laughed and clapped her hands.

"This is the traditional bridal bed." Jones sat. "I must say this bed is far more comfortable than the cot."

Darcy pulled back the covers to discover pink satin sheets and two packages wrapped in red containing an assortment of fruits and spices.

"Wow. Feel these sheets."

"Well, Mrs. Traveler, what shall we do first?"

"Hey, I've been through a lot ya know. Been waiting on this day for a while now." She stroked his cheek. "I love your eyes. They make me swoon ya know."

Jones set her down on the bed. "There is a ritual to our love making."

"Oh yeah, and what does that look like?"

"I will start with yang energy by stroking your wrists and then moving up your arm to your shoulders and neck. I will remove each piece of clothing, one at a time, while kissing the entire area until you are completely naked."

"Mmm, that sounds pretty cool." She smiled coyly. "Dude, are you making this up?"

"Not in the least. It is the Chinese instruction for the wedding night."

"And an excellent instruction it is." She extended her left hand. "You may begin."

Jones removed his *Qipao* exposing his rounded chest and strong muscular arms.

Darcy watched as he removed his leggings and pants, admiring the tattoo down his left forearm. Once naked, his thick thighs made her heart quicken.

Jones knelt and began by stroking the back of Darcy's wrists with his fingertips… dancing, glancing his way up her arms, lightly touching, causing goose bumps to rise. He lightly kissed her forearms and the back of her hands, pulling her to her feet. He removed her *Qipao* and massaged the nape of her neck using small circles as he moved to her shoulders and then to her breasts, caressing her firm flesh.

Darcy sat on the bed and leaned back on her hands. She could see sweat begin to shine on Jones's face. She sat naked from the waist up admiring her husband.

He removed her slippers and gently caressed her feet. "Lie back." He tugged the bindings from her leggings. He loosened the covering on her left leg and unwound the cloth slowly as he gingerly kissed her exposed skin with each turn. Without taking his mouth from her body, he made his way to the tip of her toes and tossed the legging to one side.

"Oh my, what do we have here?" She gripped him, moaning softly and writhed under his touch.

He continued his slow sojourn of butterfly kisses her right leg. Jones slid his powerful hand to the inside of thigh and massaged lightly, dragging his fingertips down her leg and under her calves, caressing her lovingly. "Sit up and I will undo your hair." He massaged her neck while tenderly kissing the nape of her neck. He then pulled the braided rope from her bun allowing her thick hair to fall around her shoulders. "Stand," he said as he pulled her up.

She could feel his warmth against her stomach.

Jones eased her back onto the bridal bed and lay next to her. He rolled onto his side and kissed her deeply, holding her face in his hand. The energy between them soared back and forth seeking where it was most natural to be. The room filled with panting, moaning and then the merging of two torsos into one experience as they thrashed about in a frenzy of exploration. Jones caressed her breasts as she rolled on top, throwing her head back, eyes half closed.

"Jones," she panted. "Tell me… you love me… right… right… now! YES!"

"I do… I… love you forever."

They held each other tight, sharing soft kisses and whispers of love, pulled the covers over their resplendent bodies and slept.

Sunday, 14 June 1884, 9:00 am

Jones and Darcy's room

The next morning Master Fei-hung arrived with a solution he thought would work for everyone involved should Darcy decide to remain as a student of Hung Gar.

"I have considered exceptions to the traditional expectations of my students in order to accommodate Darcy. They are in no way meant to sway your decision."

"Why me?"

"I have conferred with my top monks and we believe you have a gift that will be needed to allow the Buddha to enter deeper in everyone."

"Really? And what would that be?"

Jones clapped his hands. "Darcy, I think we are on the edge of a new adventure."

Master Fei-hung took Darcy's hand. "I cannot tell you what it may be. However, we are of one voice in sensing you have an important contribution to make to humankind. We live to serve others. That is our bliss. We are certain you will serve a greater audience than even we can reach. This is for the good of all."

Darcy sat for a moment and then blurted out, "Well when you put it that way, what's a girl to do."

"Then we are staying?"

"I want to hear the exceptions." Darcy sat on the bed.

"All have agreed you will not have to shave your head. You will, however, have to cut your hair short and wear a conical hat at all times when outdoors."

"Is that like a clown hat?"

"No, Darcy, it is the hat most Chinese wear to keep the sun off their faces. It is a wide brim hat that comes to a point."

"Gotcha. Okay, I've seen them on the guys. So that's not bad."

"And we must bind your breasts."

"Eh, okay. That sounds a bit uncomfortable, but so far so good."

"Your training will begin with a meal at five thirty each morning."

"Ouch. I just remembered you telling me that back in Snoho." Darcy took a deep breath and let it out slowly. She looked at the floor. "So don't have to shave my head but must wear a hat, no matter what, in the courtyard... bind my breasts every day. So what about an exception to the five-thirty rule... say seven." She looked over Fei-hung. "I'm just kidding. Do I still get to sleep with Time Traveler?"

"Yes, of course, you are now jing. That is the way."

"Jones? Do you have any questions?" Darcy asked.

"Master, should an incident occur with the commander, will we be expected to participate in the defense of the monastery?"

"As always the choice is yours to make. You are an exceptional martial artist and we would welcome your contributions. Life is truly about the balance of yin and yang. The choice will be yours. Darcy, your training will begin tomorrow at five-thirty."

"I guess I should think about going to bed then."

"She is jesting. We will arrive on time. Thank you, Master."

"Master Fei-hung, thank you for this opportunity. I will

do my best."

"I believe you." Master Fei-hung took his leave.

When they were alone, Jones told her, "To my knowledge he has never made exceptions like this before nor has he allowed a student to participate without following the rigors of the creed."

"I'm getting that. I'm not going to question it. I'm going to go with the flow for once."

Monday, 15 June 1884, 5:00 am

Jones and Darcy's room

In the dark sleeping quarters of their room, Jones awoke first. He rose and lit the lantern casting a shadowy warm glow against the walls. He no longer felt the need to dress before waking Darcy.

"Darcy, my sweet love, it is time to rise."

"It's barely light outside," she moaned and attempted to roll over.

"It is five o'clock by my watch. You have thirty minutes to perform whatever you need to do in order to commence with your first day of training."

"Training? OMG, did I actually say I would do this? What's wrong with me?"

"You will be fine. After a few weeks, you will automatically awaken at five o'clock. Your biological clock—

"Honey, not now." She pulled the covers over her head. "Holy crap, this is my first day of training." She jumped out of bed, wrapped the binding and dressed in the gi left for her the night before. "Why didn't you remind me?"

"I believe I did. But no matter. Are you excited?"

"I have no idea what's gonna happen to me. So I think I'm closer to being scared than excited." She turned to Jones. "How do I look?"

Jones chuckled. "You are the most beautiful Hung Gar student ever."

"Okay, just keep saying that." She hurried about the

room, hopping on one foot, pulling on one slipper, then the other.

"I must confess that is a remarkable talent."

"Let's get outta here."

They hurried to the dining hall for a quick breakfast and then to the gym for Darcy's first day.

"I am convinced that you will be a strong and powerful Hung Gar student. Good luck to you on your first day."

Darcy winced. "Good luck? I don't know if I like the sound of that."

"You will be fine. Bamboo will take good care of you."

Jones had his own training to continue and said his goodbyes. He left Darcy with Bamboo who was smiling and giggling at her antics.

"*Nihao*," Bamboo said. She pulled Darcy to the side and asked, "Are you ready for your first day? The first day is not difficult. Master Fei-hung will expect you to perform certain exercises but nothing more… and meditation, lots of meditation. Mostly he will expect you to watch carefully the work of the others who have come before you." She lay on the floor to stretch. She bent forward touching her nose to her knees.

Snow joined them "Good morning. I want to assure you that everyone works at their own level. However, most work at a pace that ordinary people would have difficulty matching."

"I was a runner back home, so I know what it's like to push your body. It's usually my mind that gives up first."

Snow sat next to Darcy. "You will find that meditation will assist greatly in approaching the most rigorous exercise as a whole person. You will become one force."

"You guys are killin' me. You sound… so intelligent.

The way you speak. I hope I can be as awesome as you are."

"We think you are awesome already. You must learn to focus your intentions for the greater good of all whom you encounter, good or evil." Snow stopped in front of Darcy and placed her hand on her shoulder. "We welcome you as one of our, how do you say, sistas." She smiled broadly. "Shall we begin? It is time."

"I am honored to be working with you. I will assist you in any way I can. You may need a massage after this day. Most definitely a hot bath." Bamboo giggled.

The three joined the many monks exercising different yoga postures, stretching out their muscles. Several at the other end of the gym were performing gymnastic aerials. As Darcy scanned the room, she attempted to discern the men from the women, a difficult task when all had shaved heads and the same uniform. She watched as a petite monk ran up the wall and grasped a bar that hung from ropes.

"Wow, that was cool. I've done that once, or at least Ling did, while possessing my body. He's a little guy."

"She," Snow said. "That is Zia. She is a formidable opponent and a long time devotee."

Darcy watched a tall lean monk lower Zia to the ground as she hung upside down. When her hands reached the ground, she did a handstand into a forward roll, and sprang onto her feet and into a stance. "That's intimidating. What's it called?"

Bamboo jumped into the same stance. "This is the Grasshopper. It requires strong legs. You will have no problem learning most of the stances. Your hard work will come when learning the Southern Fist. Your arms and hands must be like iron."

"Hmm… am I gonna come out of this all bulging with muscle?"

Snow eased her sleeve up on her left arm to show Darcy the results of many years of practice.

"Your arm is beautiful. Geeze your tattoo's so cool."

She ran her finger along the edge. "When we women are all together, naked," she laughed, "you will see the results fully."

A bell chimed at the front of the gym and all activity came to a halt. Master Fei-hung had entered the room to begin the day's class. Everyone assumed the Lotus position at arm's length to the side and front. Every movement was executed without talk. An immense quiet filled the gym.

"We welcome the new students."

In unison the group called out, "*Zhù fú.*"

"We will begin with meditation." Master Fei-hung sat at the head of the class on a covered stool. Although it was no more than a foot tall, he towered over everyone in front of him.

After five minutes, Darcy thought, *This isn't so bad.* After thirty minutes, she thought *Okay, I get it. Can we move on to something else for Pete's sake?* She began to fidget.

"You may stand. The first day is difficult." Master Fei-hung's voice soft and reassuring.

"Did you hear me? I mean, did you read my mind?"

"I read your body." He sat next to Darcy.

"When do I get my hair cut?" Darcy whispered.

"On your third day," he responded in a soothing voice.

She cupped her hands around her mouth and leaned toward the Master's ear. "Why the third day?"

"That allows you two days to decide if this is your calling. You will discover in two days if you have the mettle to run the full course. As a runner you have discipline; however, you lack focus of spirit. Our journey together will provide a plan, such that your daily routine will be a source of joy rather than work."

She nodded. "Finding my bliss. Thank you, Master."

She stood, shook her legs, walked in a small circle and then restarted her meditation. *I can do this. I'm going to do the training. That's my new mantra.*

After meditation, the group gathered for lavender tea at the back of the gymnasium. In silence, each person took a small cup and waited patiently for their fill. As Darcy approached, she leaned in close to the server and asked, "What kind of tea are we having?"

She could feel the energy in the room shift and turned slowly to see the others staring at her.

"Sorry," she whispered. She made a mock pistol with her hand, pointed it to her head and fired. She got the distinct impression, by the odd expression on their faces, that many of the devotees found the gesture disturbing. She turned back to the server and received her tea.

The training resumed with the horse stance, moving from side to side into deep squats.

"You will be seated as I call you by day, then months, then years. When seated, clear your mind of any thought that is not relevant to accomplishing balance. "We will begin by squatting to the right. *Kāishǐ* and hold. . and left... hold."

. She watched Bamboo and Snow squat to mere inches above the floor, while her legs began to tremble and ache. *Geeze Louise, this is painful.* She placed her hand on her knee for support and suddenly felt the sting of a small cane against her arm. "What the..." she mumbled, glancing back to recognize Master Fei-hung. She removed her hand and pushed through the pain. She had not anticipated the extent of this mental and physical exertion.

An indescribable half hour had passed when Darcy finally heard the rescuer's voice, "Day one, be seated."

Thank god. Darcy breathed out heavily. *Ah man, I'm gonna be feelin' this tomorrow.*

She sat, stretched forward to loosen her back, then turned onto her side and grasped her foot, pulling it behind her to lengthen her thigh muscle. She flipped to the other side and repeated. Two other first day recruits sat in a meditative state. *How can they do that? No stretching? No way.* She lay back and closed her eyes to meditate.

"You must sit up. If you do not, you will miss the opportunity to advance yourself." Master Fei-hung strolled away between the rows, checking students as he went.

Advance myself? What does that mean?

Every minute or so, he would announce another number and a group would sit to meditate. Soon, about forty monks were still holding the position as he called right and left. Each individual moved in harmony with the others in a slow dance of precision and grace.

"You may be seated.' Master Fei-hung walked casually through the students, commenting to several. Once at the front of the gym, he resumed. "Everyone stand. Choose a partner for the first kata of Hung Gar combined with Southern Fists."

Darcy grabbed Bamboo by the sleeve. Bamboo grinned and nodded.

"Using your limbs as defensive weapons requires that you harden the bone in your arm and increase your grip for full control so you do not harm your opponent. Make a tight fist at your side and on my command thrust your arm upward so that your forearm is angled above your head, like such." Master Fei-hung demonstrated by having a senior monk strike him with a board across his forearm. Master Fi-hung not only broke the board but also snatched the remaining board from the monk's hand. He bowed.

A board? No way, José. That's gotta hurt big time.

Bamboo showed Darcy the movement and then waited for the master's command.

"Ut!"

Darcy thrust her forearm skyward only to have Bamboo use her own arm to strike a blow.

"Ow, ow, ow, ow," Darcy cried as she spun in a circle holding her arm. "Man does that hurt."

"Shhh," said Bamboo, taking Darcy's arm and rubbing it vigorously.

"Ut!"

Darcy withdrew her arm and glared at Bamboo.

Bamboo giggled and grabbed her wrist. This time she hit it lightly. "You will toughen up very soon," she whispered. Bamboo repeated the exercise several more times, alternating arms at the master's command.

"You will move through a series of postures and stances. Each defense movement is intended to wear your opponent down. Use their energy to defeat them. The advanced students will teach the newer students. Begin with five elements. Move from eagle to grasshopper. Repeat slowly so that you may integrate these stances and transitions with your whole body and mind."

Bamboo took Darcy by her hand. "We may speak now while we are exercising. So the first stance is the five elements."

"Seriously, you hurt my arm. I'm gonna be bruised to high heaven tomorrow," she said as she examined her arm.

"You must pay attention. Stand with legs more than

shoulder wide. Turn your upper body to the left and drop back onto your right leg, like this. Keep your knees bent and present your left arm with your fisted hand extended and your right arm fisted at your side. Now you."

Darcy spread her legs and squatted. "Oh that hurts. I'm feeling those side to side squats. Okay, so back on right, body turned and like this?"

"Yes, that is the correct position. Now stand and repeat the movement until the master calls us to sit."

The two stood side by side repeating the movement many times before the master called, "*Tíngzhǐ*. It is time to eat a small meal."

Grateful for the break, Darcy grabbed her conical hat and jogged over to the dining hall with the hope of seeing Jones. From a distance, she could see him standing and chatting with several other monks. "Jones." She ran up next to him. "Master Fei-hung is kickin' my butt. I'm gonna be so sore tomorrow."

"What have you learned so far?"

"That my arms are going look like hell tomorrow. That upper block is a killer on this bone. Bamboo has some hard-ass, sorry, hard bones in those little arms."

Jones laughed. "I assume you will continue this afternoon?"

"Oh yeah. I may be a wimp at the moment, but if Bamboo and Snow can do this, not to mention Ling, so can I." She quickly looked away. "I miss Ling."

Jones took her hand. "I understand. We should go inside for our meal. It will keep you strong for the afternoon."

"What do you think will be my attribute?" she asked while holding the brim of her conical hat.

"I am sure whatever your feature, it will be amazing."

They gathered with the others who were chitchatting about tasks that needed attending, and who would be seeking alms later that afternoon.

"So big boy, what've you been up to? I didn't see you at the front of the class. Where were you this whole time?" Darcy eyed the meal with uncertainty. "What is that?"

"Wilted bok choy with rice and what appears to be a *gailan*, another green vegetable and fish, it would seem." Jones spooned a helping into his bowl. "And to answer your other query, I used my morning to read through the notes in my journal. I am truly amazed at the progression from spending the days with Roark in Boston, confirming my calculations to build the Atomotron and landing in your backyard. As well as the fact that you and I must have sensed from the beginning that something special was afoot. You were so incredibly kind to me... and trusting."

"Yep, I had a feelin' something good was about to happen and man, am I glad you screwed up those gears."

"I do not follow your thought."

"I liked you from the beginning, even though you looked a little weird in the goggles and dustcoat. You were so damn cute."

"May I say the same about you? But there were no screws in the gears."

Darcy chuckled. "No, screwed up means that you bent the gears and broke the time machine."

"I think I see." Jones rubbed his chin. "I did indeed *screw up* then."

The offering vessel arrived and Jones took a bit of his food, touched his fingers to his forehead and placed it in the bowl.

"But only the machine, everything else you got so right,

dude." Darcy followed suit with her gift to the vessel. "Thank you." She returned her attention to Jones. "I have a day and a half to make up my mind. I'm thinking with all the exceptions that Master Fei-hung has made, I'd be a fool not to take him up on a once in a lifetime or two, opportunity. Unless we travel even farther back and start over. I could have… never mind."

"That is an idea I need to meditate on. I will discuss it with Master Fei-hung at some point."

"What's that?"

"What could occur if we were to travel back to one's own past? Can you be present with your younger self and if so, would you not have a shared mind experience? The way that—

"No, don't say her name. Please, I don't understand how these monks can seem so indifferent to what has happened to the two of them."

"I do not believe that is the case. They want confirmation before emoting. I believe that to be reasonable course of action."

"So you guys don't believe the man who came to the gate?"

"He provided as much information as he could. The master dispatched others to confirm the identities of the two in the beheading. If the circumstances should be true then there will be much mourning. The monks will perform a ceremony to assist the energy of the deceased to find its way. If possible, we will recover Ling and Hong-li for cremation.

"I see, so don't cross the bridge before you get there."

"You cannot cross before you arrive at the footsteps of the bridge no matter what state of being you are in."

"Yeah. A hard lesson to learn."

Once the appointed monks collected everyone's bowl, everyone began to scatter to their assigned locations. Darcy waited in the hallway with Jones to steal a kiss, threw on her conical hat and headed to the gym. As she crossed the courtyard, she noticed several others walking in the opposite direction also wearing conical hats. "*Nihao*." She pulled her hands together at her chest.

"*Zhù fú*," they responded.

Darcy smiled as she walked on. She could feel her comfort level changing and a joy in her core. When she arrived at the gym, Bamboo and Snow were waiting for her just outside the door.

"You have done well." Snow patted her on her back.

"Really 'cause I'm thinkin' I'm pretty much a wimp." Darcy laughed as she rubbed her thighs and forearm.

Bamboo placed her hand on Darcy's back. "I think you have much potential. You move with grace once you understand the dance. You will be a great fighter should the occasion arise."

"Wow, thank you, Bamboo. That's a much appreciated vote of confidence."

Bamboo giggled. "This afternoon will make you humble."

"Wow, thank you again, Bamboo." She placed her hand on Bamboo's head. "I am so not looking forward to being humbled." Darcy took a deep breath and said, "Okay, ladies, let's do this." Darcy followed Snow with Bamboo, bringing up the rear.

They bowed three times to the shrine as they entered. Bamboo and Darcy took their seats while Snow headed to the very front and took a seat among monks who had changed into white leggings with black bindings and loose fitting tunics.

Master Fei-hung asked them to stand in the front of the audience to perform the first kata in full. One student would attack, while the other would defend against the onslaught.

"The first kata is a demonstration for all to remember." Master Fei-hung bowed to the group of six.

They paired off.

"Ut!"

The battle began with the attacking side using their bodies as weapons. The monks on the defense moved fluidly, making full contact with their opponents. The two closest to Darcy seemed to be handless as their movements blurred with a continuous foray of strikes and blocks. The defender backed away, little by little, in full control of his adversary. While the onslaught was fierce, the defender caused exhaustion in the aggressor without receiving a scratch. Another pair used several stances in their fight. One of the assailants demonstrated the frog leap, jumping to head height and attempting to come down on top of his opponent. The opponent assumed the drunk pose and slid from underneath, leaving the attacker to grab at air and then hit the floor.

Darcy and Bamboo turned to watch the last pair who had backed almost to the corner of the gym in a struggle that felt too real. The sounds coming from the two made her adrenaline rush. The defender turned and ran sideways along the wall, laughing. He made funny noises and pointed at the attacker. The attacker, tired from the battle, also started laughing. Then the others began to laugh.

"What's going on?"

"It would seem that Tu may have passed gas in the middle of the fight; thus, Chung is running away."

"Geeze, that's a horrible attribute," Darcy said as she held her nose.

Bamboo pinched her own nose and chuckled. "You are a funny girl."

Meditation resumed for another thirty minutes. When Master Fei-hung rang the bell, everyone stood, bowed three times to the shrine and dispersed.

"Will you be joining us for a bath? We bathe once a week and it is our turn tonight."

"Once a week? Are you kidding me?"

"How often do you bathe?" Bamboo asked.

"Every day?" Darcy cowered a bit and scrunched her face.

"You must have servants," Snow chimed in.

"Nah, what I've got is plumbing."

"Where can we get some of that?" Bamboo asked.

"Not sure. I think it's gonna be awhile." Darcy pulled on her conical hat. "I'm going to meet up with Jones and then I will join you. So, where do I go?"

Snow glanced back over her shoulder. "The bath is on the other end of the gym. I know you will hear us when you are close." She bowed.

✿✿✿✿✿

The two female monks walked away in the direction of their quarters. Darcy continued toward her room, making her way across the courtyard and through the broad doorway, without looking up at the buildings across the street. She felt proud of her discipline. In another time, she would have been unable to muster the strength to continue walking without peering underneath her hat to see who stood on the rooftops next door.

"*Nihao*!" Darcy ran straight into Jones's arms as he stood outside their room. "I'm going back to the gym to take a bath with the girls. I am so in need of a bath and did you know we can only bathe once a week? Luckily we have a few days before we start to stink to high heaven."

"I am certain the rule applies only to devotees. I will ask Master Fei-hung when next I see him."

"Oh man, that would be great. I mean I would feel guilty but…"

"Not to worry. These people have dedicated their lives to emulating the Buddha and bringing about world peace and harmony. They do not come into this life lightly. So I should think rather than envy you they will rejoice in whatever makes you happy."

"How incredibly cool is that?"

Darcy opened the door to the room and there on the bed sat a stack of gi and several tunics and robes. "That's a relief, I tell ya. At least I can change into some clean clothes. I don't suppose there's a Laundromat around the corner."

"Pardon? What is a Laundromat, pray tell." Jones took a seat on the bed next to the garments. "And do I even want to know?"

"Sure you do." Darcy bounced onto the bed next to him. "It's a place where you can wash your clothes in exchange for money. You can do them yourself, or leave them and pick them up later."

"Our garments are collected, washed and returned to us, folded and the price is a thank you for their consideration."

"Wow, okay, so that's an even better deal for sure. What's for dinner?"

"Breakfast tomorrow morning. There is but one full meal, remember?"

"No snacks? Nothing?"

"Not until we rise tomorrow morning for porridge and lavender tea."

"Dang. Those rice and veggies are lookin' really good about right now."

"Perhaps the bath will assist in taking your mind off your stomach. In a short period you will adjust and this will become your routine for the next few months."

"Yeah," Darcy said slowly. "Okay, I'm off to spa with the girls."

Darcy and Jones rose and shared a kiss. Then Darcy disappeared out the door.

Jones pulled the time machine from under the bed and checked the charge of the batteries by flipping on the switch to a low speed setting. As he turned the switch, he could hear the familiar tone coming into range and immediately backed off. After stashing the Atomotron again, he searched Darcy's bag for the remaining batteries to make sure he would know exactly where they were.

He picked up a book of the Buddha's teachings and sat quietly reading.

⚙⚙⚙⚙⚙

Darcy heard voices coming from the other end of the dimly lit gym. She jogged slowly, feeling the pain in her thighs as she crossed the floor to a small opening. She entered the crowded room bathed in the warm glow of candles. The steam from the tubs engulfed her. There before her were several tattooed women moving about, swirling the steam as they passed. The skin on one woman's back was almost completely covered with Kanji characters, while another had striking tribal symbols emblazoned across her shoulders and upper back.

"Your tub is here." Bamboo came out of the fog and took her by the hand. "How are you feeling?"

"I'm actually not feeling that bad. But, that's not to say

I'm gonna turn down this bath, mind ya. Those tats are fantastic by the way," she said as she disrobed and stepped into the warm caress of lavender oil and hot water. She slowly immersed her body, decompressing as she slid deeper. "Oh man, this is good." Darcy closed her eyes and felt the relief in her thighs and arms.

After a few minutes of relaxation, a voice filled with angst interrupted the chatter.

"We need to hurry," Snow said. "I have just come from Master Fei-hung and he is calling a meeting of all monks and wants you and Time Traveler there as well."

"Ah man, timing is everything. Not a chance that I can skip this one, huh?"

"No. You must dress quickly. If there is time afterward we will return."

Darcy stepped from the tub and received a cloth that she used to dry off. She threw on her new robe with a sash that she cinched around her waist.

"Good thing for the sash, cause this bugger is a bit big."

"It is not for looks. It is for warmth."

They left by the side door to join the many others who had gathered outside the main entrance to the gym. The monks began to line up.

Bamboo found Darcy and Snow and joined them in line for their turn to enter.

Darcy looked around and saw Jones coming toward her. "What's going on? Do you know?"

"Whatever it is, it must be very important. To gather at this time is highly unusual."

"Yes. It must concern us all," Snow added.

"I am filled with curiosity." Bamboo shuffled forward with her head bowed. "I hope this is about Ling."

Darcy felt her heart lurch. Her eyes stung as she was overcome with emotion. "I sincerely hope you are wrong." She clutched Jones's hand while glancing at Bamboo.

As each person passed through the opening, they were handed a lighted candle to place halfway between their leg and the next person. After they were seated, Master Fei-hung walked out of the shadows at the head of the gym.

"I have news that I believe you will find encouraging. In recent minutes, another monk seeking refuge approached our gate. He handed over a note from one Ling Lee and Hong-li Chun who had sent him here. I inquired as to the amount of time that had passed since he saw them last and he reported it was last night. This most certainly means the two who were beheaded were not our Ling and Hong-li. *Zhù fú* on those poor souls who were killed."

"*Zhù fú*," everyone called out.

"I feel sorrow for the two who were beheaded but I am very grateful and happy that Ling and Hong-li are alive," Bamboo said.

Snow's head was bowed and her hands were in front of her chest. She prayed quietly and rapidly.

"Jones?" Darcy stared into his eyes. "I like this bridge."

"I can safely assert that I am indeed happy to be on the other side of this span."

"In celebration of life, we shall sing Om as a way of sending our energy to Ling and Hong-li."

Darcy joined in and sang loudly while tears streamed down her face.

Jones held her close and then helped her to her feet. "We should return to our room and celebrate. I will ask for some cherry wine. We can read together or... we could make out," he said, laughing .

Tuesday, 16 June 1884, 5:15 am

Po-chi-lam gym

Darcy left early for her workout. She entered the gym determined to do better than the day before. She joined the others, stretching her legs and squeezing a ball of satin to strengthen her forearms and hands.

"You are here," Bamboo said. "You are supposed to wait for us to summon you, for your safety."

Snow did not look pleased.

"Oh. Sorry I didn't get that. But I can see how that could be a good idea since el commandante could just burst in at any time." Darcy looked up at the two who stood over her.

"It is important that you follow the requests Master Fei-hung has put forth." Snow joined her.

"No problem. I can do that. I just thought I'd get here early and get in some extra time stretching. Believe me, I need it."

Bamboo slowly spread her legs, easing her feet farther and farther apart into a full straddle split. She then brought her legs together in front of her and stretched out her lower back.

Snow leaned forward until she lay flat against her knees with her hands wrapped around her feet.

"Man, do I have a long way to go." Darcy attempted to touch her nose to her knees but fell just short. She felt a pair of hands gently pushing her.

"In the next few weeks you will be as flexible as these two."

"Jones, what are you doing here?" She lifted her head and turned to the side. "I'm so glad you... will you be working out with us?"

"Yes. I am part of a demonstration this morning."

"Who are you paired with?"

"There will be six opponents and I will be blindfolded."

"That ought to be awesome." Darcy pulled her right foot next to her hip and lay back, stretching out her thigh. "Why blindfolded?"

"Not all combat manifests in the most ideal conditions. A battle may sometimes take place as it did when we rescued you. With little or no light, you must *see* with your mind."

"Gotcha. Can you come join me after the demo?"

"I will ask Master Fei-hung."

A gong rang, everyone bowed three times to the shrine and then assumed a Lotus posture for meditation. Jones glanced in Darcy's direction and smiled.

She leaned in and whispered, "This is a total blast, thank you."

The thirty minutes passed peacefully in Darcy's mind, leaving her relaxed and centered.

There was another tam-tam and Master Fei-hung took his place, standing on his stool. "Today we begin with a demonstration of focus. The exercise will assist you in becoming one with your opponent. Time Traveler will be blindfolded. He will defend himself against six adversaries. Time Traveler, students, let us begin."

Jones rose and bowed. He walked to the front where a monk tied a headband around his eyes. He waited until his assailants slowly surrounded him then dropped into a horse stance, locking his tight fists by his sides. He moved his head slowly from right to left as he gathered energy information from his opponents and spun around just as the first assailant lunged forward. At the last second, he sidestepped his adversary and with a sweep of his foot, caused the young man to flip forward into two other opponents. Suddenly, he felt the grip of his gi pulling him backwards. He adjusted his trajectory by flipping his body over breaking the grip from his gi and pushed forward on his strong legs, causing the monk to tumble backwards.

To his right Jones heard the snap of a sleeve indicating that the aggressor intended to strike from above his head. He threw an upper block, gripped the wrist of the young man and pulled him into a bear hug, causing everyone to roar with laughter. Each warrior had tried to lay a strike on Jones but none landed a single touch.

"Ut," Master Fei-hung called out.

Jones removed his blindfold and bowed first to the students and then to Master Fei-hung. He quickly returned to his seat and waited for the next instruction.

The remainder of the day was dedicated to hand-to-hand combat, alternating between strikes and defensive moves.

"Dude, you were amazing today." Darcy flopped onto the bed. "I'm exhausted. By the way, did you ask the master about bathing?"

"I was unable to broach the subject. Devotees surrounded him all day. As compensation, perhaps I could convince you to allow me to massage your entire body, Mrs. Whitman?"

"Oh, that does sound delicious," she mumbled with her eyes closed and her breathing shallow. "Can you help me out of my..."

"Darcy?" Jones smiled, pulled the sheet over her and gazed at her while lovingly stroking her hair. "Tomorrow this

will be much shorter. I shall miss it until it grows in again."
He lay next to the bed and stretched out the day's rigorous
exercise.

✿✿✿✿✿

"Hey," she said quietly. "I think I missed my massage.
Was it good?"

"Apparently you were in need of a nap more than
anything else. I can begin now if you like."

Darcy sat up in the bed. "Can you help me out of my gi?"

"Absolutely."

"Wait. Let me brush my teeth first." Darcy returned, and
again sat on the edge of the bed.

Jones knelt in front of her and untied the square knot. He
gently opened the gi top exposing the binding that girdled
Darcy's breasts. He slipped the top off her creamy colored
shoulders, kissing each of them. "I adore you," he whispered,
his breath hot on her skin. He then pulled the end of the
binding out and raised her arms to unwrap her.

With each turn, Darcy felt an excitement growing in her
stomach.

Jones slowed as he reached the last turn, savoring the
moment and finally letting the cloth drop to her lap.

She felt vulnerable and had the urge to cover her breasts
with her hands. As she moved to do so, he placed his hands
over them and gently kneaded. "That's a great way to start a
full body massage," Darcy said with her eyes closed and her
head tilted back. "And you're not bad at it either." She smiled
coyly, placing her hands on his and looking him in the eyes
while they enjoyed the sensation of each other's touch. "This
is very sexy." She leaned forward, placing her lips on his.

He greeted her advance with enthusiasm, mirroring her
dance and kissing her deeply and passionately. He rose to his

feet and stripped away everything between them.

Darcy lay back and Jones pulled her gi bottoms off in one move, leaving her naked on the bed.

"Massage still?" Jones tilted his head, the way he had the first time they sat on the couch together in Snohomish, with that puppy dog look she so adored.

"Yes, of course. That's what we can call it from now on." She giggled as Jones joined her in the bed.

✿✿✿✿✿

"Do you recall what today is?" Jones combed her hair with his fingers.

"Don't tell me it's your birthday." Darcy was still under the covers.

"No, not exactly, but it is a day of rebirth. Today you will meet your barber. Unfortunately, he only knows one style, at which he is very good mind you, but I am not sure if he has any other ideas in his quiver."

"Ah, he's a shaver kind of guy. Well, when I was a kid my mom cut my hair for a while. I don't think he could match that humiliation."

"I cannot be sure." Jones rubbed his chin. "Perhaps we could inquire of Bamboo or Snow as a possible substitute barber. However, I am convinced that he is the only game in town."

Darcy sat up. "When're they gonna want to do this?"

"I am assuming this night. It was an evening when several consecrated monks escorted us into a small room illuminated by candles. We each took a turn under the razor. The change was remarkable."

"I could see how you would say that. My head is weird though, shaped strange. I have this flat area, it's just weird." Darcy rubbed the back of her head. "I am so glad Master Fei-hung made an exception. Talk about humiliation. Scary head methinks."

Jones approached Darcy and embraced her. "I will endeavor to query Master Fei-hung concerning bathing. I will see him before exercises begin."

She stroked his cheek. "Aww, you're so good to me."

"And you were so very good to me last night. I must admit that type of pleasure was not afforded me on many occasions and you have surprised me beyond expectations."

"Anytime, big fella."

"Really?" Jones smiled.

"I wasn't talking to you." She glanced downward then stared up into his eyes.

"We must leave. Seriously, we must take our leave in earnest." Jones stepped away from her. Darcy moved toward him and he held up his the palm of his hand. "Please. My constitution is failing me at the moment, and we have obligations. Do not act as a temptress for my sake."

Darcy halted and opened her gi top. "I'm just sayin'." She shrugged. "Some other time then?"

Jones took another step toward the door. "Soon, yes, soon would be very nice, but not now."

"Then let's go. You're just hanging around here with your mouth open and ya look funny."

✿✿✿✿✿

They went into the dining hall and found a seat. Each ate their fill of porridge, and drank their tea.

Snow and Bamboo joined them at the end of the meal and walked with them to the gym. .They bowed three times to the shrine and sat as a group closer to the back wall. Everyone continued to stretch until a gong rang, bringing all to order.

"*Zăo ān. Zhù fú.*"

"*Zhù fú.*"

"We shall work today in Tai chi chuan. We start with meditation."

Jones straightened his back and closed his eyes, while Darcy attended to a foot cramp.

She looked at the stool where Master Fei-hung usually sat but then saw he was standing next to a monk who was gesturing towards the gate. *Uh oh, crap, not again.* Darcy scanned in all directions. She reached for Jones and motioned with her head towards Master Fei-hung.

Jones immediately jumped to his feet, taking Darcy by her hand. He caught Master Fei-hung's eye and pointed to the cellar.

Bamboo and Snow joined them.

Cloud quickly caught up to them just as they were descending the stairs.

"Would you be so kind as to tell me exactly what is afoot?" Jones asked.

"There is a company of soldiers marching in this direction." Cloud offered his arm to steady Darcy while traversing the steps to the basement. The cave-like structure would once again offer them a safe retreat. Cloud and Snow pushed the door shut and quickly ran to another part of the monastery to allay suspicion of one hiding place but communicate suspicion of another. Should the soldiers take apart the suspected room and find nothing, all the better.

"This is getting ridiculous. It puts Wong Fei-hung and the rest at risk just for me to train. I feel stupid. Jones, say something or move around a bit so I know where you are."

"I believe you may be on to something important. You, I would think, should make arrangements to meet with Master Fei-hung to discuss this very issue."

"That's easy for you to say. What am I asking anyway?"

"If you should carry the burden of guilt for the choices these people make for themselves."

"My eyes are freakin' out. It's so dark. I mean blackout dark."

"Your eyes will adjust and your other senses will step forward to compensate for the lack of visual acuity. The circumstance will heighten your ability to visualize how the world must appear to a blinded person. Learn this and, should this room be filled with adversaries, you will know exactly where each is stationed and you can feel his intent."

"Is that why Master Fei-hung closes his eyes before he knocks the heck outa people?"

"When has he ever struck another, pray tell me. If one is damaged by oneself while attacking another individual, I submit to you that is the assailant's responsibility."

"Okay," she said. "Don't get your knickers in a knot."

For a moment, in the absolute dark and silence, Darcy could feel her anxiety begin to rise.

"I have decided not to ask you what that means."

Darcy laughed. She leaned back against Jones's chest and rested her head.

It was difficult to tell the amount of time that had passed but it seemed like quite a while. They heard the scraping of the stone door opening.

"What has occurred?" Jones stood at Tall Tree's side, while Ying and Silent Wind shut the door.

Tall Tree's bass voice filled the area outside the cave. "They marched right past the front gate on their way south. We thought perhaps they were coming here again, but no."

Silent Wind approached "In case, Time Traveler, you should ever have to hide when we are otherwise occupied, I want you to understand that the opening will only function as long as someone has a foot on this stone. This stone releases and unlatches, giving access to the room. That is why it is necessary to have several people to assist."

"I should think a handle on the inside would be advantageous." Jones leaned against the massive stone, rubbing his chin.

"Well?" Darcy asked.

"I have nothing. I cannot think of a single solution under these circumstances."

"Maybe grab the Atomotron and high tail it back to Snoho and McDaniel's for some super glue and a handle of some kind."

"This cave has been here for hundreds of years. It has always functioned well for us. I do not think a modification is due," Silent Wind said.

"That's the kind of guy he is, always trying to solve things. Anyway, so do we go back to the gym?"

"Yes. Classes in tai chi chuan are very important to strength and balance. It also teaches control. The slow movements, while used as exercise, can be sped up and become a powerful weapon."

With the massive stone door slid into place, everyone strode back to class, discussing the possibilities of the army invading the monastery.

Darcy listened intently and wondered if she would ever be ready to help in a fight to save the Po-chi-lam temple. Only time would tell.

The rest of the day, she worked with Jones, learning the basic routine for tai chi chuan.

"Bend your knees slightly and as you do, raise your arms in front of you, palms down. Let your fingers droop downward. Now take the full moon in your hands in front of you, right hand on top and the other cradling the bottom. Slide your hands over the surface slowly until you are cradling the moon with your left hand. Breathe in as you turn your body to the left while extending your left foot until the heel touches, rock forward…"

Darcy struggled to balance her body in the routine, not to mention her mind. She began to realize that it was important to her that she put forth a valiant effort to impress Master Fei-hung, but in doing so, her mind filled with chatter. She halted her exercise in order to meditate.

☼☼☼☼☼

After a day of moving very slowly, she was ready to sprint around the courtyard to expel some of her pent up energy.

She approached Bamboo. "So do you run? I would love to just take off for a good long run."

Bamboo giggled. "I will challenge you to a race, but it will be like no other you have ever run. Come with me." Bamboo took off jogging to the top of the monastery tower.

Darcy tied her conical hat down tight and caught her at the top of the stairs. "Okay, that felt good. But now what?"

"You must place your hands on the step below while your feet are on the stairs above. We will hand walk the entirety of the stairs to the bottom."

"Hey, wait a second. Look how tiny you are. There's no way I can do this."

"If you truly believe that, you have finished the race before you have started."

"Geeze, sometimes… Okay, so in a pushup position. I'm gonna kill myself doing this. Yeah, yeah, if I already know… let's just do this."

123

As soon as the two were underway, Bamboo started to giggle. "You look unusual."

"Oh, like you don't?" Darcy could feel her core tightening as she made it to the tenth step. "Holy crap." She lost her balance and fell to one side. "Ouch. Ah man."

"I will see you at the bottom." Bamboo wobbled down the steps. Close to the bottom, Bamboo suddenly saw a shadow cross over in front of her. Darcy had delayed waiting for the right time to jump over Bamboo to the finish line.

"You are a clever girl," Bamboo said.

"*You* are a monkey."

They both laughed.

Jones approached from across the courtyard.

Darcy said her goodbyes to Bamboo and jogged over to him.

"I have an answer for you. It would seem you have great favor with Master Fei-hung and, since you are not a devotee, he will allow you to bathe three times a week. I will be allowed to bathe whenever I like. So, on occasion, I would very much *like* to bathe with you."

"No way... that would be so cool. Hey, why me three and you get unlimited bathing?"

"As you have proclaimed before, men have not changed dramatically in one hundred years. He is attempting to allow us a privilege while maintaining certain decorum for the rest to observe."

"Hmm... maybe I'll have a talk with him." Darcy swayed back and forth.

"Darcy, on this matter, please, for my sake, I beseech you, do not buttonhole Master Fei-hung." He took Darcy's hand and started walking towards their room.

"Okaaaay, I'll behave, but my opinion of him has

diminished somewhat."

"Culture is framed by the time in which it is manifested. When we travel together, I believe it is our greatest asset to become chameleonic in our attitude about the culture we are visiting."

"When in Rome, and all that. No, I get it. So, how do I thank him for this?"

"I cannot answer that question. Perhaps by studying hard and performing at your best under his tutelage. He seems especially proud of his female students who do well."

"I'll do my best. I can see how this place changes you. It's weird, because it starts on the inside in such little ways." Darcy flipped around to Jones. "Hey, maybe we could do our first bath together tonight. Wouldn't that be cool?"

Jones resumed walking in silence.

"Not sure I like your answer. What's wrong?" Darcy asked.

"We are not here to become monks, and yet, there are times I feel we are pushing the boundaries."

"Hang on a sec. You don't trust Fei-hung to be honest. I mean that's the one thing I feel the best about. He says what he means and, for sure, means what he says."

"Perhaps you are… actually, you are completely correct. I must admit to you that in my haste to present the best of me to him, I often forget that he has always been consistently honest with me. Thank you, love. Now, with a better perspective, I feel confident that our bath tonight could be very entertaining."

"I've got a couple ideas myself."

✿✿✿✿✿

As they readied to leave, there came a knock at the door. Jones started. "Yes, who is it?"

"Snow and Bamboo."

Darcy opened the door.

"So soon?" Jones asked.

"It is time." Bamboo reached for Darcy's hand.

"Jones, I've been so wrapped up in my own stuff, are you cutting your hair as well?"

"Yes. But I will not have to shave this time. It will be cut close to my head and I will grow my beard."

"Uh oh, we may have to talk this over. I don't like scratchy beards. Just sayin'. That'll cut down on kissing," she said, wagging her finger in the air.

"The barber is waiting. He has four shaves tonight and would like to get started. He would like to begin with you, Darcy." Bamboo led her out of the room and turned left instead of the usual right.

The four followed a corridor, passing many rooms, moving deeper into the dorms where the devotees slept and studied. They reached a short set of steps leading to a well-lit room with padded chairs against one wall and another in the middle. Ancient Chinese symbols embellished the red and gold walls where a statuette of Buddha sat on a table. They performed the customary three bows to the shrine and to the barber during introductions.

"Darcy, this is Shaozu. His name means 'to honor his ancestors'. He is from a long line of barbers who have served other monasteries as well as Po-chi-lam." Bamboo bowed.

Shaozu smiled and pulled a razor from a wooden box that contained several different-sized metal knives with wooden handles. He indicated for Darcy to take the seat in the middle of the room.

Darcy released her grip on Jones and sat down. Her heart pounded, along with a ringing in her ears that took her by surprise. "What's the plan, Stan? I mean, Shaozu."

Jones watched with great interest, as did Snow and Bamboo.

Shaozu lifted her hair and ran his fingers through it. "Your hair is fine. It will be easy to razor cut."

Darcy felt the confidence in his tone and smelled mint on his breath. She decided to try to relax and let him work his magic.

He cut away lengths of her hair, stopping occasionally to step in front of her and hold her face in his hands.

"This is taking a long time," Darcy said nervously.

"Not much longer."

"Your haircut will be envied. It is perfect for your face," said Bamboo, giggling.

"I am very impressed," Jones said. "I believe this may become your choice for wearing your hair in the future. Shaozu, you have indeed honored your ancestors."

Shaozu opened a second box and reached in. He withdrew a rounded object wrapped in what appeared to be copper foil. He held it up to Darcy and turned it in his hand. Darcy looked at her reflection. Shaozu had layered her hair into a short cut, ending just above her ears and parted on the left side with a comb-over to the right. The multiple layers continued down the back of her neck, stopping just above her gi collar.

"Shaozu? You are the bomb. This has to be one of the best haircuts I've ever had." Darcy held the mirror to one side. "Whattya think there, Mr. Whitman?"

"I could not have imagined you with this style. And yet, it is most flattering."

Darcy rose from the chair and brushed away the lingering hair from her gi. "May I see myself one more time?"

Shaozu handed her the mirror and smiled. "I am happy to have brought you so much joy. Thank you for your trust."

Jones then took a seat. He knew the outcome would be difficult to embrace but necessary. Shaozu trimmed his hair close to his head leaving just enough to cover his scalp.

"Thank you, Shaozu." Jones ran his hand over the close-cropped cut and smiled. "We are twins." He rubbed Darcy's head with his other hand.

Shaozu bowed and called for the first devotee, who closed her eyes to meditate through the process. Within a few minutes, he had shaved her head clean.

Darcy said her goodbyes to Snow and Bamboo, and joined Jones on the walk to the room. "This feels so weird. My hat fits like a helmet now."

"You are adorable. I am a bit taken aback by your appearance. Although somewhat more masculine, it is also... very sexy. And I do like the way it feels when I run my hand over it."

"Jones, thank you. Thank you for everything. This is so cool."

✿✿✿✿✿

They returned to their room, gathered some clean garments and proceeded to the bathhouse. Master Fei-hung had arranged for heated water, candles, and lavender tea.

"I'm shameless, I tell ya. This is so nice. I feel like I'm on vacation." Darcy drew her hand through the warm water and began to disrobe.

"It would seem that living inside the security of these walls, where a daily routine occupies your mind, can bring an illusion of safety. It is far more difficult to live in the real world and practice a revered life. I sometimes have to check myself to make absolutely sure that I do not succumb to the illusion about myself and my place in this universe." Jones had been disrobing while sharing his ideas. He tossed his gi aside and turned to step into the tub. His glance met Darcy's and they stood naked, caressing each other with their eyes before she invited him to submerge into the warm bliss.

"Get in and I'll bathe you."

He climbed into the tub and sat with his arms over the edge and his legs spread, waiting for Darcy. "Are you coming in?"

"Oh, you betcha. I'm just admiring you for a bit." She smiled. " Jones, does this haircut turn you on?" She stepped next to the tub. "Oh my, I guess it does." Darcy climbed in and laid her head back on his chest.

"I am intrigued with your wonderful idea, but I feel certain we should wait until in the privacy of our room before lovemaking."

"Okay, I can respect that." She flopped the washcloth over his shoulder and sat up.

He saw her lip begin to pout. "Perhaps I was a bit hasty." He pulled her forward against his chest. "I believe we can engage in a tête-à-tête that would favorably increase our excitement in anticipation of what will commence upon the return to our room."

He pulled her mouth to his and inflamed her passions with a delicate, thoroughly sensuous kiss.

"You say the sweetest things. Now wash up and let's get back to our bedroom. I'm ready for some tête-à-tête."

They spent the evening exploring one another, trying different positions until they were exhausted.

Darcy lay next to Jones with her leg over his taut abdomen and her arm over his rounded chest.

They slept peacefully through the night.

As the many days passed, Darcy became more proficient at both Hung Gar and Tai chi chuan. She could sense a change in her core; even her voice sounded more grown up and confident. She loved the experience, but also found herself thinking about Snohomish, Taylor, her mom and even Crepe Escapes. She missed her coffee and music and looked forward to her return with Jones.

Jones strolled across the courtyard, on his way to return his book, and saw of Master Fei-hung sitting on the bottom step to the inner sanctum. He bowed and walked over to him.

Master Fei-hung patted the step. "Time Traveler, please sit with me."

Jones sat and waited.

"We must begin to explore Darcy's attribute. Do you have a notion of what it might be?"

"I do not, Master. Perhaps she needs reminding that discovering her attribute is all part of her destiny here at Po-chi-lam. Perchance that will push her to meditate on the possibilities."

"If you would be so kind and speak to her about her imagination. Ask her questions about power and compassion. As she meditates, she will have glimpses of her attribute and as you know, an attribute can have many faces. I would encourage her to keep her heart open for any message that might spring forth from her mental imagery."

"I will begin this very evening." Jones rose, bowed, and continued toward the monastery library. Upon his return to their room, he found Darcy returning from her second bath of the week.

"That is two for the week." He smiled. "Only one left.

Perhaps we should consider how to use your last bath and when?"

"Yeah, I know, but I really worked out hard today and I just wanted to feel the warmth of a hot bath. And guess what? I'm learning how to draw the water and start the fire. Tall Tree taught me. Sort of ironic in a weird way, right?"

"How so?"

"Tall Tree is in charge of burning wood for the baths."

Jones laughed. "I suppose so. I should think that would be a better job for Water."

"So how was your day, darling?" Darcy hung her binding on the rail of the armoire.

"I sat with the master who reminded me that it is part of your journey to become enlightened to your attribute. He has suggested we discuss your sense of the yin yang of power and compassion in human nature. Ask yourself what these terms mean to *you*. He also suggested we explore your imagination to determine what special quality you might manifest. When meditating, open yourself to messages that will assist you in that discovery."

"So when do we begin?" Darcy hopped up on the bed and sat against the far wall.

"We shall begin now, if you are in accordance."

"Shoot. Ask me questions." She leaned forward in anticipation.

"I am committed to assisting you with understanding yin as being the dark negative feminine principle that balances the bright positive masculine energy. Together they are the source of all things."

Darcy immediately raised her hand and dropped her head forward."Hold on there, bucko. So why is the *dark,* negative female and the *light,* positive male?"

"I admit the connotation is rather dubious; however, I suggest it is a reference to one half of a principle of a whole."

"I say a whole *lot* of dubious. For the sake of argument, and I mean between you and me, you be the dark part and I'll be the bright part."

"I am convinced I have failed so far to bring about a plausible discussion of Buddhism. The idea that there exists a whole, divided but integrated into…"

"Let's go to the second question." She leaned against the wall.

"An admirable idea. The second question has much to do with your imagination. When unleashed what images or scenarios come to mind?"

"Seriously? Well let's see. I used to think about time travel, but done that. People turning into clouds or snow, but I've already seen that. A guy growing into a tall tree. I think my imagination is weak compared to my reality at this point."

Jones laughed. "What about you? Do you think you might have an attribute similar in nature?"

"Dude, I really don't know. Growing up as you heard Taylor say, I collected strays. Stray animals and humans and such."

"Then perhaps that quality has an even greater purpose." Jones sat on the bed next to her.

"Like what? Like running a zoo and employing the homeless?"

"No, it will be mystical in nature."

"That's not fair. It takes a lot of understanding of animals *and* humans to…"

"Yes. Perhaps the elusive construct of your attribute may involve your extraordinary kindness toward animals who have been subjected to traumatic misfortune."

"Sure, okay, well… what the hell does that mean in the long run? I still don't get it."

"The possibilities are endless. I want to encourage you to meditate. Refrain from seeking out the answer but rather allow the answer to come to you."

"Right now?"

"We can meditate together."

"I still don't understand what meditating will accomplish, but let's do it."

They got into the Lotus position on the floor and breathed together. The meditation relieved her angst about the unanswered questions.

Darcy wanted nothing more than to receive her message. After a long while, she gave up. "I got nothing." She sighed. "I'm sorry, really I am."

"This is a process that can take some time. I did not know until Master Fei-hung gave me my name. We spoke of my imagination over the months while I resided here last, but nothing presented itself. Then the master asked me what machine I wanted to build. My reply was prophetic. I said if possible I wanted to build a time machine."

"Like Snow and her childhood memories of her favorite times with her family."

"I would assume as much."

"So, do you think I may be a shape shifter like Ying? 'Cause I'm thinking that could be really cool." She sat rocking and her mind filled with images of animals.

"Let your imagination roam free."

Wednesday, 17 June 1884, 4:00am

Jones and Darcy's room

There was a knock. Jones got out of bed and headed towards the door.

"Hey, big guy, pants?" Darcy reached to the foot of the bed and tossed them to him.

"I believe you have just saved me from an embarrassing moment."

"You mean a bare ass moment." She rolled over and pulled the covers up.

Jones laughed as he struggled to pull on his gi bottoms. He opened the door. "Bamboo? What is happening that you are here so early?" Jones leaned against the frame.

"I am here to collect Darcy."

"Why so early?"

"Master Fei-hung wants to speak to her. I am to escort her straightaway."

"Can you give us a few moments?"

"Yes."

Jones sat on the bed next to Darcy. "Master Fei-hung has asked for an audience with you."

She threw off the covers. "Doesn't this guy ever sleep? Sorry, I'm a bit cranky in the morning." She pulled on her pants. "Man, I just had a rush for some coffee from Crepe Escapes. Who's at the door?"

"Bamboo. She has come to escort you."

"Who the hell got her up to come get me? Never mind. Will you help me with my binding?"

"I can say, without a doubt, that binding these is an unfair task."

Darcy raised her arms and Jones kissed her breasts.

"Is it possible that you might consider becoming a nudist at some juncture?" Jones asked as he wrapped the cloth around her breasts.

"Only if we travel to some culture where nudity is the deal of the day. You're distracted and I need to hustle." She buttoned her top, pulled on her slippers and grabbed her hat.

"I am very curious about this visit. Make speed when you have finished. I will be waiting."

Darcy met Bamboo in the hall and quickly set out for Master Fei-hung's quarters.

"He has had a revelation about you," Bamboo said excitedly. "It came to him in a dream."

"Uh oh. Well, I hope it's a good one. My stomach muscles are feelin' the stairs."

"That will become part of your routine in a few weeks. You will be stronger as a result. Part of a strong defense is to be able to take a kick to the abdomen."

"You gotta be kiddin' me." She maintained pace with Bamboo.

"You will be so strong that you will not experience any pain." Bamboo turned quickly around a corner. "This way."

The two stopped and Bamboo knocked. The door opened and Master Fei-hung bowed.

Darcy did likewise.

"Please accept my apologies for the early hour."

"I accept."

Master Fei-hung laughed. "You are most charming."

Darcy jumped when she saw two other monks, standing behind the partially open door.

"What's this?" she asked.

"I cannot be alone with a woman without other monks present. That would cause confusion."

"Sounds reasonable." Darcy turned to them and bowed. "So you had a dream to tell me about? I don't mean to be impertinent, but couldn't this have waited until later? I'm sorry, that *was* impertinent."

"In my dream you are walking among tigers," said Master Fei-hung.

"Clearly, in your dream, I've lost my mind. What do you think it means?" Darcy eased a bit closer to Master Fei-hung and sat on the floor in front of his chair.

"What do *you* think it means? Close your eyes and tell me what you see when you imagine walking among tigers."

Darcy straightened her back and closed her eyes. "They are beautiful, I'm not afraid, I'm excited. They pay no attention. They seem calm and content. Yeah, and every face is completely different. Some are sleeping. I can pet them. Their fur is short and silky and their eyes are like pools of dark water." She sat quietly for another moment. "That's all I got." She opened her eyes.

"There is great power in your mind. There are two paths to take with the knowledge of that power. You may walk a dark path or you may walk an enlightened path. Each path is a part of the balance, therefore each serving its own purpose."

"I don't think I could choose the dark path. I barely like doing anything in the dark. So, I'm thinking an enlightened path. What do I need to do?"

"Like so many things in life, you must have the patience to allow it to come to *you*. You must open your mind and heart. Each separate and self-contained entity in this world is part of a spiritual whole but with its unique identity."

"We call it *energy* in the future. I'm sure it's the same stuff." Darcy sat wide-eyed, listening to Master Fei-hung, while the two other monks sat stoically to her right. "You guys gettin' this down, right?"

Neither moved.

"Never mind."

"You must believe in your destiny with your whole being. If you so choose, commit yourself to lightness, meditation, gratitude, honor, trustworthiness, and loyalty. I cannot be absolutely sure without your confirmation; however, my intuition has alerted me to a possibility that your attribute may be fellow feeling."

"What the heck is that? That just sounds wrong."

"It is the experience of one person to feel another's as if you are one and the same." Master Fei-hung reached down and placed his hand on top of Darcy's head.

"You mean like Ling. Wow, you think I might be another mind/body transfer girl?"

Master Fei-hung crossed his legs and closed his eyes. "It is not mind/body transfer, but as yet, I do not know in what form this attribute may manifest."

Darcy stood and bowed. "I'll let you get back to more important things."

"There is nothing more important than you at this moment. Your life will reveal a great truth. It will be resisted for many generations but in the end you will assist in expanding the Buddha nature in everyone and everything." Master Fei-hung stepped out of his chair and followed Darcy to the door. "Your attribute may be great empathy, which transcends the limitations of life's fragility. Perhaps you will bring a greater understanding of the whole for the benefit of those living in pain. The mind is a powerful driving force behind healing." He stood with his arms inside his sleeves and bowed as Darcy took her leave.

She hurried back to Jones as dawn began to lighten the monastery. The chill of the brick walls engulfed her as she entered the hallway. She scurried along the corridor and smelled porridge being prepared for breakfast. She entered their room to find Jones performing a tai chi kata.

"You're at it early."

Jones broke form. "What did the master have to say?"

Darcy jumped onto the bed and laid back. "He had a dream where I was walking among tigers."

Jones joined her. "That's rather provocative. Did he have an interpretation of the dream?"

"Not really. He had me close my eyes and asked me to walk among them to see how it felt."

"And?"

"It was wild. Every tiger had a different face. They were calm and relaxed as I walked around. It was a great feeling."

Jones lay back and turned on his side to face her. "What do you think it means?"

"Not sure, but I'm supposed to meditate on it and see if it helps me with my attribute."

"I see. The master must have been excited to have asked for an audience so immediately."

"He was or seemed to be. Sometimes it's hard to tell his happy mood from his other moods. He's pretty hard to read sometimes, ya know what I mean?"

"I have no doubt about that. Do you recall what you said to me when I arrived in Snohomish regarding strays?"

"Yeah, that I'm known for picking up lost animals and people and finding them a new home. Maybe I *am* meant to be a zookeeper."

Jones smiled broadly. "I do not imagine that being employed as a zookeeper will turn out to be your attribute. An attribute is far more powerful than a daily routine of caring for animals."

Darcy sat up. "Exactly what is that supposed to mean? Taking care of anything is really important."

Jones pulled her down next to him and gently stroked her cheek. "I have offended you and I did not mean to. I quite simply meant that when you discover your attribute it will be far greater than what you may be imagining."

"Kiss me."

"It would be my pleasure." He caressed her neck, allowing his hands to sculpt lightly along her shoulders and torso. "Your skin is lovely to touch." He raised the covers to allow her to snuggle in close. "I do love kissing your lips," he said as he devoured her mouth.

When they broke, she threw the covers back.

"I think your skin is lovely too..." She grasped him firmly in her hand.

"That is quite exquisite." He lay back and closed his eyes.

They made love in the shadows and light flickering on the walls cast by candles. Wrapped in his arms, they spooned and drifted off.

Jones awoke with a start and jostled Darcy. "Darcy, we must forego breakfast or we will be late for our daily routine. I have never been late. Make haste." He bounded from the bed and immediately pulled on his gi.

"Wow, that sounded a lot like what my mother used to say to me when I was in high school. But not those words exactly...at all," she said as she threw the covers back.

Jones handed over her gi, poured a small amount of water into the washing vessel, and quickly brushed his teeth. While

Darcy dressed, he squirted a small amount of toothpaste onto her brush and waited. She brushed, tied on her conical hat, and they left for the gym.

"Be open today for a sign concerning what power you may possess."

They stood facing one another just outside the gym.

"I will. And if it comes to me you'll be the first to know."

"I will miss you. I have a task to perform on behalf of Master Fei-hung." Jones scanned the area and gave her a peck on the lips.

"That was brave, you little trouble-maker. Now I'm all hot and bothered."

"I shall see you at the end of the day," he said with a wink.

Darcy watched as he strode toward the inner sanctum and wondered what task he might be required to perform. She pushed through the door into the gym, and greeted Bamboo and Snow.

Snow rushed up to Darcy. "I have heard you were summoned to Master Fei-hung's quarters this morning. That is the conversation among the monks today."

"Really? Wow, who'da thunk it. So monks gossip? Hmmm."

Bamboo approached from her other side. "So what did the master dream?"

"About me walking among tigers."

Bamboo scrunched her forehead. "What does that mean?"

"I haven't the foggiest."

Bamboo laughed. "You say the strangest things."

"Yeah, I'm trying to be aware of slang but it's not easy at all. Anyway, I'm supposed to meditate on the tigers and see what comes up for me."

Snow stood close to Darcy and looked her in the eye. "When I was a child I loved the snow because it brought my family together for happy times. It was wonderful and relaxing. Peace and joy reigned during those times. Perhaps a situation from your childhood will bring enlightenment."

"I can't really think of anything. I love animals and people, but not to keep, just to find them new homes, other than Jones, that is. I've been picking up strays since I was a kid. I wouldn't go as far as to say my folks were terribly excited when I came home carrying a puppy."

"We must make our way to our seats." Bamboo took Darcy's hand and pulled her through the throng of monks. "Let's sit here."

After the ritual of bowing to the shrine, everyone adopted the Lotus posture and prepared for meditation. The ominous sound of Om began quietly in one corner of the group but soon the room filled with a round of continuous vibration. As it had begun, it also ended, quietly, down to the lone bass voice of Tall Tree, trailing off into silence.

Darcy took a deep breath, straightened her back and waited. She felt weightless. Parts of her body seemed to disappear and her mind calmed. In the quietude, she could see tigers and many other animals. Africans and East Indians also flashed across her mindscape. She glided through her thoughts without judgment, observing her own place in each scenario. She felt whole and complete.

"*Zhù fú,*" Master Fei-hung called out.

"*Zhù fú,*" the monks responded in unison.

A full day of exercise and meditation did not bring Darcy any closer to understanding what her attribute might entail. She left the gym with the intention of bathing with Jones that evening. On her way to the room, she stopped at the entrance of the hallway. She suddenly felt compelled to turn around. In the courtyard sat a monk on the steps to the inner sanctum and not more than a few yards away stood a magnificent wide faced tiger, staring straight at him.

Darcy felt spellbound to join the two at the bottom of the steps. As she approached, the tiger took a couple of steps back and locked eyes with her.

"OMG, this is wild beyond my imagination. Is he dangerous?" She sat cautiously next to the monk who continued to stare.

"He is trying to tell me something but I am unable to decipher his message."

Darcy stilled her mind and looked the big cat in the eyes. "He's in pain. He says he has an arrowhead in his shoulder that has been there for a while and recently has begun to hurt him."

"I was not sure what he needed, but I could feel his distress. Which shoulder?"

"He says it's his left. At least that's what I'm hearing. It's not like he speaks, but at the same time he's telling me. You probably think it's just bullsh—silly, but I swear to you, I can hear him."

The tiger padded forward within arm's reach of Darcy and lay down. He chuffed and rolled onto his right side.

Darcy scooted onto her knees next to the animal and gently touched his left shoulder. "His shoulder is hot. Master Fei-hung needs to hear about this. He says he is willing to do whatever it takes. He says he trusts the people here and would like for us to help him."

Jones sidled up next to the two and sat quietly next to Hu, whose name means tiger.

Hu remained calm as he observed Darcy stroking the big

cat. "I will summon Master Fei-hung," he said, standing.

The tiger started and sat up, his eyes full of angst.

"It's okay. He'll get someone who can help you. Try to relax," she said as she stroked his head.

"Darcy, are you confident concerning this situation?" Jones watched the cat cautiously. "This may be an awkward question; however, I feel I must ask where you came by this ability? Have you always spoken to animals and perhaps did not realize it?"

"Maybe, I really don't know for sure." She continued to soothe the shoulder of the massive cat. "I mean, I do remember looking into different dogs' eyes and feeling a certain way, but never heard a... not a voice but more like OMG... empathy." She turned quickly towards Jones. "Is this it? Is *this* my attribute? That I can speak to animals? Or more to the point, they can speak to me?"

"I am very excited for you. We have so much to learn. It would be most impressive to know their point of view regarding history. How our two worlds have collided."

"He likes you. He says you also have a warm heart and are trustworthy."

The master approached and said, "I see you have met our resident tiger. He has visited for many years. We call him Hao, meaning very clever. He has been able to seek us out on numerous occasions without stirring attention from the townspeople. What can we do for him today?"

"He's in a lot of pain. He tells me that he has an arrowhead in his left shoulder. I think he wants us to take it out... yes, that's what he wants. It must be infected somehow because his shoulder is hot."

"I am very happy for you." He gently patted her on the back. "This would seem to be your attribute after all." Master

Fei-hung joined Darcy on his knees.

Hao lay once again on his side and flipped his tail a couple of times.

Master Fei-hung gingerly touched the tiger's swollen area and made his assessment. "This will have to come out. I fear that if we do not extract the object, it could mean the death of our friend. Ask him if I make a potion that will help him sleep during the surgery will he drink it."

"He says as long as I stay next to him with my hand on his head." Darcy leaned in and wrapped her arms around his big cat.

"Then we should take him below and prepare a table where I can perform the procedure."

Hao struggled to right his body, but once on his feet he steadily strolled next to Darcy as the group escorted him to the basement. Master Fei-hung retrieved his herbs to prepare the potion to help Hao sleep.

"He says it tastes terrible. I'm assuring him that's what medicine is supposed to taste like. The worse the taste, the more powerful the cure." Darcy paused. "He says he doesn't believe me, but he will drink it anyway."

He consumed the small bowl, containing the liquid concoction. Everyone waited anxiously, as he slowly succumbed to the powerful elixir. He began to waver and his eyes became heavy. He yawned, exposing aged yellow canines that pointed to the potential danger should he awaken and not remember why he was there. He staggered, sat on his haunches and rolled onto his side.

Four monks lifted Hao onto a table and laid him down on his right side. Master Fei-hung opened a box and removed a short razor. He then smoothed the area with his hand while drawing the razor in a straight-line over the swollen shoulder, cutting through the skin into the area where the bulge was most prominent. The sound of metal on something hard alerted everyone that the arrowhead had been located. Master Fei-hung carefully carved around the sharp pointed head and removed the source of Hao's pain. He then placed several acupuncture needles around the wound to enhance the healing of the area.

Everyone watched as he sewed the wound closed.

"You can tell him upon awakening that he must stay here with us for a few days to allow me to treat against further infection." He patted the tiger on his head. "I believe he will be fine."

"That was amazing. No blood. How... never mind." Darcy looked back at Jones. "I'm so excited... and I just can't hide it. I'm about to lose control, and I think I like it." Darcy suddenly realized that everyone had stopped to listen to her sing.

The group stood, stared at her for a moment, and then started to laugh.

"You guys don't know that song? Where ya been hidin'?"

She and Jones remained with Hao while the others took their leave. Later, when he began to stir Darcy placed her hand on his forehead to reassure him. He attempted to sit up but fell back onto his side. Jones reached out and cautiously stroked his back.

"He wants to thank you. He finds that very comforting."

"Truly it is my pleasure," he said and smiled. "How do you know what he says?"

"I don't know... it's almost like a feeling or a knowing, but my tiger is a little rusty."

"What does that mean?"

"What I mean to say is that I don't speak tiger as far as I know, so I have no idea how I know what he is saying, but I do."

"This attribute could serve us very well in the future or past, depending on where we travel," Jones remarked.

"How so? Do you think this could also work with humans?"

"There is only one way to find out. Now that you have integrated your attribute into your mind, let us have Snow speak to you in Chinese. We can assess whether or not it works for human's too, if you are able to understand her words."

"As soon as Hao is able to walk. I want to stay here for now."

"Shall I prepare us a meal and return?"

"You're so sweet. Yeah, I think that's a great idea. I'm starving."

The tiger shifted.

"Did he say something? I am somewhat concerned for your safety. So perhaps I should wait here with you."

"He said that his stomach doesn't feel well and I pointed out that the surgery and sleeping herbs might be making him feel queasy. But trust me, if this big boy wanted to eat us, he would have no trouble. He is my friend now. You don't need to worry."

Jones nodded and left for the dining hall.

"You have such beautiful and kind eyes. How are you feeling?"

Hao raised his head, looked at Darcy and chuffed.

"Maybe some water will help?"

He licked his lips.

"Okay, wait here and don't try to get up. You don't want

to reopen the wound."

Darcy left the basement and found Jones returning with three bowls.

"That was fast. Did you use the Atomotron?"

"No." he said and laughed. "I assumed Hao would need water. I have filled our bowls and one for him."

Darcy took the bowl of water Jones had balanced between their food dishes and led him back to the basement. "Here ya go big fella." Darcy placed the bowl in front of Hao. "You're welcome."

He lifted his head and shoulders upright and sniffed before taking his first lick. His massive pink tongue lapped up the water until the bowl was dry.

"Do you want more?" Darcy pulled the bowl away and stood.

"Perhaps he is hungry. What would he like to eat?"

"Oh, that's not nice. He says he would like to eat the villager that shot him with the arrow."

"Surely he is jesting." Jones laughed.

"He says no." She paused. "He says he really doesn't want to eat him. He doesn't understand why they are so frightened of him. He has lived in these jungles for many years without harming anyone. He regrets that he allowed himself to lose his instincts. He's feeling old these days." Darcy lay back with her head on Hao's side, feeling the rise and fall of his labored breathing.

Jones in turn laid his head on Darcy's stomach. The bowls of food sat uneaten as the three of them drifted into a nap.

✿✿✿✿✿

Darcy felt a gentle tug on her shoulder. She opened her eyes to find Bamboo and Snow, standing with their hands extended, offering to pull Darcy to her feet. "Where's Jones?" Darcy smoothed her robe.

"We saw him go into the men's toilet," Snow said.

"That boy's as regular as the sun coming up." Darcy bent down to stroke Hao. "Look at this magnificent beast."

Hao sat up on his haunches, pushed to his feet and walked out of the basement.

"Hey! Where're you going?"

Snow and Bamboo stood at Darcy's side, watching the tiger.

Hao stopped and looked back. He then growled a low chuff.

"But wait. Master Fei-hung wanted you to stay for a few days."

Hao stopped and waited for Darcy to catch up.

She jogged up next to him and took his face in her hands.

"I see. I'll tell Master Fei-hung. But I'd think a poultice on your surgery would help."

Hao continued his slow ambling walk toward the back of the monastery where he could escape unseen into the forest twenty yards away, disappearing into the dusky scattered light and shadows.

"What did he say?" Bamboo asked.

"He said he has a cub he wants to watch over. He can't leave her for that many days. He will try to return soon."

Snow joined the Darcy and the tiger. "How are you able to understand what he says?"

"I don't know. I just listen and it comes to me."

"But how do you know if it's the right interpretation?"

"When you look into someone's eyes, even if you can't speak their language, you can tell how they're feeling. This just seems to take it one step further. I can tell what they're thinking too."

"Can you tell what I am thinking?" Bamboo giggled.

Darcy concentrated for a minute. "No. Weird. I have no idea. So why does it work with tigers but not you guys?" Darcy started walking toward the dorms. "This is way cool though. I can't even believe it."

"OMG, what the hell?" Bamboo said.

"Bamboo, what're you doing? That does *not* sound right coming out of your mouth."

"But you say it. Is it not right to use these words?"

"Yeah, well... the answer is *no*. You're too cute for words like that. I 'm not trying to be mean. Just refrain from using them and I will too."

Bamboo stood before Darcy with her head bowed. "I do not understand."

"I do. You're like a kid sister, a little sister, and you want to be like me... but there are some things I do that you shouldn't do. Like using some of the words that I just blurt out, okay?"

"Can I say 'what the fu...?'"

"Especially that."

"What does 'fu' mean?"

"We can't be having this conversation. Strike that stuff and I will too. Listen to the new way I speak, okay?"

"Okay. I can use that word. Okay? Okay."

Snow laughed. "She *is* like a little sister. You have chosen well. She will do her best to bring harmony back to your relationship. In her zeal to emulate you she did not realize what she was doing."

"Oh, trust me, I know. I'm such a dufus, I should be more aware... like you guys. I promise to—"

Jones walked up. "You promise? This must be an

interesting turn of events. Pray tell me what I have missed."

"It's complicated. Hao returned to the forest, Bamboo has a potty mouth, not really but... and I'm responsible for bringing a trash mouth to the eighteen hundreds."

Jones pulled her into his arms. "They will forget. When we take our leave for Snohomish we will be but a memory, and a myth, no doubt, but only among the monks."

"So if we visited Po-chi-lam in 2012, you think the monks would tell us stories of us being here?"

"I feel very confident the story of a young woman who could speak to tigers will be among their favorite tales."

"That is so cool to think about. Maybe we should think about it in the tub."

"Is it not too late for bathing?" Jones took Darcy's hand and kissed it.

"I couldn't possibly go to sleep right now. Let's crank up the fire and take a bath. By the way, what did you have to do today in the inner sanctum?"

Working as a team, they filled the tub with water, lit the wood to heat it, and climbed into the warmth, relaxing quietly in each other's arms.

Thursday, 18 June 1884, 5:00am

Jones and Darcy's room

In the shadowy hours of morning, they rose to dress for the day's workout and meditation.

"I think I'm losing weight." Darcy tugged on her drawstrings

"Yes. I should think so, considering the amount of exercise and the type of food we have been consuming. Your muscle tone is beginning to show itself. I think it's very handsome." Jones pulled open her gi. "Your abdomen in particular."

Darcy closed her garment. "Then that's where your eyes should have been, don't you think?"

"Ah, yes, I was momentarily distracted." He reached for the placket to open her top, smiling broadly. "If I may?"

Darcy tightened her stomach. "This is my six-pack such that it is. Now, let's take a quick look at yours."

Jones opened his top and lowered his pants a bit. "I know you like this side muscle that trails to one of your favorite locations."

Darcy traced his physique with her finger, and leaned in close, drawing in his scent. "I could never get tired of this." She grabbed the sides of his pants and pulled him into her. "I am of the opinion, Mr. Whitman that you are in need of special attention this evening. What say ye?"

"On all accounts, Mrs. Whitman, I shall defer to your superior judgment concerning my need for prodigious tending. Thank you very much."

"Smart man. Bind me please and don't get any ideas."

"I will never get used to this part."

"Good job, dude. Let's get out of here." Once she had exited the room, she turned to Jones. "And you still haven't told me what's going on with you and why you spent the day away from me, doing who only knows what."

"I can assure you that as soon as I am allowed to share it with you, I will. Suffice to say, I believe you will be very excited indeed."

They parted company at the door of the gym. Aromas of various and sundry potpourris, from locations outside the wall filled the cool damp morning air.

She watched Jones with a new perspective that morning. She had claimed her attribute. Other than Hao, she really had no idea how to use her newfound skill. Nevertheless, she realized that in their travels her attribute would certainly come in handy.

Snow stepped up next to Darcy. "*Yŏu xiao wŭ shì.*"

"Who me? I think I have a long way to go."

"What do you think I said to you?"

Darcy shrugged her shoulders. "You sort of implied I am an effective warrior."

Snow grinned. "Yes I did, *in Chinese.*"

"Okay, that's confusing, because I heard English and most definitely *not* Chinese."

"So that is also a part of your attribute. Bamboo and I were wondering. Languages come to you in your native tongue no matter with whom you are speaking. I should think that could come in very handy, particularly if they have no idea you know what they have said. I like that." Snow rubbed her hands together like a mischievous child.

"Seriously? Say something else. I want to know if I'm

really hearing this."

"You are *miǎo, le*, and a *měi nǚ.*"

"Snow, you think I'm beautiful?"

"And clever and cheerful. I understand why Ling cared for you so much."

"Thank you. And you were definitely speaking Mandarin?"

"Trust me. You can understand Mandarin even if you cannot speak it."

"That is crazy cool." Darcy laced her fingers around the top of her head. "I love Ling. I miss her. I can't believe we got arrested, went to jail together and then broke out. She is my new sister. Not sure Ella would approve."

"The situation brought together a formidable team for your rescue."

"Even when I think back on that night, I still think it feels mostly like a dream, or a movie of some sort. I can't believe I stood next to Jones and Roark with my back pressed against Ling with all kinds of crazy goin' on around me. And dang it, I can't tell anyone about it."

"I wish I had your attribute so I could understand some of the things you say." She took Darcy by the shoulder. "Let us go in." She looked back over her shoulder. "Where is Bamboo?"

"She has kitchen duty this week, so she may run a bit late. Who's gonna be my second body guard?"

"Xia, also known as the Reader."

"Is she one of those perky, right out of bed, types?" Darcy groaned. "I hope I like this girl. I'm not exactly cheerful first thing in the morning, but I am getting better."

Darcy and Snow sat after bowing before the shrine, waiting for the ringing of the gong to signal the start of meditation. A striking young woman with a clean shaved, round head, and beautiful dark eyes sat next to Darcy.

"*Zǎo ān,*" she said energetically as she leaned into Darcy's shoulder.

"You have to be Xia. Am I right?" she said with a chuckle.

"Yes. How did you know?" She flashed her white teeth through a broad smile.

"Why haven't I seen you before?"

"I am the librarian; my schedule is different than most. So it is possible we have not crossed paths except at a distance."

"You're like a light under a basket. You just have this glow." Darcy leaned a little closer. "Hey, just curious… what's your attribute?"

"I can see a drawing or read a document and commit the entire content to memory and replicate it. I am the Reader."

"So, wow, that's pretty cool. How do you use that?" Darcy asked.

"Well, let us assume that a message needs to be carried from one monastery to the next that is top secret. The master would write the text, I read it, commit it to memory and leave right away for the appointed monastery. Upon arrival, I would write out the entire message for the master at the new temple."

"Holy crepes suzette." Darcy laughed. "Sorry, that's all I could come up with in the moment. Wow, wow, wow, that is so very cool."

"I'm sorry."

"Oh no, I do this all the time. 'Cool' in this case means exciting, great, very acceptable. Not cold, nothing to do with air temp."

The ringing of a small bell brought their attention to the front. Everyone rose to their feet and bowed to Master Fei-hung who stood in a ring of incense smoke, billowing above his head.

"*Zhù fú.*"

"*Zhù fú,*" bellowed the simultaneous response.

"We are too humble to comprehend the vast web in which we are but a small part. Each morsel of knowledge adds to the never-ending pursuit of answers to satisfy our craving to perceive our one great attribute as human beings. One must learn that yin and yang are equally important to the balance of all life. Let us begin our meditation."

"Whoa I think I need to hear that again," Darcy mumbled under her breath.

As the illusion of time evaporated, a lightness and calm filled her, adding to the serenity of the moment. Wholeness enveloped her as she realized, even in a brief instant, how this wholeness contributed to the ultimate dance of life. The elation charged her chi, giving her great physical and emotional strength, transforming her into a self-proclaimed peaceful warrior.

"I have observed a vast shift within you," Master Fei-hung said softly as he neared.

"Do you know my new name? My Hung Gar name?" Darcy remained seated with her eyes closed.

"Your name will be Listener. You will know the deeper truth of what others experience. You will have the ability to hear beyond words and sounds to include thoughts of others if they wish. You will exhibit a high standard of ethics, respecting the notions of those who you will encounter. This will be your Hung Gar name. This will be your tattoo on your left forearm… 听者. " Master Fei-hung held out a piece of parchment.

Darcy jumped to her feet. "Really? I can't believe it. Does that mean that I've graduated? Woot, woot."

"You will receive your tattoo later this evening. You must seek out Jones. He will be pleased to hear your name."

"Thank you so much." She stood, bowed and then stepped in for a hug. "I promise to do my best to honor the name you have given me."

Master Fei-hung returned the embrace. "I have given you a name, but the universe has bestowed your attribute. Go now."

Darcy charged out the door at full speed to find Jones. She waved as she passed Tall Tree and Wu still in a full run for Jones.

She rounded a corner and met up with Ting. "Have you seen Jones?"

The older monk smiled at her excitement. "You seem very happy."

"Crazy happy."

"He is in the inner sanctorum practicing."

Darcy continued her way up the stone-carved steps, taking two at a time. She slowed her pace to a fast walk as she entered the sanctum, snaking through the tables and figurines until she stood before Jones. She stopped and bowed.

Two mysterious monks in dark burgundy robes retreated into the shadows, leaving Jones behind.

"What were you doing? Never mind." Darcy waved her hand dismissively and said, "I've got great news. Betcha can't guess my Hung Gar name."

"Beautiful Lotus flower… or angel of the universe. I am hard pressed to come up with a name on such short notice, which would suit what I believe you to be."

Darcy moved in close, watching his expression in the flickering candle light. "My name is Listener. I am a listener. Like an interpreter. I have this crazy ability to hear in some kinda special way. Dude, I am so excited. And I'm getting my tattoo later this evening." Darcy shuffled away a few steps and then back, trying to expend the excited energy that had accumulated in her body and mind

Jones waited patiently for her to come around to hug him.

When she did, she sighed into his arms. "I can't wait to use this skill. I wonder if it's any language? Wouldn't that be cool? I wonder if I can turn it off when I want to."

"The answers to your questions lie in the not so distant future. I sincerely hope they are the outcome you desire." He stroked her cheek with the back of his hand. "I do look forward to traveling with you."

"Yeah, me too. When we get back to Snoho, I want to stick around for a while. I can't wait to see how I feel after going through all of this. Oh, when we get back, the first thing I want to do is go for a run along the river."

"That is an excellent idea. And perhaps we could eat a meal outside at a cafe."

"I'm getting excited. Well, I've been excited for about twenty minutes now but even more excited when we talk about going home."

"I am looking forward to sleeping in your bed."

"Our bed, dude. It's our bed now. That'll be awesome. Total privacy." Darcy smiled demurely. "Hey, by the way, what's this secret thing you're doing?"

"You may want to sit down for this explanation."

"Uh oh… did you get into trouble or something?" Darcy sat on the floor and watched as Jones paced back and forth.

"Where shall I begin? At the beginning, of course. I wanted to understand why the others were able to manifest their attribute without the aid of a device. I wanted to know the purpose the Atomotron serves."

"That seems obvious to me. It's the way you travel across time and space."

"Yes. I surmise it was necessary for me to spend seven years designing the machine in order for us to meet at that particular point on the time space continuum. The chances of repeating those exact circumstances, statistically speaking, would be virtually impossible. Therefore my entire life led me to your backyard, on a warm summer's day in Snohomish, Washington, to discover the truth of love."

"My heart is starting to race a bit." Darcy patted her chest. "This must be somethin' really big."

"Yes, I should say so. Perhaps a demonstration is in order." Jones assumed the Lotus posture and closed his eyes. He began to glow and then disappeared, only to reappear, sitting next to Darcy.

"Jeeze Louise. What did you just do?"

"Master Fei-hung explained to me that the Atomotron is for you. I did not realize I had the ability to time travel as my attribute."

"What the hell? You can time travel anytime you want to? Just by closing your eyes? So why can't I do that?"

"Because, my most lovely person, your attribute is empathy. I am certain that you will demonstrate extraordinary feats as we live out our lives together. And truth be told, I now can see clearly that the Atomotron is for my traveling companion."

"So you can travel back to the future, to Snohomish or anywhere by just thinking of where you want to be?"

"Well, I am learning how to do that, thus the secretive meetings with the two monks you saw here earlier."

Darcy leaned against Jones. "This is a bit scary. Hey, wait a second, those two, are they time travelers too?"

"Yes. Apparently, many time travelers lead secret lives. The band of time travelers has maintained strong ethics concerning the intervention of events. However, some of the miracles we have experienced are the result of travelers assisting in changing micro seconds in events for a more positive outcome."

"You've got to be… this could take me a few days figure out." Darcy scratched her head. "So when I travel, I need the Atomotron, but you don't. I don't like the idea of traveling alone. I like it when you hold me."

"That does not have to change. I will hold you as long as you wish." His chiseled face filled with a warm smile reflected in the candle lit room. "I must complete my training for today. I will see you in our room. I would like to request a bath with you this evening."

"Oh for shur. You betcha…" Darcy said in her best Fargo accent.

Jones looked puzzled.

"Yes, that would be a yes." Darcy took her leave in pursuit of Bamboo and found her washing bowls in the kitchen. "I have so much to tell you." Darcy grabbed her arm.

Bamboo turned, tears staining her cheeks.

"Bamboo, what's wrong?" Darcy reached under her chin and raised Bamboo's eyes to meet her own.

"I am sad to say that my father has died."

"Ah man, that's terrible." Darcy waited for her to respond.

"He could be a kind and gentle man, but he also drank

too much at times." Bamboo resumed wiping the bowls dry. "He would become angry and beat us, my sister, mother, and me. Master Fei-hung taught me how to forgive him, not for his sake but for my own." She stopped drying the cup in her hand and dropped her head. "However, in doing so I became vulnerable once again. I will miss the kind and gentle side of my father very much."

Darcy drew her into a gentle embrace. "I am so sorry for you. You seem sad that you didn't see him one last time. That's how I felt when my dad died. I loved him very much, but he didn't really like to show his affections. He would bend over backwards to help me out when he could." Darcy stepped back and folded her arms over her chest. "My mother lost her mind when he died. They were incredibly close."

Bamboo wiped her eyes and began to clean again in silence.

Darcy picked up a cloth and worked alongside her.

✿✿✿✿✿

After leaving Bamboo, Darcy found Jones in their room, lying on the bed.

"What're you up to?" she asked as she began to undress.

He held up his hand. "Wait. I am to escort you to the tattoo room."

She closed her robe again. "Oh boy, I'm kinda scared I might not live up to your expectations when it comes to pain, ya know? Will you leave me if I cry like a baby?"

Jones sat up and pulled her to him. "You will do fine, I am sure of it. While it is a somewhat painful process, your training and new ability to summon your chi will see you through to the end."

"You mean in spite of the whimpering?" She huffed. "I'll do my best."

They walked, hand in hand, into the room where Jones had been not too long ago by a time traveler's clock. The candles flickered shadowy images on the walls as the artist prepared his concoction.

Darcy found the silence unnerving.

"Please have a seat," the artist said and walked over to her.

Darcy sat in the Lotus posture, closed her eyes and presented her left arm.

He rolled up her sleeve and laid her arm on a small wooden stool.

She opened her eyes for a moment and saw the bamboo stick that would ink her arm. "Oh mama, that looks like it could hurt." She took a deep breath and let it out slowly.

"In your mind, you must visit a place that is comforting. Focus your thoughts on that image. Become timeless and this will be over before you know it."

She focused on Snohomish and her friends, on Crepe Escape, coffee, her music, Taylor, her mom and last, her dad. She could feel the emotions well up in her heart as she remembered how she played with her dad as a child, and when she thought about his death, a tear escaped down her cheek and dropped onto her arm. She recalled her recent wedding and Jones's wonderful vows. Before she knew it, the silence was broken.

"We are complete. You have done well. Far better than Time Traveler." The artist laughed, looked at Jones, and smiled.

"Wow. That looks awesome. What ya think, Jones?" She held her arm toward Jones.

"Listener, I am very proud of you."

"Ah, I see we have completed your initiation," Master

Fei-hung said as he entered the room. "Listener, you must be very proud."

"I am. I'm so stoked. I really like my tat."

Master Fei-hung looked at Jones, shrugged and laughed. "I have made you a potion to wipe onto you tattoo five times a day until you have healed properly."

"That's so kind of you. I'll make sure to follow your instructions to the t."

Tall Tree hurriedly approached his side.

"Master Fei-hung, the commander is at the gate with a small group of soldiers." He stood quietly awaiting a response.

"Show him in. Take Listener and Time Traveler out through the back gate to the adjacent forest. Wait there until I send someone to escort you back into the monastery."

Tall Tree joined two other monks at the gate and invited the commander to accompany them. The monks opened the passageway wide to allow easy entry for the group and followed the soldiers in single file. The aroma of soaped leather wafted from the soldier's uniforms as they marched in step behind Tall Tree and the commander to Master Fei-hung's quarters.

"Why so many monks?" the commander asked as he surveyed the room.

"It is our policy to eliminate confusion when we are conversing with anyone from outside of the monastery."

"I see." The commander took a seat and removed his helmet. "I have come on behalf of Empress Cixi. Although you and I have had our disagreements in the past, the Empress has ordered me to summon you on behalf of the empire to train soldiers in hand-to-hand combat to fight in the southern regions."

"Am I to understand that this is an offer, not an order?"

"At this time, but it is a request that you should consider with great deliberation. Empress Cixi knows the ranks could swell with notice to villagers that you will be training the new recruits."

"I am humbled by your compliment, but my training would be purely defensive in nature. That cannot be of assistance to you." Master Fei-hung stood.

The commander slowly rose to his feet, anger etched on his face. He had failed in his commission. "I hope you will reconsider. The Empress Cixi does not take lightly to being turned down."

"But she is wise. She understands our circumstances and our relationship with one another. There need not be friction between us."

✿ ✿ ✿ ✿ ✿

Tall Tree had gathered Bamboo, Darcy and Jones and left by the back entrance to the adjacent forest. Between the wall and the forest lay a parcel of deserted land with no cover. A small group of soldiers now stood between them and the entrance to the monastery. They waited patiently, hidden amongst the foliage.

"What do you think they're up to?" Darcy asked.

"They are a reconnaissance team. They are looking for signs that we have hidden you from them." Tall tree sat on the ground as the others knelt peering through the bushes at their possible fate.

Jones whispered. "I do not know the exact situation in the courtyard but perhaps I could travel inside to warn Master Fei-hung that there are troops outside the wall."

Darcy turned to Jones. "Have you practiced enough? What if you end up in the pool again? That's gonna bring a lot of attention. I'm not lovin' this at all."

"Well said. Then I could endeavor to travel to the master's quarters."

"Jones, I'm not really feeling very good about this."

Bamboo put her hand on Jones's arm. "You must conjure your chi like never before. Your focus has to be razor sharp. Any distraction and you could lose your ability to travel and therefore you would have no means of escape.

"Another plan would be for me to go through the forest and back through the front gate," Bamboo said. Bamboo stood, intending to sneak past the soldiers through the outskirts when she felt Darcy take her arm.

"No. I couldn't bear to see you arrested because of us. We can just wait until the coast is clear. What's the hurry? Right? We can just wait here," Darcy said.

"I fear it is not about us. We are committed to the safety of the monastery and at this moment, it would appear it may be in jeopardy. I am given to believe that I alone have the solution. I am going to time travel to the master's quarters and hope that all is clear."

Darcy jumped to her feet. "Then take me with you," she whispered. "Why should I stay here without you when there's a possibility you could get caught? If you're going, so am I."

Bamboo smiled. "You have become a real warrior. I think you should go. Tall Tree and I will enter through the back gate and join whatever commotion occurs."

Tall Tree stood and parted the foliage. "Bamboo, you wait here for my signal. I will distract the soldiers. When their backs are turned to you, slip in through the back gate."

Jones embraced Darcy and closed his eyes. "I am not sure I am far enough along in my training to take you with me, but I am willing to try." He visualized Master Fei-hung's quarters, took three deep breaths and waited but nothing happened. No white noise occurred and no ringing in his ears. Jones opened his eyes to see Darcy's panicked face. "I am unable to make this happen. I am baffled."

"Concentrate harder." She pressed her cheek against his chest and waited.

He once again summoned his chi, following the procedure taught to him by the monks, but again, nothing happened.

"This is beyond frustrating to me."

"You're thinking too much. You're trying too hard. Just relax and let it happen."

"*Cǐ dì*, over here," a helmeted soldier called out. He had knelt down and picked up a broken limb to show to the others.

At that moment, Tall Tree stepped from the bushes startling the three.

"*Zhàn, sēng rén!*" one of them shouted.

Tall Tree halted and waited as they approached.

"Why are you returning from the forest?"

"Part of my meditation is to commune with nature."

"Have you seen any strangers?" another soldier asked.

"Other than yourselves? No." Tall Tree stepped past the three and turned back to them. "Are they dangerous?"

One soldier turned and said, "Not to us. You should be careful. It has been said they are ghosts."

"If they are ghosts, how will you see them?"

The three looked at one another and scanned the area.

"Move along before we change our minds and arrest you."

With the stealth of an owl, Bamboo had slipped past the three soldiers fifteen yards farther down and made her way across the open land to the back entry. Jones and Darcy lay in wait to make their escape.

Darcy suddenly felt the urge to sneeze. She pinched her nose and held her breath but to no avail. She squeaked out a small muffled, "Hachew."

Jones whipped his head around to see her with her hands covering her face.

"What was that?" one soldier asked, looking in the direction of the noise.

The three then rushed to the area, drawing their weapons and slashing through the brush.

Jones felt his pulse quicken. "This could be most unfortunate."

Darcy grabbed his arm. *Hao, help us*! she pleaded in her mind.

"Please travel! You can come back and get me."

"This circumstance does not lend itself to my traveling and I would *never* leave you here." He reached out and touched her face as he felt the sure grip of the first soldier to reach them. A growling second soldier grabbed his other arm, while the third pulled a struggling Darcy away from Jones.

"Let go of me, you asshole," Darcy screamed as he pulled her arms behind her. She stomped his foot and tried to free herself.

"We are from the monastery. Perhaps you could escort us to Wong Fei-hung?" Jones said calmly.

"And perhaps not." The soldier then pushed Darcy forward into a bent position, pulling the robe back to expose her neck. He lifted his sword above her head.

"Not in this lifetime." Jones focused the intensity of his chi on saving Darcy. As he started to move, he caught a glimpse of what seemed to be fire flashing through the air.

Hao's elongated body flew over the top of Darcy, knocking the soldier to the ground and pinning him with his giant paws. The tiger's eyes filled with fury and he growled one inch from the face of the soldier who now pleaded for his life. The other soldiers jumped to their feet and started to run for the monastery. Two young female tigers leapt from the bushes, quickly gaining on them. Running low to the ground, they caught up and dragged each to the ground.

"Bring them back," Darcy called out. "Oh my god, Hao, thank you so much, but please, don't hurt him."

Hao glanced in her direction with his canines bared and his eyes wild with anger. He then slowly relaxed and lay down on his captive. One of the two females bit into the back of one escapee's leather uniform and began to drag his fainted body to join Jones, Darcy, and Hao.

"Hao, if we may take advantage of this situation." Jones rested his hand on Hao's head.

"Would you be so kind as to guard these three until we make our escape?" Jones looked at Darcy.

She was listening to Hao. "Yes. We can't thank you enough for saving us. I'll always remember you." Still holding the tiger's gaze she said, "He says he is quite comfortable and may take a nap." Darcy smiled.

The two females lay lazily, guarding the other two men.

Darcy hugged Hao's neck and held his big head in her hands.

The soldier started to utter and the tiger placed a paw on his face, rendering him silent once again.

"Hao, you've got to let them go without hurting them."

The tiger laid his head on the soldier's chest.

"I understand, but if you hurt them they'll hunt you down as a man killer. That puts you and all your family in danger."

"What is his response?" Jones asked.

"He's willing to let them go but may toy with them a bit."

"I am confident that he will make the right decision. We must make haste."

Darcy took Jones's hand and they sprinted across to the back gate. "By the way," Darcy said as they arrived at the back of the temple. "What's the plan once we are inside?"

"How would you feel about returning to Snohomish as soon as possible?" Jones waited on her response.

Darcy stared. "I don't know. Yep, of course, that's exactly what we should do for the sake of the monastery." A grin lit up her face.

"We shall make our way to our quarters, secure the Atomotron and leave immediately."

"I'm very happy about that."

"One quick question if I may."

"Ask while we are moving."

Jones matched her stride. "What did you call the guard?"

"Oh man, I was hoping you'd missed that. I'll explain when we're back in Snoho. Cool? Is that okay?"

"Absolutely."

They came to the corner that led down the hall to the dorms. On the left, a few short strides away, the door to Master Fei-hung's room flung open and the commander stepped into the hallway followed by several monks. Master Fei-hung appeared in the hallway with his back to Jones and Darcy and his hands folded behind him. He used his pointer finger to motion them towards their quarters. They moved quietly but quickly until they arrived at their room.

Jones fell to his knees and reached under the bed for the Atomotron. "I do not understand," he said, as he swept his hand under the bed, finding empty space.

"You don't understand what?" Darcy joined him, lying flat to peer under the bed. "Where the hell is it? What are we gonna do, Jones?"

"Perhaps this is a test. Perhaps this is to force me to conjure my chi to travel with you in my arms."

"That's not what I understood. I need the Atomotron to travel. We've got to find out what's happened."

A light knocking on the door startled them both. Jones jumped to his feet mentally prepared for whatever might happen. He took the handle and snatched the door open. Bamboo and Snow both dropped into a Dragon stance.

"That is no way to open a door under these circumstances. Come with us." Snow motioned for Darcy to hurry.

"But the Atomotron is missing. We can't go home."

"Master Fei-hung felt sure the commander was up to no good. He scanned the area and saw soldiers outside the wall. In the event that they may have searched the rooms, he had Ting shape shift into Black Eagle and carry the Atomotron high into the sky. He is circling, waiting for us to appear next to the commissary. The commander and his men are outside the gate so we must say our goodbyes on the way. We cannot take any chance they will return, and to be sure, they will station men on the buildings across the street."

The four jogged through the hallways, past the kitchen and the aromas etched forever into Darcy's mind. They ran past the gym and came to a stop against the commissary wall.

Jones looked up at a small dot soaring on the winds. The dot stopped and began a rapid descent, coming closer and closer.

"Jones, hold out your arms," Bamboo said.

The eagle spread his wings and slowed his dive, pulling

up to hover only a few feet above, where he opened his talons and dropped the Atomotron into Jones's hands. Ting screeched and flew back into the sky.

"I must run back to the room. I need my journal." He sprinted off in the direction of the dorms.

Darcy began to pace. "Oh man, can we go back inside? I'm freakin' out again."

"Yes. We can stand inside the kitchen doorway and call to him when he comes by."

So as not to bring attention, the women walked casually, shoulder to shoulder, into the food prep area as Jones approached from the opposite direction.

"I overheard Wu and Yun whispering of a return of the commander. It would seem that three of his soldiers have yet to rejoin the ranks."

"Oh, no. Hao, you better not have killed those guys." She turned to Jones. "Damn it. Can we go to the back gate and take a look, please?"

"I should think we would be at risk in doing so." Jones shortened the straps on the time machine. "We can at least be ready to travel in the case that an unacceptable event should arise."

He toggled in the coordinates for Snohomish 2012 and pulled the Atomotron on. He and Darcy ran back through the monastery to the back gate. Jones cautiously pushed a crack in the opening to get a look at the scene outside.

Darcy scrunched down below him. "OMG. Hao," Darcy called in a hoarse whisper. "Let them up."

Hao climbed to his feet and stood next to the stilled soldier.

"No," Darcy called out, wagging her finger.

"May I ask what he is saying to you?"

"He wants to chase them when they get up and run. He's mischievous, that one is."

Hao said his goodbyes and the three big cats sprinted back into the forest, disappearing into the foliage in seconds. The soldiers ran for their lives around the corner of the temple walls.

Jones pulled the door shut.

"Should we leave from here?" Darcy asked.

"I am sure Master Fei-hung will send a message to us."

A noise from behind had Darcy's heart bumping against her ribs. She then recognized one small voice—Bamboo.

In single file they approached, arms crossed, hands tucked into their sleeves, eyes cast downward.

"We have come to say goodbye," Bamboo said.

Tall Tree, Snow, Cloud, Silent Wind and Master Fei-hung encircled the two. Everyone bowed, exposing a lone figure smiling.

"Ling!" Darcy squealed. "You've come to say goodbye." Her eyes filled with tears. "I'm so glad you could make it." She held out her arms and they embraced as long lost friends.

"Across time you will always be my sista," Ling said and laughed. "It has been a great pleasure knowing you. Take good care of my adopted brother."

Jones stepped forward to hug Ling and kissed her on her forehead. "I will miss you terribly, but I also remain committed to return to see you in your future and my past."

"I am certain you will know where to find me. I am happy for you and the life you will lead. I will always hold you true in my heart." Ling stepped back as Master Fei-hung moved closer to Darcy and Jones.

"You are welcome in this temple anytime you should have an urge to commune with us again." Master Fei-hung opened his arms to embrace Darcy. "The world awaits you both. Use your attributes wisely and maintain the utmost integrity in doing so. Until now again."

The group filed in behind Master Fei-hung and disappeared down the hallway.

"Are you ready? I mean, am I gonna wake up and find out this was all a dream?"

Jones embraced her.

"Would you do the honor of taking us home?" He closed his eyes.

Darcy turned the switch and heard the familiar whirling reaching the ascendant pitch, the white noise rising in her ears. She could feel her body expanding as they left Po-chi-lam Temple, Foshan, China in 1884 for the year 2012.

Wednesday, 27 June, 2012, 6:30 am

Snohomish, WA

They materialized, swept up in each other's arms, their breath mingled in their closeness.

Jones opened his eyes first and beheld Darcy's smiling face and lips.

"I know you're staring at me. I'm afraid to open my eyes. I'm scared you'll be gone and that you never were. I think that would kill me. Seriously, dude, say something to me."

"I have never loved another the way I love you, Mrs. Whitman. Open your eyes now and tell me how you feel as well."

Her eyes fluttered as they focused. "This *is* real. Oh my god." She threw her arms around his neck and pulled his lips to hers. "I'm exhausted. I'm excited. I'm actually a little horny, if ya know what I mean."

"First things first. We must change out of this garb and back into Snoho attire. Perhaps we should shower first?"

"How many *first* things are you gonna list? They can't all be first." She broke free from his embrace and ran over to the refrigerator. Jerking the door open to check the food left in containers, she reeled at the sight of so much abundance for two people. She realized how much her point of view had changed because of her time in Foshan. "Let's get a shower. You're right. We need to get out of these clothes. And I'm goin' to throw on a long sleeved shirt for a day or two."

"You seem disheartened. I thought you would be thrilled to return." Jones gingerly took her hand in his. "Ah, yes, grand idea. Could prove difficult to explain the kanji characters and the new haircut at the same time."

She leaned against the counter, pulled her hand away, and folded her arms. "I am thrilled but I'm also blown away."

"It is culture shock. Not unlike what I went through when I first arrived here. Each age has its own distinctions. This new age will someday appear as primitive as Foshan did to you when you arrived."

"Yeah, I'm sure. But I think it's gonna take me a few days to unwind from our little trip to Po-chi-lam."

"I have no doubt." Jones stroked his chin. "I feel as if I am a man from the planet earth. Time travel has stripped away the veneer of here and now. We are mates from different ages and yet love still reigns. I cannot imagine what the future will bring."

"Lucky for us we can go find out, right?"

"I can truly say that I would not want to travel too far ahead at one jump for fear that locations might have shifted and we could end up in the middle of an ocean. Traveling forward could be very risky."

"I think I'm through with traveling for a few weeks... months or maybe even years."

"I understand." Jones smiled. "Shall we shower?"

"Sure." Darcy pushed away from the counter and ambled to the bedroom where all her of clothes were in exactly the same place she had left them. "I'm gonna miss our baths in the wooden tub."

After the shower and dressing, they returned to the kitchen. Nothing had changed, except for everything. Darcy felt a wave of confusion and sadness.

A knock on the door surprised her and she panicked.

"Darcy, your chi. Remember, this is the same day we left.

Act as normal as possible." Jones touched her hand as she passed.

"Helloooo. Darcy, you here?" Taylor strolled into the room and Darcy could not refrain from hugging him. "Okay, who are you and what have you done with my sister?" he said, holding her away from him, scrutinizing her appearance.

"Oh, sorry. I'm just really glad to see you. How's mom?"

"Have you joined some kind of cult?" Taylor circled her, looking at her hair.

"What?"

"Eh, the hair?"

She ran her hand over her short-cropped cut. "A new look. Whatta you think?"

"I don't know Dar. It's kinda short. Hey, Jones." He waved. "Whatta *you* think man?"

He joined Jones at the table.

"She has captured my imagination. I do believe Darcy would glamorize any haircut she chose."

"Oh man, you're hittin' it hard, buddy. If I were guessin' I'd say you guys have gotten to know each other a lot better these last couple of days."

"You don't know the half of it. Wait a minute, what time is it?"

"It's eight, why?"

"Because I have to work today. This is crazy. Maybe I should call in sick."

"Are you sick?" Taylor pushed away from the table, walked over to Darcy and placed his hand on her forehead. "No fever. What's wrong with you? You seem jumpy, weird. Hey, what's goin' on here. Do you need to tell me something?"

"No. Everything is fine." Darcy pushed past Taylor.

"Whoa. That was weird. Déjà vu. I been havin' some really messed up dreams lately too," Taylor said as he stepped away from the counter.

Darcy looked over at Jones who was watching Taylor pace around the kitchen.

"Taylor? How can we be of assistance?"

"Oh yeah. They called last night to say mom's not feeling well and they need one of us to sign for medical care."

"What's wrong with her?" Concerned, Darcy joined Jones and Taylor at the table.

"Hell, I don't know. If I knew, they wouldn't need a doctor. Can you go over today and sign?"

"Sure. I'll do it." Darcy laid her face in her hand. "Just like ole times."

Taylor halted and cocked his head sideways. "What have you been smokin'? Ole times? I just saw you on Sunday. Why are you acting so...so—"

"No, it's just I'm feeling you know... that time of the month?"

"Whoa, TMI! Ya know what I mean?"

"Taylor, if I may," Jones said. "What I mean to say is, if you have the time right now, I have a sum of money that I would like to present to you."

"You may and be prepared for lots of praise and groveling."

Jones went to the bedroom and brought out four ten dollar eagle coins to Taylor.

"Eh, I don't mean to be rude, but this ain't gonna make much of a dent in the startup."

"Taylor," Darcy reprimanded.

"No, I'm appreciative. I just thought we understood how much I was looking for."

"Ah, I see. Yes, but four coins, they do seem wildly short as they are. However, if you cash them in they are worth approximately fifteen hundred dollars each. My math indicates that comes to six thousand American dollars."

"No way. Six thousand is a huge help. Dude, how can I ever thank you?" Taylor eyed the gold with the delight of a young boy discovering a Babe Ruth baseball card in his packet of gum.

"I will be rewarded by the success of your shop, I assure you." Jones sat stroking his chin.

"Maybe you can design a cycle for him?" Darcy prodded.

"Absolutely. That's exactly what I'll do. How does that sound?" Taylor said, grinning from ear to ear.

"I look forward to your expertise. Perhaps we can spend some time sketching out the design in the near future."

"Alrighty then. This is awesome. I'm blown away right now. I've gotta run, but man, thank you one last time. You won't regret this. By the way, I'll take care of mom. It's the least I can do." Taylor hugged Darcy and shook Jones's hand.

"This hugging thing is kind of nice," Darcy said. "Give my love to mom then and tell her I will see her in the next couple of days."

Taylor left, walking taller than when he came in.

"It is wonderful to see him experience independence. Seeing Taylor in this manner brings Roark to mind. I have a notion that, after we have been settled in for a few days, we should make a quick trip to Hiva Oa to see him."

"Can I make a decision about that later? The idea of traveling right now makes me queasy."

"In a couple of days then. May I add that my proposal is to return three years in his future? That way we can see how he has fared."

Darcy stood and walked around to sit on Jones's lap. "Okay you got me. Man, wouldn't that be cool. I bet he's gonna be a fat and happy islander. I wonder if he's had a kid yet. A little Roark. Wouldn't that be awesome?"

Jones laughed. "I suspect there will never be anything little about a Fogerty child."

"Yeah. Hey, I gotta get going. I can't believe I have to work. This is gonna be really weird. Sarah is gonna flip when she sees my hair."

"It will not only be your hair that intrigues her. Your demeanor has shifted. Your confidence has increased markedly. Perhaps we should meditate prior to your departure."

"How about you just hold me for a few moments. I think that'll help me focus."

He pulled her in close and kissed her cheek, trailing down to her neck.

She pushed him away. "Oh, no big boy, don't get me started."

"We have enough money. Perhaps you should consider resigning from your work. And—"

"Not sure that's a good idea. Snoho is a small town. We've only been together for a week or so. That would seem strange, don't you think?"

"Time travel *is* complicated. Keeping one's story straight could become a rather cumbersome task. You and I have shared a tremendous adventure, declared our love, you went to prison, escaped from prison, and can now converse with your strays at will."

"Not to mention, I can seriously defend myself like never before. I meditate, do Tai Chi, and I can bathe in a matter of minutes. That's a miracle. I've seen things and experienced

178

things I could never tell anyone, 'cause they'd have to lock me away."

"Just prior to your entry into Crepe Escape, take a deep cleansing breath, focus your chi, and allow the natural consequences to evolve." He kissed her again on her forehead and hugged her tightly.

As she opened the front door, Darcy looked back over her shoulder at Jones. "I miss you already."

"I will see you soon." He waved.

✿✿✿✿✿

She opened the front door and basked in the wonderful feeling of being in familiar surroundings. A bright clear blue sky greeted her, causing a glee in her soul. She strolled up Cedar and crossed over 1st Street walking up to the front window of Crepe Escape.

She could see Sarah in the back preparing the batter for the crepes they would be serving in less than twenty minutes. Darcy knocked on the window.

"We're not open yet." Sarah glanced in her direction but continued working.

What? Darcy knocked again.

This time Sarah looked straight at her and pointed to the clock. "We're open at—Darcy?"

She flipped her hands out to the side and made a beeline for the front door with a surprised look on her face. "What did you do to your hair? I didn't even recognize you."

"Sarah, you're a sight for sore eyes, I tell ya. Ya know, I have no idea what that saying means. Anyway, how's it going?"

"Eh, well, since a couple of days ago? Let's see. Wow, where do I start." She laughed and went back to her batter. "It's going the same as the last time we worked together. Not much." She had an inquisitive expression on her face. "You sound like you've been on vaca or something."

"Really? Oh sorry. I'm just in a great mood."

"Guy from the past?" she asked raising her eyebrows.

"You could say that." Darcy smiled broadly while tying on her apron.

"Somebody got laid," Sarah teased.

"Sarah!" Darcy laughed.

"Hey, we're the only ones here, ya know." She flipped the button on the coffee grinder just as Darcy began to speak again. "Go on, tell me everything." She dumped the ground coffee into a canister.

"Oh my god that smells so good. I can't... nope, I won't wait to have a cup." She packed the portafilter, cranked it into place, and pushed the timer to pull a double shot to make the Americano she had fantasized about back in Foshan. "You have no idea."

"You're *really* acting strange this morning. What's up with you?"

"Okay, okay, just between us girls... I got laid in a major way." Darcy gently and slowly poured in her cream, bringing the color and aroma to exacting perfection. She cradled the cup in her hands like the face of a baby and lifted it to her nose. "Ahhh, this is going to be sumptuous." She placed her lips on the rim of her cup and pulled a small amount of the concoction into her mouth with an approving groan. "Oh man, this is heaven."

"So who cut your hair? I'm gettin' used to it already. It's cute... different but cute." She reached out and fingered the layers.

Darcy headed toward the sidebar to fill her station. "An Oriental dude. He's not really affiliated with a shop. He only does this cut and a couple of others."

"Well, I like it. Makes you look thinner in some weird way too. That's always a good thing, right?" Sarah pushed through the swinging doors to the kitchen. "The scones should be out in a few," she called out. "We're supposed to get a delivery of organic granola bars later this morning."

Darcy turned on the griddle to be ready for the first orders.

It was Wednesday and, as usual, the hungry patrons lined up at the door, waiting for them to open.

Darcy straightened a couple of chairs and adjusted the tablecloths and flowers on her way to the front door. "Bon jour, everyone," she said with a smile. "You know the drill… place your order at the counter and we'll bring it out ASAP. Bon appétit!" She greeted several regulars and then took her place at the griddle where she ladled out the first of many crepes for that day.

The air quickly filled with all the breakfast aromas of rich coffee, crepes—sweet and savory—prepared to order, and the fragrance of flowers and perfumes carried by the wind from the open door. Chatter and laughter blended with the clinking of flatware and plates.

Darcy sighed with satisfaction just as soon as she was able to stop long enough to appreciate the beauty of her life.

"Order up," Sarah called out. "I'll grab these three plates if you can take the fourth and the two cups of coffee."

Before Sarah had a chance to pick up the plates Darcy said, "I got it."

She layered the three plates on one arm, covered with a small towel, and placed the coffee and remaining plate on a tray in her other hand.

"Holy crap, Batman, when did you learn to do that?"

Sarah stood with her hands on her hips as Darcy glided to the four-top table.

"I have a Cedar special… my favorite so somebody better claim it quick."

"Right here," a fiery redhead said, as she patted the table in front of her.

"Great hair. You remind me of a big ole friend of mine. And who's havin' the strawberries and cream? A delightful choice if I do say so myself. Snoho Veggie, hold the onion. There ya go. And lastly, you must be Strawberries and Chocolate."

"And one of those coffees belongs to me."

"The cream is on the coffee bar." Darcy held up the second cup.

"Me. Mine. Thank you very much. I've been waiting all morning for the first sip. Oh yum."

"Right? Okay guys, have fun, and if you need anything let me know." Darcy smiled, bowed slightly, caught her body and jerked upright. She rolled her eyes and headed back to the crepe station.

"We make a good team, Sarah. I like working with you."

"Yeah me too. Makes the time go by really fast."

"Time is a funny thing." She glanced over at Sarah. "You can never know exactly what will happen next. Then again… maybe you can?"

✿✿✿✿✿

"Hi honey, I'm home." Darcy slowed her pace and waited. She raised her voice. "Jones? Jones, why do I have this funny feeling? Something just isn't right."

A voice from around the corner in the living room spoke softly. "Do not be frightened. We are your friends."

The pulse in Darcy's neck throbbed as she eased around

182

the doorjamb. "Who... how?" she blurted out. She stared for moment. "Hey wait a second, I recognize *you*. You guys are the monks who were training Jones. What're you doin' here?"

"We have come to complete his training, but he is not here. So we have remained to ask you where he might be?"

The two monks stole a look at one another and then turned their expectant gaze back to her.

"He should be here. I was at work. Maybe he's out walking." Darcy dropped her things on the couch. "You guys are scaring me. You don't think something has happened to him?"

"We do not. You have a great listening ability. Focus your chi and open yourself to hear from him."

Darcy reluctantly closed her eyes and breathed in a deep breath. Images began to flash across her mind in rapid succession. After a moment she blurted, "Holy crap, he's at the grocery store with Taylor! You two scared me. What were you thinkin'? And how long have you been here?"

"We arrived a short time ago, and waited."

"I can see that. Take a load off." She pointed to the couch.

One of the monk's eyes widened.

"I mean have a seat. Please sit down." She shook her head.

They both dropped to the ground into a Lotus position. "We shall wait for Time Traveler."

"So would you like some tea? I don't have lavender, but I do have green tea?" Darcy called out from the kitchen. The silence drew her back to find the living room empty. The two monks had disappeared. She sat on the couch scratching her head when the two reappeared in the same spot as before with a small bundle.

"We prefer lavender tea. We have brought you enough to last for a while. You can always return to Po-chi-lam should you require more." They handed it to her with a smile.

"It took the two of you? Dude, I can just go around the corner to Everything Tea. How do you do that so fast?"

"We went to the commissary. I know where the tea is kept. And yes, as you know we cannot be alone with a woman without another monk present." The monk spoke quietly and calmly. "Perhaps later we could visit the tea shop?"

"Really? That's what you're thinkin' about. I'm thinkin' how do I explain you guys?" Darcy sat on the end of the couch with the tea bundle in her hands.

"We are monks from China. We are visiting you or perhaps we could simply take our leave should the need arise."

The front door opened and in walked Jones and Taylor carrying bags of groceries.

"Hellooo, Darcy. We have chow for you." Taylor placed his two sacks on the table. "So, what ya up to?"

Jones, carrying the last bag in his hand, sauntered over for a kiss. "How was work?" He brushed a layer of hair from behind her ear.

Darcy leaned against the kitchen counter and nervously pointed toward the living room. "We have...viz—" she peered into the empty room. "Okay, that's just not right," she mumbled.

"Alrighty then, I'm gonna take off. Jones if you ever need a ride again just let me know. Dar, catch ya later." Taylor walked to the front door and waved above his head.

"Thanks for helping out, Taylor," she called out. "Owe you."

Jones took her by the shoulders. "If I may?"

"Yeah, so, the two guys that were training you? They showed up here today. Freaked me right out."

"Really, they came here?" He stroked his chin. "Perhaps they will stay with us for a couple of days and continue my education, such that it is."

"Are you crazy? Think about it. First, there's you… and now two full-blown Chinese monks staying here? I'm starting to feel like a universe flop house." Darcy flounced onto the couch. "This is too weird. Maybe you could meet up with them somewhere, like in… eh, Egypt. Or maybe in Hawaii. Yeah," she said with a smile. "That could work, and I could come along too… nah, we can't afford that and 'oh yes we can,' he says."

Jones laughed heartily. "I am assuming I could take my leave and be fairly well represented in this conversation."

Darcy laughed. "Sorry, I just know you. You would say we have the money, right?"

"To luxuriate in a hotel suite? We could entertain ourselves with food and other sensual pursuits? I should think so." Jones nudged her shoulder and she blushed.

"Jones Whitman, you naughty boy." She laughed, grabbed his hand, and placed it between her breasts, kissing his fingers one by one. "So whatta ya say fella? Ya wanna take a little trip to Hawaii for some training?"

"I believe that can be arranged. I am of the inclination to return briefly to Foshan to discuss the matter with Wu and Dun. I do not think it will present a problem."

"So should I check on a hotel? I mean I assume we are staying for a day or two." She stood, hopped upwards and slid her legs around his waist. "So what's the budget for a night?"

"I am sure the rates have changed dramatically, so I will

leave that portion of the trip up to you. I believe we can afford a more upscale room."

Darcy dropped to the floor and scurried to get her computer. "I think I can find a good place for a decent price."

Jones followed her into the kitchen. "We should endeavor to find suitable out of the way sleeping arrangements, regardless of the cost. I should amend that to say within reason." Jones smiled. "And make the arrangements such to accommodate visitors, say two monks? And I must stroll around to see Mr. Evans about selling a couple of Eagles."

"Right, very good idea." Darcy scanned the hotel prices and locations. "We might have problems getting a room on such short notice."

Jones laughed. "Perhaps you can simply inquire as to when there will be an opening and we can travel to that date." Jones sat next to Darcy at the table.

"Brilliant," she said with a mischievous grin. "How about this B & B? Whoa, it runs $429 a night."

"No matter, it would seem perfect." He ran his finger over the screen. "Can we see these photographs in a larger venue?"

"Sure."

Before they arrived at the fourth photo, Jones said, "That is one amazing location. I think you should book us as soon as I know that Dun and Wu can meet us there."

"We will teach you all you need to know," Wu said.

Darcy jumped to her feet with her hands on her hips. "You guys have got to stop doing that. You scared the crap out of me *again*!"

Jones laughed.

Wu and Dun bowed.

"That was not our intention I assure you. However, I

know of no other solution," Dun said.

"Can ya call ahead or text or something?" she said, sounding a bit frazzled.

"Where would you like for us to appear?" Dun asked.

"How about at the front door and then knock for ..."

A knock at the front door startled Darcy and Jones.

"Oh no, who could that be?" Darcy's voice rose at the end. She left the three men standing in the kitchen. "Yeah, who is it?"

"It's Cars."

"Cars? What are you doing here?" Darcy leaned against the door on her forehead.

"Just checking in."

"What? Has she barricaded herself in?" Taylor sauntered up next to Cars.

"Taylor? What the hell?" Darcy opened the door a crack.

"What's going on?" Taylor asked. "I left my beer in the bag."

Cars looked from one to the other. "Should I leave?"

"Gentlemen," Jones said calmly. "Darcy, it's fine to allow them to join us." He winked.

Darcy opened the door wide and followed the men into the living room.

"Nice cut," Cars said as he flopped onto the couch.

Taylor scanned the adjacent rooms suspiciously. "Why are you acting so strange? What's gotten into you?"

"Nothing. I just wasn't expecting company or you coming back."

"Somethin's goin' on around here." Taylor squinted his eyes. He walked into the kitchen and pulled his beer out of the grocery bag.

"I just stopped by to say that déjà vu thing happened

again. What's up with that?" Cars said. "I keep dreaming about this little box called Adventurer." He pointed at Jones and Darcy. "And it seems to have something to do with you two."

"Interesting, that is a great name for a sailing vessel." Jones raised his palms out. "Perhaps we are acting oddly because we were otherwise engaged." He smiled.

"Ahhh," both men sighed in unison.

Cars hopped to his feet. "Oh man, okay then. I'll stop by another time." His face flushed red.

"Eh, yeah, me too," Taylor said as he walked toward the front door with his beer under his arm.

"Doesn't anyone call ahead these days?" When the door was once again closed, Darcy sat on the couch with her head in her hands.

"Darcy," Jones reached out and lightly massaged her neck. "They are gone. Shall we continue?"

"So Wu and Dun just popped out again?" She looked around toward the kitchen.

"Yes."

A knock at the front door brought Darcy to her feet.

"Holy cow, Taylor, this is…" As she jerked the door open, she laughed hysterically. "You two get in here," she said as she opened the door wide. She followed the two chuckling devotees into the living room.

"Look what the cat dragged in." She plopped back down onto the couch.

Jones stood and bowed. "It is so nice of you to pop in again." He smiled. "We have a proposition for you. Would it be to your liking if we were to meet up for training in Hawaii? We have yet to secure the exact date; however, it would be of no consequence to meet you anywhere at any time you would prefer."

"We are not bound by time. That being said, we will leave those arrangements to you," Dun said.

"Excellent. How should we proceed?" Jones asked.

"We simply need a location," Dun said.

"I can show you the place." Darcy pointed toward the kitchen table and made her way to the computer with the rest in tow. "This is Orchid Tree B&B. It's located on the island of Hilo. Do you need coordinates?" She glanced back at the three men hovering over her shoulders.

"No. That will not be necessary. We will find you once we have an idea of the area and an image of the habitat." Dun leaned in to peruse the photos.

Wu stood quietly next to Jones. They looked at one another and smiled.

Darcy watched intently as the slide show faded from one image to the next. "Not sure what room it will be."

"We only need to know that you will be there. Once we have arrived, we can find you. Should we knock on your door?" Wu chuckled.

"Oh a wise guy I see. How do you find us?" Darcy turned to Wu.

"We can ask at the front desk," he said.

Darcy laughed. "You're kiddin' me right? You must have some kinda mystical thing you do."

"We locate your chi and it guides us to you." Dun folded his arms and slid his hands up his sleeves.

"Ahhh, see, now that makes more sense."

"I am amazed you would find it more believable they use chi location over the assertion that they would simply ask for us at the front desk." Jones shook his head. "What have we done to you?"

"You've made me a time traveler... and I have my attribute. Nothing can stop me now but linear time and I plan to live a long life. I do live a long life, don't I, Wu?"

"I am not familiar with your outcome. I cannot say with certainty." Dun returned to Wu's side. "We shall leave you now."

They bowed and dematerialized. The energy shift in the room became apparent in the absence of the two monks.

Darcy glanced at Jones. "That was weird. You'll be able to pop in and out like that?"

"I assume as much. I still find myself puzzled by the Atomotron and the necessity of its use when we travel together. I am hopeful that at some point I can simply embrace you and we can be on our way."

"That would be nice. So here's my proposal. We prepare dinner, shower, watch a program, *not* baseball and then a bit of spoonage before sleep. Oh, maybe we could make out before we fall out. Whadda ya think?"

"Sounds like a marvelous plan." He smiled warmly.

"So let's get this party started."

Thursday, 28 June, 2012, 5:30 am

Snohomish, WA

Morning light filled the room as they opened their eyes and gazed at one another.

"You're a handsome lad," Darcy said softly. She delicately stroked his cheek with her finger.

"That would be Roark, I'm not Irish." He smiled and propped himself up on his elbow.

"Kiss me anyway."

"Do you express your longings in this manner with just any man who comes along? Irish or Bostonian does not factor in the matter?" Jones pulled her to him.

"Nope. Just one good-looking time traveler who just happens to have a certain charm about him."

Jones bent down to kiss her.

"Wait!" Darcy threw back the covers. "I have to brush my teeth first." She held one hand over her mouth and pushed him away with the other.

Jones called out. "We must endeavor to pack a toothbrush each and every time we travel. I would be sorely disappointed to be in another time and space and find that I am unable to kiss your sweet lips because you have no toothbrush."

Darcy bounced back into the room and onto the bed. "There, now it's your turn," she said beaming.

Jones stared at her for a moment, flipped the covers off his naked body and planted his feet on the floor.

Darcy reached out, grabbed his hand and pulled him back

to her. "Oh what do we have here?"

"This is my way of expressing how beautiful you are to me."

Darcy laced her hands around his neck, pulling him in close. "Then you must think me gorgeous. Ha! I did a Jones there. Hurry up. I want to get this party started."

Jones jumped from the bed in a rush to return from the bathroom when he heard Darcy yelp. He rushed back into the room with his toothbrush still in his mouth. "Dun, Wu, you cannot simply show up unannounced," he mumbled. Suddenly, he realized his state of undress. "Hold your thoughts, I shall return momentarily."

The two monks stared at one another while Darcy spoke from underneath the sheets. "A little bit later and you guys would know what it means to renounce celibacy. You have my permission to show up, but keep it in the kitchen, will ya?"

Jones returned in his PJ bottoms and bowed. "To what do we owe this visit?"

"Master Fei-hung has suggested we meet at Po Lin Monastery on Lantau Island, Hong Kong. We have made arrangements with the abbess for you to meet one another when you are ready to leave."

"They are expecting both of us, right?" Darcy slid the sheet from over her head, revealing her expectant eyes.

"Although we understand your attachment to one another, you will not participate this time." Dun bowed. "We will use the monastery to practice the dynamism of self-determined time travel."

Wu stepped forward. "Listener, you have the ability to remain in constant contact, should you wish, with Time Traveler throughout his training."

"Really?"

"Time Traveler simply must provide the path of least resistance by meditating on you and you on him. When you connect you will know what the other is thinking."

"Is this like some sort of mystical thing I don't know about?" Darcy asked.

"Actually, it is a part of every human relationship. However, some are less skilled than others in opening to the information. The ability to share mind thought grows as you walk great distances with one another."

"That's cool. So, how long will you be gone? Ha! That's a stupid question." She wrapped the sheet around her body as she stepped from the bed. "When will you be back? Ha! Another silly question."

"When I leave," Jones started, "you should meditate. I will return moments into your reflection thus having the appearance of a momentary lapse in time. Wu, what amount of time is needed to secure my graduation?"

"I do not have an answer, but the truth *is* that it does not matter because you can return at any time." Dun placed his hand on Jones's shoulder. "Shall we take our leave?"

"Am I to travel with one of you?"

Wu spoke first. "You will need the Atomotron until you no longer need it to travel."

"We will assist you, but your success will depend entirely upon you." Dun said.

"So why can't you guys do this here?" Darcy asked.

"We want the isolation of a monastery to protect ancient secrets. It would be devastating for the average person to realize that time travel is not only possible but has been exercised for thousands of years by a chosen few."

"So why Jones? Why did you choose him?" Darcy asked.

"He has been chosen because of his integrity. Master Fei-hung assisted us in finding a replacement for a traveler who moved on."

"Jones, that's gotta make you feel really good," Darcy said.

Jones blushed and smiled at Darcy.

"I shall toggle in the coordinates." Jones retrieved the time machine and placed it on the kitchen table. He fixed in his destination and strapped it on. "I love you, Darcy Whitman, and I shall return in a matter of moments."

"I'll be listening for you," she said with a smile. "See you soon."

Jones turned to Wu and Dun. He flipped on the switch and glanced back at Darcy. As he disappeared, he felt a stagger in his heart when he realized he did not want to leave her behind.

Thursday, 28 June 2012, 10:00 am

Po Lin Temple, Hong Kong

Jones materialized and beheld a statue of a shimmering bronze and gold Buddha, ten stories high. His body quivered in its presence, his gaze fixed on the face that expressed the warmth of unconditional acceptance and serenity. It was no wonder to him why so many made their pilgrimage to sit in the spirit that emanated from its eyes.

"You will join us in the dormitories where you will be introduced to the abbess." Wu turned and walked slowly toward the entrance with his head bowed as he passed underneath the Buddha.

The monastery housed the nuns who came from a long line established in1906.

"Your training will commence tomorrow morning. Today I will escort you throughout the monastery. Should you have any questions do not hesitate to ask." Dun reached over, lightly placed his hand on Jones's shoulder and smiled.

"I am honored to be here. I will do my best to perform at my highest level of focus. I actually feel the power of my chi pulsing through my body. This is very exciting."

Dun and Jones followed closely behind Wu through the catacombs of Po Lin to the sleeping quarters.

"We will start with a meditation and gift giving to the abbess," Dun said. "Tomorrow we will begin with the continuation of the training from Foshan. Shall we meet the abbess?"

"But I have nothing to give. What should I do?"

"You are not expected to give this time. We have gifts from Master Fei-hung and others, primarily consisting of tea and this red envelope."

They entered a room with minimal furnishings where a woman sat in a Lotus posture. She wore round spectacles, a golden colored tunic, and a deep red cloth draped over her left shoulder. She smiled without opening her eyes. "You must be Time Traveler." Her voice was melodic and calm. "I have heard a great deal about you. I am honored to meet you." She opened her eyes. The warmth of her expression immediately caused Jones to relax. "My name is Xia Lee. I am related to one Ma Chun Lee who resided in Boston with whom I believe you may be familiar."

Jones nodded and smiled broadly. "I should have guessed. He was, is a wonderful master in his own right. It is truly a pleasure to meet you." Jones bowed and sat cross-legged in front of the abbess. "Thank you for your gracious hospitality."

"We want you to feel as one of us, Time Traveler. Take as much time as you need to perfect your attribute. Everything you need will be at your disposal so that you may concentrate on your skills. The daily practice of Tai chi is at sunrise. Wu and Dun will escort you tomorrow."

"I look forward to participating." Jones rose and bowed, as did Wu and Dun.

"Master Lee," Dun handed over a bundle of tea and a red envelope while in a deep bow. "These are from Master Fei-hung in appreciation of your cordial reception."

"It is my bliss to provide comfort to you and Time Traveler. I am joyed to participate in his evolution as a peaceful warrior."

They exited the room in quiet, and made their way to

Jones's room through the virtually empty halls.

"We will leave you for now. I would suggest you meditate on your time travel purpose. You have a great gift and it must be used for the greater good of all."

"I will." Jones found a tunic folded neatly on his bunk. He changed his clothes and sat upright, on a meditation mat, with a straight spine to align his chakras. He closed his eyes and breathed deeply, allowing his mind to center on the task that lay before him.

For what purpose do I travel? Jones waited. The thoughts and visions began to accumulate in his mind. He would travel without expectation and live in the present moment with an open mind, ready to influence an unjust or unfortunate event. He realized that his purpose necessitated the spread of kindness and comfort amongst the people of all eras. His daily purpose was to effect calm where once there was chaos, one person at a time.

Jones allowed his thoughts to wander to Darcy. In that moment, he could feel her presence. *I miss you being by my side.*

Darcy smiled. *Hi, I miss you too. I can't stop thinking about you. As long as my eyes are closed, I can feel you inside me... like, you are right here even as I meditate.*

I cannot tell you how grateful I am that we are able to share this time. I am learning more every moment of the determination of my attribute. My meditation seems to indicate that our travel will take us across time for the purpose of influencing the greater good.

How do we do that?

We are to spread the message of kindness and acceptance. I do not know how that will manifest yet. It would seem I would be teaching in some manner. Not formally, I should think, but rather, individually.

Well, you have taught me a bunch of stuff. I think I'm a better person for it, don't you?

I submit that you were already a wonderful person and I am very fortunate to have met you.

Awww, you're so sweet. Come home and see me. Like right now. Just kidding. I mean I wish you could.

This gives me great mental energy to hone my skills quickly, which will allow me to return to you sooner.

You're coming back at the same time you left, right? So how can you come back sooner?

You are quite right. A paradox, I suppose.

Does that mean we'll lose these talks from our memory? I mean that's fine as long as you come home.

And I will, no doubt. The plan is to arrive ten minutes later than my departure. I will visit you while you are meditating and let you know later in the day tomorrow how I am progressing.

I want you home but not at the expense of you hurrying through a travel and leaving behind a leg or something. Ya know whatta I mean?

I do. My heart-felt love and adoration is yours forever. I so look forward to being in your presence once again.

Awww You say the sweetest things. Love you. Talk again soon.

Jones stood and began to perform his favorite tai chi chuan kata. He felt the firmness, yet suppleness of his muscles as he swayed to the ancient rhythms that had been practiced for thousands of years. He embraced the powerful surge of his chi, narrowing his focus and sharpening his mind. He could envision the accelerated use of tai chi chuan in battle as an unnerving defense. He moved smoothly, fluidly, flowing from the beginning to the end as if it were one movement.

A light knock on the door drew his attention.

"Zhù fú. May I help you?" Jones asked, holding the door open.

Wu bowed and stepped forward. "I hope you find your accommodations suitable."

"Yes, very much so. Kind of you to inquire." Jones returned the bow.

"It is time for the daily meal. If you are so inclined I will show you the way to the dining hall." Wu's round face filled with a warm smile, his eyes playful.

Jones slipped into his bamboo sandals, taking up a stride next to him.

They walked past the ornate shrine of three Buddha surrounded by many gifts, smoking incense, and offerings. The bright red and gold tapestry, accentuated by flowers, filled the antechamber. Lanterns hung from the vermillion ceilings where dragons and other mythical creatures of Chinese lore stared down at them. They entered the hall where hordes of monks, from all over the world, had gathered for a retreat. Dun joined them at their table.

"Where are you from?" Wu asked a young monk.

"Viet Nam." He smiled and nodded.

"We are from Thailand." An older monk extended his hand in greeting.

"We are from Beijing, China. Where are you from?" another monk asked.

"Snohomish, Washington." Jones saw a look of confusion on the others' faces. "The United States? I'm originally from Boston."

"Ah, Boston. The marathon. I am Nattapong from Thailand," he said. "Have you ever run the marathon?"

"I'm unfamiliar with… that is to say… I am not much of a runner myself." Jones paused. "Do you know when the first marathon was run?"

Chu surprised everyone when he pulled a smartphone from his robe. "It says the first Boston marathon was run in 1897."

"I see. That is precisely why the run is unfamiliar."

A full-bearded monk from Beijing turned to Jones. "You must be a time traveler?"

"I am indeed."

The group moaned an approval with nodding heads and bright smiles.

"I am here for the training provided by Dun and Wu."

"We are familiar with both Dun and Wu. They visit us on occasion. They are itinerant time travelers." Nattapong laughed. "We have become used to them popping in and out of our lives."

"Darcy, my wife, seems to have an issue with that event,

though I think we have worked it out. We spend a large portion of our time at the kitchen table, so we decided that location should be the entrance and exit for Wu and Dun."

"We want always to accommodate you and Listener as best we can." Dun raised his right hand in a gesture of blessing.

"Nattapong, what is your attribute?" Jones asked.

"I am a shape-shifter. Although, I've not had any great cause to use my attribute of late."

"Under what circumstances would you be called upon to activate your ability?"

"I use it to investigate, mostly government or military intentions involving our monastery. Cats are almost always ignored and even petted on occasion." Nattapong smiled. "Although that can be comforting, I prefer being a biped with opposing thumbs to four paws."

"Am I to infer from your statement that there are those who would prefer to remain in their alternative state?" Jones stroked his chin. "That might explain some of the reports of highly unusual animal behavior."

Nattapong laughed. "That is most likely. I've read stories of cats dialing 911 when their owner has had a heart attack and dogs running into a burning house to retrieve a loved one. Or dolphins protecting a swimmer from shark attack. Those occurrences are most likely shape-shifters who have decided not to return to their human form. Have you ever suddenly realized your pet is staring at you with adoring eyes and you thought, wow, if he could only talk?"

"That would be Darcy's department. She is a Listener. I do not want to seem obtuse but what is 911?" Jones asked.

"You haven't been a traveler for long have you?" Nattapong moved to one side as a devotee placed the dinner vessel next to him. "Have you only recently traveled forward to this time?"

"Yes," Jones said. "I am still very confounded by the liberties taken with the spoken word." He smiled thinking about the verbal exchanges he and Darcy had traded since his arrival. "My wife, Darcy, uses the word "cool" to express so many different points that I often wonder if it is recognized when used in the proper context."

"911 is to report an emergency by telephone to local authorities like firefighters or the police."

"Ah, I see."

A monk approached Nattapong and whispered in his ear.

He said calmly, "I must excuse myself. I need to meditate and pray."

"What has happened?" Jones stood and bowed as he asked the question.

"My brother has used self-immolation to protest the present military government of Thailand. I want to wish him well on his journey."

"By what method?" Jones asked in a surprised tone.

"Fire." Nattapong walked away.

Jones then turned to Wu and Dun. "I must admit that leaves me experiencing much confusion. I am uncertain of the benefits of sacrificing oneself in such a violent manner."

Wu closed his eyes and began to speak. "This method is unusual and therefore brings about a great deal of interest, spotlighting the issues his people face."

"It is not a choice I would make," Dun said. "However, I can understand how he could have come to that decision."

They sat in silence until Jones pushed his meal away.

"I cannot eat. I am returning to my room. I will see you tomorrow morning." He rose and bowed before making his departure.

Friday, 29 June 2012, 5:00 am

Po Lin Temple, Hong Kong

Jones awoke at the appointed time in order to exercise tai chi chuan with the group in the courtyard. A gentle breeze greeted the many monks who had gathered and taken their seats in rows and columns at the bottom of the steps below the Tian Tan Buddha. Three monks stood in front and the group followed, executing the Yang first form with precision and fluidity. They moved slowly, embracing the serenity surrounding them and experiencing the power of Tian Tan to focus their chi. Time seemed suspended as they re-created the twenty-four forms.

"That was very intense," Jones said as he walked beside Wu and Dun. "The idea that no matter where I travel, it gives me great comfort knowing tai chi will remain the same."

Wu slapped him lightly on the back. "Are you ready for some training?"

"I am indeed." Jones followed Wu and Dun into the Po Lin inner sanctum and then past several doors to one large windowless room. He shuddered against the stillness as he and Wu sat cross-legged on mats, and Dun closed the door. Jones attempted to adjust to the total darkness until he simply closed his eyes. He could hear their breathing and found himself inhaling harmoniously with the two monks. He allowed his thoughts the freedom to still as he concentrated on his breath. His mind easily relaxed and a newfound composure flowed over him.

Jones recognized Wu's voice.

"As you breathe, be mindful of your purpose here today. The time will be spent practicing your Om, focusing your chi, and opening your mind."

Jones drew a deep breath. "Ooommmmmmmm," he sang, blissfully, allowing the sound to escape from his upper body. "Ooommmmmmmm," he repeated several more times.

"Time Traveler, you must perform the first form in tai chi chuan," Dun said. "This is your first experience as a person who has lost their sight. You should allow yourself to see differently."

Jones rose unsteadily and centered his body. His former training with Master Fei-hung allowed him to know exactly where Dun and Wu sat. "I shall begin." He waited a moment in the silence and then slowly, began to move through the first form, his body surrounded by a faint light-blue spherical energy force field. His mind's eye saw the colorful aura in the absolute darkness.

Dun approached. "You will notice a change in color of your shield as I enter. This change reflects my energy combining with yours. Lighter colors are a reflection of harmony and darker colors are reflections of a disquieted spirit and possibly danger."

"Wu, what purpose does this serve?" Jones asked.

"These exercises will assist you in learning to focus your chi under stressful circumstances, giving you an advantage over anyone who might want to do you harm. You will be able to travel at a moment's notice."

"Who would want to harm me and for what reasons?" Jones folded his hands in front of his chest.

"There are travelers who want to take advantage of the knowledge they have acquired and they sometimes introduce conflict. They have succumbed to worldly desires. Some have been used as assassins in the past and perhaps even in the future," Dun shared.

"Let us continue your training," Wu said. "Put in these earplugs when I have finished speaking. This exercise teaches you how to cope with deafness. You must hear with your mind and body. Perform the second kata of the Yang Tai Chi. You may plug your ears."

Jones inserted the sponges and started the movement realizing at once how much he depended on his sight and hearing in his everyday life. After finishing the form he once again returned to his mat and assumed the Lotus posture.

Flashes of faces of loved ones began to appear in rapid succession. A rush of noise and voices in familiar locations from two different centuries flooded his brain. He felt present for a microsecond and then back in this room.

"Am I dreaming, Wu? Or… am I traveling?"

"You are not dreaming. In this achieved state, you are able to move along timelines at will. However, you must learn to control your thoughts. It is in this way that you may cross the linear time barrier to eternity. Practice will be of the greatest importance, taking small steps to achieve the confidence necessary to control your attribute."

"Do you recall the inner sanctum?" Dun asked.

"Yes."

Wu leaned in. "Focus your attention on the chair next to the shrine. At a given point when you are ready, chant Om and you will travel to that seat. Once there, open your eyes to confirm your experience. Close again and return to us here in this room."

"I understand." Jones closed his eyes and focused his full attention on his destination within the walls of the monastery. "Ommmmm. Ommmmm," he chanted until he heard the familiar white noise, experienced the vibration of his body expanding, listened to the familiar swooshing sound, and then found himself surrounded by silence. When his eyes opened, he recognized the seat he sat upon and the shrine next to him amongst the flowers. He used all of his powers of concentration to remain in his travel state of mind and closed his eyes again. Nothing happened.

After several attempts, Jones rose from the chair, ambled to the far door and knocked lightly. "Wu, Dun, I am unable to return." He reached for the handle, opening it slightly.

A calm voice came from behind him. "This is of no consequence and is to be expected, but your practice shall remain local until you are able to control thoughts and the resulting excitement," Dun said with a smile.

"I must admit I am *very* excited. I was able to travel and that means a great deal to me."

"The purpose of the room is to habituate your mind and body to a specific state of being, so that you are able to return to that state at a moment's notice, thus having the property of appearing to pop in and out," Wu said and laughed.

"Then I shall spend the rest of the day meditating in here."

"We will see you at the daily meal."

Jones stepped into the room, found his mat, closed his eyes and focused on Darcy meditating. It did not take long. Darcy suddenly became aware of his presence.

Hi! I miss you,

And I you. I have the most amazing news. I traveled today from the room I am in now to the inner sanctum where the three Buddha are enshrined.

206

That's so cool. How did it feel?

To be honest, it felt the same as utilizing the Atomotron. However, I must also say that I failed to return to the room from the sanctum.

Oh my god, what happened?

I lost my concentration. An event occurred similar to our experience when trapped in the woods outside the monastery in Foshan. That was very frustrating.

But you're alright, right? You still have both hands and feet?

Yes. I am safely in the hands of Wu and Dun.

Maybe we could have them over for some rice and veggies.

I fear they will not accept. They are not allowed to accept anything that is prepared specifically for them.

They have a lot of rules. When are you coming home? I'm trying to be patient but failing miserably. Sorry.

In a few moments... or at least it will feel that way.

I love you. Hey, what's the possibility I can pop around to see you. I could use the Adventurer.

I would be most delighted by that but I would not feel comfortable until I have had a chance to examine the system further.

Gotcha. Okay, I'll see you in a few minutes.

I adore you and I cannot wait to be in your arms again.

Love you.

Jones chanted Om for several minutes, concentrating on being still and avoiding, as well as he could, the faces and places of his past so as not to accidently *trip the lever* once again.

He spent the next several days meditating and practicing tai chi chuan in the mornings, returning to the training room to take frequent trips in time, popping in and out of different areas of the monastery. On two occasions, he appeared behind tourists who were visiting Tian Tan, inadvertently startling them and sending hands in the air and laughter all around.

Wu and Dun intervened at times to protect the anonymity of the ancient ones as Jones' proficiency progressed. Assigned monks spontaneously threatened harm or physically attacked Jones as he walked from one area to another. He had learned to use the sudden rush of adrenaline to focus his mind for the instant teleportation to another location.

Saturday, 30 June 2012, 5:30 am

Po Lin Temple, Hong Kong

The following day, Wu approached Jones as he was exiting his room.

"It is time for you to leave us. You will carry the Atomotron in your hands for this journey."

Jones bowed. "I am forever grateful for your teachings and training. I will do my best to honor you and Dun no matter where I am in time." Jones gathered the Atomotron.

Dun sidled up next to Wu. "We are leaving for Foshan. Master Fei-hung will no doubt have other assignments for us. It has been a pleasure working with you. *Xingshi* to Listener."

"And blessings to you as well." Jones closed his eyes, smiled, and focused on home.

Thursday, 28 June 2012, 10:10 am

Snohomish, Washington

"**D**arcy, would you do me the honor of allowing me to kiss your sweet lips?" Jones moved in close to her face where he could feel her hot breath against his own.

She smiled, opened her eyes and kept her back straight, her breathing easy and steady. She pouted her lips and leaned against his. "Welcome back. Seems like you haven't been gone long at all. And I really, really liked our mind talking stuff. That was seriously cool."

"I assumed that returning five minutes later would give us enough time to remember our first conversation. I am thoroughly enthralled with the possibilities for our future. We should spend the night together and then consider what direction we want to explore."

"I'm way okay with that idea. We're still going to go see Roark, right? I can't wait to see him older."

"Hellooo, Dar are you here?" Taylor leaned in through the front door.

"Yeah. We're here. What's up?" she asked as she rounded the corner to the foyer.

"I picked out a bay this morning and made the first and last payment on a lease. And I'm working with a sign painter on a design for the shop. *Taylor-Made Bikes.*"

"That's way cool, dude. I bet you are flippin' out inside." She smiled and grabbed him for a hug. "I'm so proud of you."

"Thanks to you guys for believing in me. I wouldn't have

stopped, but man does this make things so much easier and faster. Maybe you guys could come by and check the place out?"

"Congratulations, Taylor." Jones took his hand in a firm grip. "I am very happy for you."

"I also want to show you something." Taylor strolled over to the kitchen table and unfurled a white sheet of paper. "So whatta ya think?"

Jones's eyes filled with excitement. "Is this? Could this possibly be your design for my motorcycle? This is fantastic. The yellow and orange flames on the purple tank are... formidable."

"You are correct, sir." Taylor had drawn three perspectives of the bike: front, rear and side. "Can you see yourself on that machine?" Taylor laughed. "And the added benefit of a similar color bike to Darcy's, except for one small difference, but it's up to you. It's electric. When you told me about your steam-powered ride, well, I just thought you might get a kick out of having an electric bike. It's the Zero S electric motorcycle."

"That would be fantastic." Jones slapped Taylor heartily on the back.

"They do cost though, but I'll customize it for free." Taylor extended his hand. "I really do appreciate your support."

"I feel grateful that I am fortunate enough to be able to aid. I may have to return to Boston for a bit of financial adjustment. Not to worry though, that won't take but a second."

Darcy smiled as she walked back to Jones and took his arm. "Electric motorcycle. Ha! That just makes so much sense to me. Maybe we could stop by the bay on our way back from seeing Mom."

"Am I to understand that we, as in you and I, will be visiting your mother today?"

"Not to worry, she doesn't bite. I really wish I could tell her the good news about us." Darcy pulled him in close. "She would be very happy for me."

"I should think at some point that would make sense, but right now I think it might confuse her." Jones wrapped his arms around her waist.

Taylor looked up from his drawings. "Hey you two, get a room. I'm outta here. I have work today. Meet up around two?"

"Sure, cool. We'll see you there. Where is there, by the way?"

"Oh yeah. The bay is at the end of Lake View. Darc, you know it. Check ya later." Taylor whistled as he left.

"So would you like to see a demonstration?" Jones asked, beaming.

"Sure. Where are you going?"

"To the bedroom."

"Cool," Darcy said and laughed. "I guess I'll have to walk."

She took two steps back and waited.

Jones closed his eyes, chanted a single Om and, like so many times before, simply disappeared.

Darcy sprinted to the bedroom. "That is so flippin' excellent. Do you think I'll ever be able to travel with you?" she said as she slid in next to him and pulled his arm around her neck.

"Only time will tell. Until then, you will be using the Atomotron."

Darcy sat on the edge of the bed. "But what if it's an

emergency? I'd have to hang around for nine seconds to take off."

Jones laughed as he joined her. "I would never ever leave you behind." He sat next to her and took her hand. "Should we find ourselves in unsavory circumstances, I shall make sure that you are on your way before I take my leave."

"Alrighty then. Let's go see Roark tomorrow."

"If that is what you want, that is what we shall do."

"In the meantime, Mr. Whitman, I am due some serious cuddle time with you. I don't know what you called it in the past but nowadays we call it an afternoon delight."

Friday, 29 June, 2012, 5:30 am

Snohomish, Washington

Jones toweled off as he walked from the shower into the bedroom. He whispered in Darcy's ear, "Good morning my sweet. Would you be available for a short visit to an island today?"

Darcy pulled the covers over her head, and then suddenly popped out. "Yes. I almost forgot. We are traveling today. Yay!" She jumped out of bed, threw on a robe, and pitter-pattered her way to the kitchen. "First things first," she said as she gathered the items she needed for her coffee pour-over. "We should maybe shower, run over to see my mom, and then get outta here."

Jones joined her. "Should we not take the motorcycle?"

"Of course." She scrunched her face and then chuckled. "Oh, you thought I literally meant... *run* over. No, we'll take the bike."

"Excellent. In addition, I am thinking we should use the Atomotron to travel today. I would be highly disappointed to teleport and discover that one of us is not at the correct location."

"Yeah, no kiddin'. And we know who that would be." She grabbed the kettle just as the whistle began to blow. "I would be crazed, landing in Hiva Oa if you got stranded somewhere between here and there." She carefully poured the hot water down the side of the filter cone in a circular motion. "That's a scary thought. I mean what if you are headed to one place and think about another, and bam, you show up somewhere weird."

"Yes," Jones lightly stroked his chin. "Like Snohomish, Washington in the year 2012."

"Yeah, just like that." Darcy laughed. "You wanna fix, I mean *prepare* your own, or shall I *prepare* it for you?"

Jones grinned. "You are making light of my cultured speak."

"Now, what would give you that idea?" she said as he picked up a coffee cone. "Nah, I'm just busting your chops."

"I should remember what that means, but it escapes me at the moment."

"Jesting? Remember?" She poured in cream and brought the cup to her lips. "Oh, yeah, baby, now that's a good cup of coffee."

"I will *fix* my own." Jones laughed as he scooped in the coffee. "How would you expect your mother to respond when she meets me?"

"She's gonna love you." She placed her hand on his chest. "She'll flip when you speak to her with that Bostonian accent."

"Shall we bring our coffees to the bedroom and dress then?" Jones put his arm around her shoulder, leaned in and kissed her forehead.

"Yep." Darcy halted. "It feels like it's been months since I've seen her. But really it's only been a week or so. This is a very freaky place to be in."

"You must remember that you have aged a bit, and you have changed physically and mentally, so it would not be surprising that she may have a reaction to your new self."

"I almost forgot how different I'll look to her. I hope I don't scare her."

Darcy pulled the motorcycle into a space right outside the front of Americus and parked.

Jones dismounted, removed his helmet and reached for Darcy.

"I gotta tell ya, I'm a little nervous," she said looking up into his eyes. "She hasn't been hugely responsive the last couple of times I've been here. She's been really depressed, so I'm not sure what to expect."

"Perhaps I should wait here for you to return?" Jones placed their helmets on the handlebars.

"No. Are you crazy? I want my mom to meet you even if she doesn't know exactly what's going on."

Jones took her hand and gave her a gentle squeeze.

The doors flew open automatically as they approached.

Jones halted in surprise and stepped back. "Completely unexpected." The doors closed and he stepped towards them, causing them to fly open once again. "I am so interested to know what precipitates this phenomenon. This must be a child's joy."

"Ya think. Maybe a traveler's joy, too. Come on, let's get this party started." Darcy sidled up to the reception desk. "Hey. How's it goin'?"

"Hi Darcy. I'm doing fine and yourself. Wait a second, something's different. You cut your hair. It looks great. Has your mom seen it yet?"

"Nope, not yet." She glanced back over her shoulder. "Sylvia, this is a friend of mine from Boston. This is Jones Whitman. Jones, Sylvia."

"It is my pleasure." Jones shook her hand.

"Nice to meet you," she said. She looked up at the clock on the wall. "Darcy, your mom is probably sitting next to the fountain about right now. You don't need an escort. I'll see

216

you when you leave."

They signed the visitors form, and Darcy slid it back to Sylvia. "Thanks. Be back in a few."

They left through the side door and continued along a narrow walkway to an open area with benches. Next to a water feature sat a gray haired lady, staring into the pool.

"Mom," Darcy said as she sat next to her. "How's it going?" She stroked her back gingerly.

"I'm fine. As well as can be expected. He said I need to cheer up and socialize more."

"Is that something you're willing to do?" Darcy moved around to face her mother.

She looked at Darcy. "As far as I know."

"I see. Well, sounds like good advice." Darcy stood and reached for Jones's hand. "Mom, I want you to meet a friend of mine. His name is Jones Whitman. Jones this is my mother, Ella Champagne."

"Mrs. Champagne," Jones said as he bowed slightly.

Ella smiled. "You don't seem to be from around here. You sound more like an easterner, maybe?"

"You are very perceptive. I am indeed from Boston. I have only recently met your wonderful daughter."

"What's your job? Where do you work?"

"Mom," Darcy interjected.

"Those are fair questions to be sure. I am an entrepreneur. I graduated with a degree in engineering from Lawrence School of Engineering Harvard. And I am now an inventor and a traveler slash explorer."

Ella narrowed her eyes. "I see." She stared for a moment.

Darcy took her mother's chin and guided her back to her line of vision. "Mom, do you need anything?"

"No, Taylor has been by a couple of times with things I

needed. He says you've been busy. Now I know what's been keeping you."

"Ella, it was very nice meeting you." Jones reached as if to tip the brim of his hat and realized he was not wearing one. "That was awkward." He chuckled. "Darcy, I will meet you in the reception area." He followed the path to the front.

"Are you dating? How old is he? He seems like a nice enough guy," Darcy's mom said.

"Yes, we're dating. He's twenty-eight and a very nice man. You seem tense today."

"Some days are better than others." She rested her chin on her hand. "I still miss him. I wish I could go back in time and redo some of the things I didn't do right back then. Spend even more time together."

Darcy felt her heart ache. "I wish I could make that happen, Mom. Maybe someday we can revisit that idea." She leaned down and kissed her mother on her head. "Memories are very close to time travel." She touched her cheek. "Listen, I need to get going. You can always call me if you need anything. I'll see you again soon. I love you, Mom."

Ella flashed a faint smile and turned back to the fountain.

Darcy caught up with Jones, thanked Sylvia, and headed outside to the bike. Her eyes suddenly filled with tears. "I hate this part... leaving her here, but she needs to be constantly watched. She has never recovered from the loss of my dad."

"This situation must leave you feeling helpless," Jones said as he wiped a tear from her cheek.

Darcy straddled the bike, pulled on her helmet, and keyed the engine. "Yep, that's the right word for sure." She sat for a moment and then sighed, wishing she could take her mother back in time to see her Dad. "Hang on," she called out over her shoulder as she tried to brush off the pain that the loss of her father had caused all of them. She decided she needed to focus   on   the   present. "Let's run by Taylor's bay real quick. I really want to see what he's up to."

They pulled onto Lake View and rode to the end bay. The last fasteners of the new sign were being screwed into place by two skinny guys on ladders. The sign read *Taylor-Made Bikes* in bright purple lettering, bordered by flames.

"Taylor! You scored, dude. That looks great." She shut down the bike and rocked it over on to the kickstand.

Jones stood, admiring the creativity. "This was a good, no… great investment. How can one not come here for a custom motorcycle? Hats off, Taylor."

Taylor grinned from ear to ear. "Thanks a million, Jones. I'm feeling good. So good, I may have to go for a wild ride just to blow off some steam. HA! Get it? Steam?"

"So we'll see you on the flip side, Taylor. Give me a hug." Darcy pulled him in and hugged him fiercely.

"Whoa, what's wrong?" Taylor held her away from him, looking down.

"I'm okay. I just saw Mom and you know how that is."

"Yeah." He nodded and stepped toward Jones.

Jones took Taylor's hand in his two and bowed. "I see really marvelous things coming to you. I am looking forward to what the future will bring."

As they pushed off and Darcy wheeled through the back streets, Jones fondly recalled his Columbia steam-powered motorbike from 1891, and memories of taking the long way home from the train station. Upon arrival, he jumped off and raised the garage door. "You should get the device that opens the hospital doors," Jones said as Darcy entered the garage.

"Yeah, it's called a garage door opener. Just haven't looked into it. Hey, guess what... I'm excited about zipping over... and back, to Hiva Oa. So, I'm going to pack a couple extra batteries and a toothbrush... just in case, and I think I'll be ready."

"Perhaps we should stay overnight? Do you have a preference?"

"Sure, that's cool, and we can come back at the same time we leave. So I'm gonna take an extra pair of shorts. Wait, no, I'm going to bring a sarong instead. When in the islands, ya know what I mean?"

"I do not."

"Another time then. Let's get our stuff together and get out of here." Darcy pulled her backpack from the coatrack and dropped several AA batteries in. She then went to her closet and picked two sarongs as Jones loaded an extra t-shirt.

"No undies?"

"Will I need them? I had planned to wear my tunic." Jones held up the top.

"Goin' fresh. I like that." She slapped him on the butt. "Just don't be making me crazy."

"I assure you I do not intend on doing anything of the sort. That is until we get back." Jones then pulled his t-shirt over his head and dropped his blue jeans to the floor.

"Whoa, dude, you gotta stop just dropping trou like that."

He quickly retrieved his clothing from the floor and began to fold his pants. "My apologies. I would not have just left them piled on the floor."

"That's not even close to what I was referring to, big boy." She threw her arms around his neck and they shared a deep kiss. "I'm ready for some fun in the sun. Hiva Oa, here we come."

He donned his tunic, toggled in the coordinates and the date Sunday, 19 June 1895 12:00 pm, adding the info to his journal. He pulled on the Atomotron, adjusted the straps and recorded their departure time, 2:05 pm. "If you would be so kind," he said and held out his arms. He pulled her into a tight embrace, reached back, and turned on the time machine. The whirling pitch of gears continued to rise but slowly.

"You must step back," Jones yelled and pushed Darcy away. He then quickly unloaded the Atomotron and struggled to turn it off in time.

"What the hell is going on?" Darcy asked from across the kitchen.

"The batteries. They must have lost power and I feared that perhaps we would forever disappear as atoms scattered across the universe. We must, from now on, check the cells prior to strapping on the Atomotron."

"That's a great idea. Dude, we can pick up a battery tester for a few bucks."

"We should take it with us."

"Absolutely, and a couple of fresh extra batteries." Darcy stroked the side of the time machine. "You'd never intentionally hurt us, would you?"

He chuckled. "I am fairly certain that the machine has no intentions either way."

"Yeah, I know. Hey, let's take the bike around the corner, pick up the tester and a pack of AA bats and get back here ASAP."

"Can I wear my tunic?"

Darcy looked him up and down. "Wait here. I'll only be a few minutes."

"What?" Jones said with his palms out.

"Definitely not motorcycle attire, dude, for *so* many reasons." She plucked her leather jacket from the coatrack and headed out the side door.

Sunday, 19 June 1895 12:00 pm

Atuona, Hiva Oa Island, French Polynesia

They materialized on a cloudy summer's day as a strong wind blew onshore. The waves crashed in a thunderous roar, spilling sea foam at their feet.

"Looks like a storm's coming in," Darcy said.

"The appearance is rather ominous. We should make haste to find Roark." Jones unloaded the Atomotron and stashed it in the same place they used the last time they were on the island.

They clasped hands and hurried up the beach to the path that led to the village. As they approached, several village women ran up, smiling broadly. They took Darcy's hand and pulled her along, giggling as they pointed to a hut just off the path.

"Oh my god. Jones, look at this." Darcy pointed to a child with wild curly red hair.

"Just as I postulated. This can be none other than a young Fogerty." Jones approached the young boy and stuck out his hand. "My name is Jones Whitman."

The boy stood and stared up at him with his head cocked to one side.

"He can't be more than two and he's so cute. He's an interesting mix of Roark and whichever one is the mother. Do you speak at all?"

A deep resonant voice shouted, " 'at's me son."

Darcy wheeled around and ran straight at him. "Roark," she called out. "Oh my gosh, it's so great to see you. And your son is adorable." She threw her arms around his chest and hugged him as hard as she could.

When he broke the embrace, Darcy caught a glimpse of Roark's new scar that ran across his forehead and nose.

Jones took Darcy's place for a hug of his own. "Roark, my friend, it is without any doubt whatsoever that I am extraordinarily happy to see you."

"Ya come at a good time." He smiled broadly. "Me second wife is about ta make me a dod again. I could use a good man friend about now."

"Really? Is this a good thing?" Darcy asked.

Roark reached down and pulled his son to his shoulder. "Ya, I like bein' a dod. Not mean like me dod was."

"I'm sure you're a great father," Darcy said as she played with the baby's toes. "What's his name?"

"Kieran, Kieran Fogerty." Roark rubbed his fingers through his son's curly hair. "He takes afta 'is mom. It means little dark one."

"That's way cool. So where is everyone?"

"Most women are with Amura. A few watching the kids. The men are drinkin' kava at the gatherin' house."

"Are you still with the same three women?"

"Methinks 'at's enough." He raised Kieran above his head and placed him on his shoulders as they strolled toward the beach. "Puroto and Temoe stayed with Amura."

"Where is Gauguin?" Darcy leaned against Jones.

Roark pointed out over the water. " 'e's on 'at little island over there."

"Roark is this your second that is to be born?" she asked.

"In some ways ya. It's me second child with Amura."

"Am I to understand you have children with the other two as well?"

"Ya, I do. Two lassies. Me daughters. Babies 'ey are. Happy babies."

"That's a lot of kids, bud."

"None seem ta mind."

Jones pointed to Roark's face. "What pray tell did this to you?"

Roark touched his forehead with his massive hand. "We 'ad visitors 'at turned out ta be bad men. Wanted ta do harm to our women. Methinks they won't be comin' back anytime soon."

"So how'd you get the cut?" Darcy stared up at Roark.

"A bad man started yelling at me. Made a voice like me dod's. 'e said ta me ta shut up. 'e grabbed Temoe by the arm and she screamed. Me ran up ta him and hit 'im so hard he never got up. 'at's when da bunch of 'em jumped me. One yellow-skinned fella took a swipe at me wif a sword. Me stopped 'im, but he still cut me."

"How did you manage to repel the likes of these men?"

"Been showing da men how ta box since ya left. 'ey learn fast. Fair at fightin' I kin say."

"You have become a great figure in their eyes then. Congratulations on a fight well done."

"Can I hold Kieran?" said Darcy.

"Methinks he'd like 'at," he said and lifted the baby from his shoulders into Darcy's arms.

"You're so cute," she said, tickling him under his chin.

"I can see the mother in you coming forth." Jones placed his hand on Kieran's back. "Coochy coochy coo."

Darcy laughed. "Coochy coo? Where did you hear that?"

"I think it might be fair to say my childhood? And to be precise it is coochy *coochy* coo."

"Are you sure. Not one or three but two coochies."

224

"Exactly." Jones wrestled Kieran from Darcy and lifted him high in the air. As the child came down, he began to laugh.

"Yabady yabady." And up he went again cackling like an hyena.

"Methinks you'd make a great dod. Ya got a way with people big and small."

"Thank you, Roark. I take that as a true compliment."

" 'ow long ya here for?"

"Just the night I'm afraid. We've got some things to do back in Snoho." Darcy stopped in mid stride and looked out over the bay. "Have you seen a storm like this before, Roark?"

"Methinks this 'ere looks meaner 'an most."

"It would seem this wind is a forewarning," Jones said. "It appears to be steadily gaining in force."

Darcy took hold of Jones's hand. "I think we should get to the village and get ready for this sucker."

The clouds had turned black over the Pacific and tumbled toward the small island, foreshadowing impending fury. The sea churned into an inky soup, topped with whitecaps, while darkness crept into the village.

"What about Gauguin?" Darcy called out over the wind.

In the distance, they saw the villagers had gathered and started the walk to the cave Hanapete'o.

"Methinks ya should follow the rest ta higher ground. Gauguin should be good ridin' it out."

A sudden fierce bolt of lightning lit up the village huts followed by a voluminous clap of thunder that shook the ground.

"We need to get out of here," Darcy said as she pulled her body in close to Jones.

"Travel?" he asked.

"No. We can't leave Roark and his family… and we can't take them with us."

"I am going to run down the beach and retrieve the Atomotron. I have no idea how high the tide might be this afternoon. I will return quickly."

"That's a short distance so maybe you can travel." She laid her hand on his chest. "I know you can. Try it. Here, come over here behind this tree."

Jones closed his eyes tightly and took a deep breath.

"Ommmmmm. Ommmmm."

He stood still as the noise around him change to chaos. He opened his eyes to see the ocean boiling and sliding over the sand to the edge of the Atomotron. He quickly rescued the time machine and held it in his arms. He smiled and once again closed his eyes. He took one deep breath, "Omm," and he was teleported back to Darcy.

"You did it," she said as they fell in behind the rest of the tribe heading up the mountain. "Dude, you are so cool I can't stand it."

"I am truly indebted to you for your confidence in me. I am not always completely convinced that I am as capable as you think me." Jones pushed back the foliage as they stepped up the volcanic rock path.

Darcy ran into Temoe. "Where is Roark?"

She stopped to look around the group. "He decided to stay with Amura. I am to go into the mountains with the children and Purotu."

The rain had begun to fall and the strong winds pushed the trees about. The clouds rolled onto the island and the darkness shrouded them in fear.

"Temoe, which of these girls belong to Roark?" Darcy

called out.

"This is Moehau. She is my daughter with Roark. We must keep moving."

"She is so beautiful." Darcy reached out and took her other hand. "And where are the others?"

"Purotu's daughter Aata and Kieran are with Purotu just ahead of us. This storm is angry." Temoe looked skyward shielding her eyes from the rain. "We must get to the cave. Hanapete'o will keep us safe for the night."

Jones pushed past the tall ferns to stand by Darcy's side. "Darcy, I want to check on Roark and Amura. Take the Atomotron for safekeeping. Should an emergency arise do not hesitate to travel. I will toggle in Snohomish."

"We must get the children to the cave first."

"Observing the tide gives me great cause for concern for Roark and Amura's safety. We must relocate them." Jones wiped the rain from his brow.

"She's in labor. How could we possibly do that?"

A sudden intense wind caused everyone to halt and protect the children.

Jones huddled with Darcy, covering her head with his arms and chest. "I will travel back and assist them. I would think that Roark could easily carry her."

"Wait until no one's looking." She turned to make sure of their timing. "Okay, go."

Jones closed his eyes and began his chant, "Omm." He could feel the teleportation process beginning in his body and opened his eyes. He stood just outside of the hut where Amura and Roark remained.

As he pushed open the thatched door, he caught a glimpse of Roark lying over Amura. In the darkened hut, Jones could see where a palm had fallen, crushing the corner and apparently striking them both. Jones pulled at Roark. "My friend, are you hurt?"

Roark began to stir and pushed Jones away. "Methinks they could be dead." He looked at Jones.

"Let me examine her." Jones checked Amura's pulse. "Faint, but she is alive."

"We're in trouble," Roark said as the waves began to strike the side of the hut.

"Wait here. I must travel to Darcy. I have an idea." Jones stepped out into the wind and rain. He centered his mind and conjured his chi. "Ommm."

As his body vibrated, he thought of Father Carlini, Emily, Master Lee and Master Fei-hung. Jones appeared in front of Carlini, sitting on his bunk in the Danvers Asylum. Father Carlini's eyes bulged and his mouth dropped open. An image of Emily came and he ever so briefly stood by her bed, then he was in front of Master Lee, sleeping in his office at the university. He flashed to Master Fei-hung and in another instant, he was back on Hiva Oa. He took a deep breath, concentrated fully on Darcy's face and once again chanted *"Ommmmm"*. He opened his eyes and took her by her shoulders.

"We must travel to Snohomish and return at exactly the same time as we did before. A tree has struck Amura and she is in peril. We must come back to warn of the storm in order to secure her safety," he called out to Darcy.

"Temoe, I've got to go with Jones. I'm sorry."

"We will move ahead with the children. It is not far now." Temoe took Moehau by the hand and waved goodbye.

Jones strapped on the Atomotron and wrapped his arms around Darcy. She laid her head against his chest and closed her eyes as the white noise enveloped them.

Friday, 29 June, 2012, 2:05 pm

Snohomish, Washington

They appeared in the kitchen of Darcy's house and Jones unstrapped the Atomotron.

"We haven't a moment to lose." Darcy watched over his shoulder as he toggled in the coordinates and the time for Hiva Oa.

"I am toggling in the exact same time as before. However, this time we must approach the situation carefully. The tribe could become suspicious if we disclose too much information too quickly."

"I'll follow your lead. This is so weird. Hurry!" She waited with her arms out.

"Come to me," said Jones.

Once they embraced, Jones turned the switch and they disappeared.

Sunday, 19 June 1895 12:00 pm

Atuona, Hiva Oa Island, French Polynesia

They arrived to the now familiar cloudy summer's day with a strong wind blowing onshore. The waves crashed in a thunderous roar, spilling foam at their feet.

"Déjà vu," Darcy said.

"I believe I was correct in saying it appeared rather ominous. We should make haste to find Roark. We will take the Atomotron with us."

They clasped hands and hurried up the beach to the path that led to the village. As they approached, several villagers ran up, smiling broadly. They took Darcy's hand and pulled her along, giggling as they pointed to a hut just off the path.

"This is so freakin' weird," Darcy said as she pointed to a child. "Is it possible for him to be even cuter than before?"

Jones approached the young boy and stuck out his hand. "My name is Jones Whitman."

The boy stood and stared up at him with his head cocked to one side.

A deep resonant voice shouted, " 'at's me son."

Darcy wheeled around and ran straight at him. "Roark," she called out. She threw her arms around his chest and hugged him as hard as she could. "We have something to tell you, privately."

"If you would be so kind as to give us a moment of your time, it is quite possibly a matter of life and death."

"Ah, this feels like Boston. Have ya already been 'ere taday?"

"We have and there is a storm brewing that will cause great harm to Amura should we not move her from her present location."

"I know fer sure ya been 'ere cause you dun't know how my wives are called. Ya didn't say nothin' 'bout me scar. Do ya already know me son?"

"Yep and he is a real sweetie. Kieran, right? You're very brave to take on so many women and children. The tribe must be very proud of you." Darcy smiled and patted his chest.

"My friend, we have but a few minutes before we need to make arrangements to carry Amura to higher ground. This storm that is approaching is more dangerous than it appears."

Roark placed his hands over his head. "Ya savin'me agin? And Amura?" He picked up his son.

"Yep, but we need to get goin' like right now."

"Ya know already she is in labor. Dunt know how long afore the child is here." Roark ran his fingers through his son's hair. "Will the girls be okay?"

"As far as we know. Only you and Amura experienced danger when we were here last."

"We kin ask the women who bring in babies what to do." Roark lifted Kieran over his head and placed him on his shoulders.

They quickly made their way to Amura and the women of the tribe who birthed children. The cries from inside the hut made it clear that her labor may have progressed beyond the point of easily moving her to another location.

"The women say she's close," Roark said as he looked up at the darkening sky. "Ya already know what happens. Maybe we can do something to make it not happen."

The wind picked up speed as the dark menacing clouds moved closer to the island. A cool drizzle began to fall while the others gathered to make the trek to Hanapete'O cave for safety.

The four birthers took their leave when the waves began to splash against the sides of the hut.

" 'ey want me ta bring 'er ta the cave."

"That's crazy. She could give birth at any moment. But we've gotta do something quick 'cause this storm is right here." Darcy suddenly jerked around to Jones and took him by his hands. "What if you take her up the mountain using the Atomotron?"

"That is brilliant," Jones called out. "The thought does however give me pause. What if something were to happen during teleportation? And how do I explain to her what is about to happen?"

"Methinks I should do 'is. I kin take her and the baby in my arms and you kin turn on the machine."

"Brilliant again. I must calculate the new coordinates or they will end up by the palm where I stash the time machine." Jones squatted under the fronds over hanging the hut, and drew a picture in the sand of their point of entry to the island. "Allow me to think this through. We land here and it is approximately three hundred yards from this point south by southwest meaning it to be…" He laid the Atomotron on its back and began to quickly toggle in the coordinates and time. "This will, at the very least, take you to higher ground. And I am assuming you will be in a location that is somewhat on or near the path to Hanapete'O."

"How sure are you?" Darcy asked.

"I am sure of one thing… this is far better than the circumstances we find ourselves in at this moment."

The rain increased as darkness rolled over the island. The winds began to toss the trees, causing the palm fronds to

233

stream horizontally while the waves splayed no more than a few feet from where they stood.

"Okay, so we are footin' it up the hill?" Darcy said.

"Yes. If I am interpreting your meaning to be that we will be hiking to Hanapete'O. Roark, strap the Atomotron on and come inside with me."

Jones held the time machine in place while he bent backwards to slide his arms through the straps.

They entered where Amura lay in labor. As Roark went to slip his arms underneath her, she squealed painfully, causing him to stand upright.

"Amura, I'll pick you up easy. Ya tell me if I do anythin' to make you hurt. You and me are going for the cave. I need fer ya to close yer eyes tight and don't open them until me says it's okay."

"*J'ai peur*," Amura whispered.

"She says she is frightened," Darcy said and shrugged her shoulders at Jones.

"Scared," Amura said and moaned.

"Put yer arms around me neck." He scooped her up into his arms like a child. "Close yer eyes tight," he whispered close to her ear.

Jones turned the knob and watched as the two disappeared.

"They have been transported up the mountainside," Jones yelled. "We should make haste and join the others."

"Look out," Darcy screamed as a palm tree uprooted and fell toward them, crushing the very side of the hut as before. She turned and ran, hanging onto Jones's hand as tightly as she could.

"We are fine," Jones said and pulled her back towards him. "The path is over there. Follow me."

They trudged up the volcanic rock through the thick wet foliage, Jones stopping to call out, "Roark!"

"Wait, I've got an idea. Let me see if I can hear him." Darcy stood still in the pouring rain and relaxed as much as she possibly could. "Okay," she shouted. "He's not far from here. This way." She led Jones farther up the path and then off into thick leafage. There, no more than ten yards off the beaten path, was Roark, with Amura in his arms. When the next contraction started, he marched towards them, holding Amura as closely as he could.

The winds swirled around them as they were pelted with large, cold raindrops. The lightning struck closer and closer, illuminating the entire rainforest. Earth shattering thunder quickly followed.

" 'is way. Not much more ta the cave." Roark effortlessly carried Amura to the opening. "Manutea, I need the women who bring babies."

The older woman motioned for him to follow her, past the men huddled at the front of the cave, to the back where a group of children and women were gathered.

"Leave her here on these mats. We will take care of her." Manutea then ushered Roark back to the front where they touched noses and breathed in the breath of life. "I will return with news of your child when he or she has arrived."

"Roark, do other men have more than one wife?" Darcy sat on a mat next to the cave opening.

"Don't know. Methinks I get ta do things other men don't. Maybe they like me."

"Of course they love you. You work hard. Look how you have fought beside them. You've taught them to protect themselves and their families. You have a strong son, two beautiful daughters, and another almost here... and, apparently, three happy wives. Plus, you help to keep Gauguin in line, I'm sure."

"I never heard me story before. I like me." He grinned.

"And I like you very much," said Jones. "You have been a great friend to me and to Darcy. It was fortuitous and maybe even fated that we chose now to stop in and see you. I must tell you I am certainly ecstatic that we did."

"Not sure what ya sayin'." Roark ran his fingers through his curly red hair and folded his arms across his chest.

"Only that we are happy that we were able to help out with Amura. What is the new baby's name?" Jones asked.

"Dun't know yet. The baby ain't here. Babies dunt get the name 'til they show themselves."

"That is remarkable and very pragmatic, sensible… a really good idea."

"Ya, methinks so."

"A child who expresses his ways for a nominal period will reveal a suitable name for his or herself. I like that. Darcy." Jones stroked his chin. "We shall have to remember should the need ever arise."

"Whaaat?" Darcy laughed. "Dude, did you just talk to me about babies, as in you and me having one? You never cease to catch me off guard. Man, what a… a… a… freakin' surprise."

"Have I offended you? I dare say that is the last thing I want to do." Jones leaned against the cave wall.

"Offended? No way, José. I'm excited. I mean this needs some discussion for sure 'cause we don't know what the future will bring… but, oh my god, I'm so willing to talk about it."

"Perhaps your skepticism about the future could be quelled with a short trip to a time to come."

Manutea stumbled along, steadying herself on the cave wall. She took Roark's arm. "Hoanui, I have come to say you have a second son." She smiled as she pressed her forehead against Roark's. "Tomorrow we will hold a feast and the village will meet your new boy."

"Roark, you gotta go see them. We'll wait here." Darcy waved him forward.

Roark followed Manutea as she pressed through the men standing to congratulate him as he passed.

"What did she call him?" Darcy asked.

"I cannot be sure, but from past experiences I would surmise the name has a connection to the adjective large." Jones laughed.

"I'll bet you're right. Should we be looking for a good spot to sleep?"

"Or we could travel home for the night and return tomorrow."

"I could use a shower and I'm cold." Darcy took a couple of steps and stopped. "That seems so wimpy."

"What is *wimpy*?" Jones asked as he set the Atomotron against the wall of the cave.

"Sissy, eh weak, uncool. Like, I'd be avoiding the pain of staying here, when everyone else has to stay."

"I see. You have empathy." Jones leaned in close to her face. "I will support your decision one hundred percent."

"I was afraid you'd say that." She leaned back against the wall and then sat on the ground. "I guess we're staying."

Roark's pride lit up the cave upon his return. "A real Irishman 'e is. 'e's already makin' a fist. Punchin' like a boxer. 'e's a cute one 'at one is."

"Ohh, I can't wait to see him. How's Amura doing? Is she okay?" Darcy extended her hand for Roark to pull her to her feet. "Whoa, easy big fella."

"Your excitement is evident." Jones slapped him on the back. "Another son." He looked into Roark's eyes. "You must be very happy indeed."

"The thunder and lightning has stopped but there's still a drizzle. Are folks planning to go back to the huts?" Darcy asked.

"I can ask," Roark said and turned to the men gathered. "*Allons-nous revenir à la maison*?"

"*Non*," said one man. "*Les huttes sont endommagés*."

"*Merci,*" Roark turned back to Jones and Darcy. " 'ey say the huts are damaged. We can wait 'til the light of day. Morning will come bright and clear."

"I guess we should get some sleep. We have a party to go to tomorrow and I brought a great sarong to wear." Darcy smiled and winked at Jones.

"Maybe we should check on the huts. Check the beach for damage."

"Oh, you naughty boy."

✿✿✿✿✿

The tribe gathered their belongings and began the short trek down the steep slope to the beach where they did indeed find most of the huts damaged. The blue skies, calm lazy waves, and warm sun belied the dangerous thunderstorm with winds that had thrown trees to the ground and washed away the huts closest to the shoreline.

"Wow, what a mess." Darcy surveyed the area with her hands behind her head. "I guess we won't be going home today."

"We will return at the same time we left, correct? So it will be as if we…"

"Forget it. I've heard it before, but this time I'm torn

about going home until we get Roark's *house* in order."

"Then I submit we start at the beginning." Jones cupped his hands around his mouth and shouted. "Roark, where shall we begin?" Jones then noticed a young woman with long dark hair, naked from the waist up, carrying what appeared to be a swaddle. Walking beside her, with his arm across her back, was Roark.

"Amura?" said Jones. "Should you be up? Where will you stay while we repair your hut?"

"Methinks she'll be fine." Roark called out with a grin. "Come see me son."

Jones and Darcy joined the two at the opening of their damaged shack. Amura unfolded the bark cloth wrap. There in the folds were two hazel green eyes staring out. The child's round face and dark skin were a testament to both proud parents.

Jones leaned in and stroked the little cheek.

Amura looked at everyone with a smile.

"His name will be Teina. This means little brother." She handed Teina to Jones.

"He is a handsome young man," Jones said as he swayed back and forth.

"You've got quite the way with babies, ya know." Darcy held out her hands for the baby.

"A natural inclination, I suppose."

"Methinks it's time to get to work."

Several villagers had gathered next to the fallen tree. Each took one palm frond in hand and pulled it free from the hut, exposing a gaping hole.

Jones stood assessing the situation. "I believe we can have this repaired in no time at all. We will need a rope and several new palm leaves to cover the hole."

"People know how to pack dirt together ta make a wall. Should be ready ta move back in taday."

"What time is the ceremony for Teina?" Darcy asked.

Amura offered to take the squirming baby from Darcy.

"I think he is hungry."

She found a spot near the creek that ran next to the village and sat down.

" 'is afternoon. Lotta food and drink fer everyone," Roark said twitching his eyebrows. "Methinks I'm happy yer here."

"Certainly we are as well. I want to visit you in your future to experience your children as adults. I am sure they will contribute greatly to the wealth of the community."

The community had begun to pack an earthen wall to replace the damaged corner. With everyone's help the tribe's people restored all the huts in time for the afternoon feast. The sun shone brightly accompanied by a cool breeze that came over the ocean. The gleeful sounds of women and children gathering coconuts, bananas, and breadfruit added to the growing excitement. The men brought *poisson cru* fresh from the ocean, cleaned them, and cut them into bite size pieces.

Darcy peered over the shoulder of one of the men cutting fish. "Sashimi is on the menu. That's awesome. This is gonna be fun."

"And what pray tell do we have here?" Jones stood next Roark at the underground oven and watched as three women wrapped chicken, breadfruit and taro with coconut leaves. Several men built a fire to heat the pumice rock. The cooks placed the wrapped food on the heated rocks and covered it with banana and purao leaves and a layer of dirt to keep the heat trapped.

Dancers practiced their moves while the drums carried

the rhythm. Everyone in the village played a role in preparing for the celebration.

The tribe walked to the open-air temple as the ceremony drew closer. Teina, along with Roark and Amura greeted everyone and accepted their well wishes for the child, who, unbeknownst to the tribe, had come close to death only hours before.

Amura handed Teina to Roark who raised him high in the air for all to see. The crowd rumbled their approval and began to move back onto the sandy beach for the rest of the ceremony, which began with food.

The villagers dipped their food in coconut cream, using their fingers to eat. They also served kava kava as they celebrated the arrival of Teina to the community.

Darcy laid her head against Jones's chest. "Between the kava kava and the dancing, I think I'm pooped... tired."

The day had lasted well into the evening.

"I must agree. Perhaps we should travel now that all is well."

"Nah. I'd like one more beautiful morning on the beach. I have my second sarong in the backpack... and I'm going topless tomorrow. That'll be a rush."

"That being the case, I shall remove my shirt as well." Jones laughed.

"These women seem so innocent in their ways." Darcy sat up abruptly. "That voice sounds very familiar."

"*Bonsoir,*" Gauguin said, grinning as he approached from the beach through the evening dusk. "You are glad to see me, no?" He threw his hands up. "What an *incroyable*, how do you say... incredible night of wind and rain. *Qui?* I was in fear for my life at times but I am here once again safe and sound."

"It's good to see you. It's been a while. Sort of. So how's the painting going?" Darcy stood.

"I am presently painting a friendly woman. I think I will call it: *Where are you going?* That has been a *thème* of mine the past few months... asking questions." He flipped his hand up to his ear. "So, I am thinking kava kava is calling to me. No? Do you not hear it? Listen intently. Ah *oui,* there it is again. I shall return *momentanément.*" Gauguin stalked off into the evening where the villagers greeted him as a celebrity. Not to be deterred, he pushed on towards his cup of kava.

"He's growing on me." Darcy watched him as he meandered through the crowd. "It seems like he lives in another world. Nothing seems to faze him in the least." She laughed. "He just starts in like we were always here. He's a freak, but I kind of like it."

"He leaves not one doubt that he has found his dharma. This is where his potential to paint continues to gush forth on whatever canvas he can find. This scenario for Gauguin is timeless."

"Are you ready for bed yet? This dancing could go on for a while and I'm too tired to hang out. I think time travel messes with my inner clock or something."

"Then I believe we should do exactly that. We can attempt to right our circadian rhythms."
Jones took her hand and pulled her to her feet.

"I'm rhythm-ed out. I just want to cuddle up and sleep like a baby."

They walked hand in hand to the guest hut where they had stayed the last time they visited.

"I find it fascinating how slowly environments change," Jones said as he unbuttoned his tunic.

"Maybe here in the eighteen hundreds, but man wait til we're hanging out back in Snoho. New models of everything are coming out constantly. It's hard to imagine so many changes happening so fast. At some point, it gotta run out, don't you think? New ideas, I mean."

"As long as we have imagination, I do not believe there is an end to what we can do. Until just recently, I thought I had discovered time travel. Now I know it has been around for a thousand years or so. I can only imagine what we are fully capable of as human beings, both positively and negatively."

With her pointer finger, Darcy traced his abs, down to the top of his tunic pants and wrapped the drawstring around one finger. "This conversation is too heavy for the island."

Jones laughed. "I am sure that has a meaning to you. I guess one could say that certain conversations do carry weight."

"I see what you did there, bad boy," she said with a grin. She loosened his pants and allowed them to slide to the top of his hips. "I just meant this is how we should spend our time on an island." She tugged on his pants and they dropped to the ground next to the mat.

"I see. I like the way you think."

"I can see that." She clasped his forearms.

He drew her up to her feet, untied her sarong, letting it fall to the mat, and embraced her nakedness against his own. Their kiss had Darcy's head swimming. Jones lowered her gently to the mat and covered her with kisses.

"Oh, Mr. Whitman, you do the greatest things to me. Oh my, you *are* a naughty boy."

✿✿✿✿✿

White cotton candy clouds slowly morphed into interesting shapes against the crystal blue skies as Darcy and

Jones emerged from the hut into the cool morning air.

Jones stretched his arms above his head. "Ahhhh, yes. Oh, that does feel good. Tai chi on the beach?"

"Wow, sounds perfect. And don't be shocked, but I'm tying off my sarong around my waist." Darcy folded the material in half and tied it off.

Jones stood staring with a smile on his face.

"This may be inappropriate but since we are married as such I want to say…"

"Yeah, they look good don't they?" Darcy said and laughed.

"Yes. Indubitably so. I am under great pressure to contain my urge to cup them in my hands," he whispered.

She noticed several children had gathered and were staring at them. "Not a good idea. Well at least not in front of an audience. Maybe later."

"Audience?" Jones glanced from side to side.

"Behind you."

"*Bonjour*," Jones said and waved.

The children laughed and ran away.

"To the beach for tai chi, some breakfast and then we can lay out for a while. No tan lines. Woohoo! Well at least up top. That'll have to do for now."

"Perhaps we can ask about an area to sunbathe in the nude?" Jones put his arm over her shoulders.

"I'm sure there are plenty of places. Why would they care anyway?"

"We can ask Paul."

After performing their katas and meditating, they took a dip in the cool waters of the bay. They sat on the beach to dry, as a group of men came to pull in the fishing lines and nets they had left in the shallow waters. Two noticeably different characters stood out against the natives; Roark, who assisted by pulling in the lines with fish on the hooks, and Paul, who assisted by shouting instructions.

One of the younger boys had swum out a ways to untangle a line when a shark fin cut through the surface of the water and headed straight for him. While the others on shore yelled for him to return, the shark made a pass very close to the boy.

"Darcy, quickly, you must talk to him." Jones jumped to his feet and, with Darcy in tow, sprinted to the water's edge.

Darcy stopped in the shallows of the ocean and calmed her mind. She watched the shark intently as it made a second pass, even closer to the boy, and listened carefully.

"She says not to panic. She was only curious. She does not intend to harm him."

Gauguin called out to the group. "*Tout est bon*. Calm yourselves. It is good."

Roark had waded waist-deep to reach the young native and lifted him onto his back to bring him back to shore. The shark made one last pass in front of the villagers, flipped her tail and bolted through the sea, surfacing one last time to flash her fin as she left the bay.

Paul approached Darcy. "What do you say about hearing *le requin*... the shark? Do you have a special *cadeau*... eh, gift?"

"Something like that. I trust you'll keep this between us?" Darcy untied her sarong from her waist and tied it around her neck. "Not that anyone would believe it anyway."

"The Fiti Nui tribe was more accepting of *esprit* before the Catholic church. Mystical spirit travel made up much of their traditions." Paul stopped speaking, staring out over the bay. "The church has quelled? Is this the right word? They quelled much of their ideas and *douane*... customs."

"Quelled? Jones, what does quelled mean exactly?" Darcy called out.

"To suppress or do away with, why?"

"Paul and I are talking about my attribute and the Fiti Nui tribe. He thinks they would be open to the idea of talking to the animals."

Jones walked through the sand to Darcy's side. "I am unfamiliar with their customs and spiritual beliefs, but having spent time at Foshan with Master Fei-hung I am more than ever convinced that the ancient ones understood far more than we give them credit for."

"*Oui.* These people have super... superstitions from the ancient ones. *Particulier* to death."

Jones stroked his chin. "Correct me if I am wrong but a superstition is an irrational fear. Perhaps we are drawing conclusions without the benefit of ancient experiences."

Paul placed his hand on Jones's shoulder. "It is too bad for us we cannot experience those events at the time of their occurrence. No?"

"Hmm, kind of a cool idea there, Jones. I mean you know the concept." Darcy bowed her head to hide her smile.

"It would seem that time travel would be of benefit," Jones said.

Roark had sidled up behind him. "Ya mean ta say that ya gonna—"

"Whoa, Roark, we're just talking not really sayin' anything. Having a talk with Paul here," Darcy said. "Would you like go with me for a walk, Roark?"

"No. I need ta get ta work on pullin' in the rest of the lines. We need fish fer ta-night."

"Okay, but we still want to talk with you about our

plans." Darcy took Roark's hand, feeling it close in around her own. Jones joined them and strolled with Roark back to the group of fishermen.

"Roark, we are leaving today. I… we would like to see your entire family in one place before we go. Would that be possible?"

"Methinks 'at's a good idea. Sometimes it's hard ta find 'em all at one time, but I kin tell others to send 'em home."

Roark took hold of the fishing line and pulled with great strength until flipping and flopping fish emerged from the waters. The others quickly unhooked the catch and placed it in a basket.

An elder came over to examine the catch. He pointed to the smaller fish and then to the bay.

"*Libere ces petits,*" he ordered. "*Nous allons attendre jusqu'à ce qu'ils soient gros comme Hoanui.*"

Everyone laughed.

"Paul, what did he say that was so humorous?" Jones asked

"Ah, he said the little fish should be liberated until they are as big as Roark."

"Okay, that's a scary thought," she said as she watched Roark loom over the rest.

"Indeed. The advantage is not having to fish but on one or two occasions a week." Jones asked.

"Once a month, ya mean." Darcy took Jones by the hand. "Let's eat and then round up the fam. I'm starting to feel the pull of Snoho."

Surrounded by children eyeing their every move, they ate a breakfast of coconut meat, mango, and milk.

"They're so cute. Look at those big brown eyes. Oh and look who we have here. Ole green eyes himself. Hi Kieran,"

Darcy said smiling. "What've you been up to?"

"To be honest," Jones said as he stared at the boy intently. "I am not sure he speaks as yet."

"If there was a way I could try to hear him, but that seems wrong. Maybe he doesn't want me to hear his thoughts." Darcy leaned on her elbows and studied the boy's face.

Kieran looked away, then ran as if called by someone, though they had heard nothing. After a moment, the rest of the children scurried over a small dune towards the village.

"Wonder what that's all about," Darcy said, looking in the direction of the path.

"Perhaps we should follow and observe for ourselves?" Jones stood and buttoned his tunic top.

Over the dune and farther along a path, the children were huddled together with several women attending them when Roark joined them.

"Roark, what's this all about?" Darcy asked.

The women seemed to be counting.

"When the bad men came everyone didn't know they were bad. The people now kin hear a sound that means gather where ya were told ta so we kin count heads."

"Kinda like a fire drill."

Both men cocked their heads.

"It's this thing where... never mind. So this is pretend, I hope?"

" 'is is to teach." Roark stood straight with his hands on his hips.

"Had this been a real emergency," Darcy said and laughed. Again, Jones had an inquisitive look on his face. "Eh, it's something we say when... forgeta bout it."

"A preventative measure to be sure," Jones said. "Where are the others?"

248

"The women head fer the forest. The men fer weapons."

"And is everyone participating in this exercise?" Darcy asked.

"Ya so Methinks I should leave now," Roark said as he headed down the beach.

"So what was the sound?"

"I should have asked Roark. Perhaps you could stay here with the children and I can go find the men."

"Okay. See you in a few," Darcy said and joined the group of children huddled behind the dune. "Hi, kids," she said.

"Shhhhhhh, *on ne parle pas*," they replied.

"Wow," she whispered. "No talking. I get it."

Darcy's face flushed. She sat twiddling her thumbs and noticed she had drawn the attention of the younger children. One by one, they moved forward to watch in amazement and quietly attempted to mimic her.

✿✿✿✿✿

Jones reached the men who had gathered at the marae community square to affirm procedures, should an actual attack prove imminent. They also practiced the sound of the lorikeet as a way of signaling to each other their location. Roark had taught them the art of boxing should they have to fight hand to hand.

"If I may," Jones asserted. "I too have a weapon that if used diligently will greatly increase your chances of survival. It is referred to as the shadowless kick." Jones dropped into a horse stance, stepped forward and kicked the end of a banana leaf away from the body of the frond.

"I did not see your leg move," a young warrior said.

"Form a line and I will demonstrate. I will teach you that the determined mind is the most important asset you may acquire." Jones set about teaching the technique for two hours and then had everyone assume a Lotus posture for mediation.

Darcy, along with the women and children had joined the ceremony around the edge of the marae. They laughed and pointed as the men learned the move. Although it was odd to them, the men embraced the teachings in the same spirit as when they had learned to box. After multiple hours of training, everyone took their leave to go about their daily life.

"Are you ready to meet up with Roark's family?" Darcy asked, shielding her eyes from the sun.

"I am, and you?" Jones looked back over his shoulder. "Roark," he called out. "Is it possible to gather your family together?"

"Ya. Now would be a good time ta do that meetin' ya was talkin' about. Why we meetin'?"

"We just wanted to say goodbye to all of your wives and children," Darcy said.

"We will stay in touch over time. You must tell the younger ones about us as they grow so when we do visit they will not be upset or frightened."

" 'ey will know all about ya ta be sure."

Jones and Darcy said their goodbyes to Amura, Temoe, Purotu, and the children.

"As always my friend, you have a true command of my affections and gratitude for simply being the person you are."

"We love you Roark. And we're very proud of what you have done here. Take good care of yourself and your family. We'll see you again. We have to. I would go crazy not knowing what you're up to in your life. And with my attribute, I'm pretty sure you could call me across space and time."

"You're good people, ya know. Methinks ya deserve a

bigger thank you then I kin offer." Roark lowered his head. "Jones made me life worth livin'. I'll miss ya hard."

Roark reached for Darcy and gently pulled her into an embrace.

"Ah man, here we go again." Her voice broke. "You seem to be the one man I can count on to start my waterworks." She laughed through the tears.

"Ya cryin' makes me sad. I want ya ta be happy that ya come to see me and me kids." Roark rocked her back and forth. "Me wives like ya a lot. Jones only a little." He laughed heartily.

"I find that incredibly difficult to believe. I am a very likable man."

"Yer a great man. Me family loves ya. Ya welcome here anytime." Roark embraced Jones in a bear hug. "Ya me best friend ever."

"Why are we talkin' like this? It's not like we'll never see each other again." Darcy scooted under Jones's arm. "I just hate leaving but we've got to go. Kieran, come give me a hug."

She held out her arms.

"Kieran, *un câlin,* a hug. Come give her a hug." Roark made a gesture of wrapping his arms around Darcy.

Kieran looked at Temoe and back at Darcy, then ran into her arms.

"*Merci*, Kieran. I'll see you again soon," Darcy said, holding him by his shoulders. "He has no idea what I'm saying does he?"

"Methinks I'll tell 'im when yer gone."

"We should retrieve your backpack and the Atomotron." Jones drew in a deep breath. "This is difficult," he said as they trudged through the sand back to the hut.

"I've never broken down this many times in my life. Methinks Foshan has dun somethin ta me," she said.

"I must say that was a really convincing impression of Roark's voice."

They arrived at the guest hut with heavy hearts.

"I will strap on the Atomotron and you the backpack."

"Gotcha."

They took one last look at their habitat, hugged, and disappeared.

Friday, 29 June 2012, 2:05 pm

Snohomish, Washington

"**I**'m so happy to be home, but man am I goin' to miss those guys. We're gonna have to make a trip to see them around the holidays."

"Serendipity seems to play a strong role in time travel." Jones placed the Atomotron on the kitchen table and patted its side. "You have made a remarkable difference in our lives."

"Now who's giving out human characteristics?" Darcy laughed.

"What if taking different elements and bringing them together for a singular purpose renders some type of sentience? Ha! I believe I have stepped over some type of line here."

"And into some... eh never mind. Do you want coffee?"

"No thank you." Jones took a seat at the table. "I enjoy watching you as you move about preparing coffee or whatever else. Perhaps you could adjust your sarong to the earlier style?" He placed his chin on his closed fist and smiled.

"Ah, I see. You want me to set the girls free so you can watch me walk around naked."

She pulled the coffee cone from the cabinet, set the kettle on the stove, poured grounds into the filter and then leaned back against the counter. She untied the sarong and let it drop to the floor.

"Around your waist, please. That is wonderfully sexy and

very stimulating."

She picked up the wrap and tied it loosely around her hips.

"So you liked the island girl look, huh?"

"Yes. I am also fond of the Snohomish girl playing the role of an island girl." He stood, walked over to her, cupped her breasts in his hands, and kissed them.

"Ah, so this is what you were avoiding this morning. Well… feel free to express yourself in whatever way you want." She reached over to the stove and turned off the burner.

✿✿✿✿✿

Darcy rolled over, placing her bent leg across Jones's waist. "What time is it?"

"I would be guessing. Shall I retrieve my pocket watch?" He made a move to leave the bed.

"Nope." She pulled him back. "It's more of a rhetorical question. I'm getting hungry though. How about you?"

"I believe sustenance is in order." He paused. "I am losing a sense of linear time. I made a note of it earlier today. It would seem that here and now is all there is."

Darcy snuggled up to his chest. "Yep. That's the big babble going on these days."

"Babble?"

"Well, that you, we, need to learn to live in the here and now. People make big bucks… money, telling other people how to live in the here and now."

"I think I understand. We may be speaking of two different postulates. I am referring to the confusion, both mentally and physically, that seems to manifest because of time traveling. After all, we traveled back in time, then forward and now farther into my future, but your present day

254

remains here and now. So yesterday, even one hundred twenty years ago, yesterday, is fully a recent memory. Therefore, all time is simultaneous, at least where time travel is concerned. Of course, it is just a thought." Jones turned to kiss Darcy on the forehead.

"And a deep sucker at that. Not sure I followed all of it but it sounded really cool." She sat up. "Hey, maybe we should make tomorrow a bed day."

"On my honor, I have never been exposed to a bed day." He laughed. "Are you submitting that we remain in the bed for a full day? I cannot even imagine."

"Don't worry about it. I'll teach you everything you'll need to know. We'll have food and drink and movies. We can watch TV or just talk."

"All day, in bed?" He looked up at her. "Oh, that pouty bottom lip will get you anything you want, I suspect. Tomorrow then, all day spent in bed. This should prove to be interesting."

"I'll do my best to keep you entertained. What would you like for dinner?"

"May I see the menu?" Jones laughed.

"It's a buffet. Whatever's left in the fridge." She bounced out of bed and pulled on her PJs. "Why don't you pick out something to cook?"

Jones tied his robe. "That sounds like a fine idea. However, you do not think I can cook, do you?" He twitched his eyebrows.

"Show me whatcha got."

Jones turned around and opened his robe.

Darcy laughed loudly and applauded.

They walked hand in hand to the refrigerator.

"What is that smell?" she asked.

"It would seem that *some* elements are still subjected to linear time after all, even as we travel and return. What shall we do with this?"

"Jeeze, compost. Ugh. That's more than an odor, that's an o-dear." Darcy pinched her nose and pointed at the compost bin. "Wait. Can you take it outside to the big bin? Please. Oh my god, gag me with a spoon." She continued to pinch her nose as she escorted Jones to the back door.

Jones glanced back. "A rather dramatic affectation, if I do say so myself."

"Kiss your what?" she yelled out from the back steps. "Hang on there's somebody knocking." Darcy returned through the house to answer the door. "Yeah, who is it?"

"Darcy?"

"Mom, what the hell are you doing here? How'd you get here?" she said as she jerked open the door.

"I'm feeling better, so I thought I would come home for a visit," Darcy's mother said as she walked past Darcy into the house. "You haven't changed the house too much. That's thoughtful."

"Ella, you are an unexpected surprise," Jones said as he approached her with an extended hand. "If I may, how did you manage a ride from the center?" He cinched his robe in tight.

Darcy's mother sat on the couch absent-mindedly rubbing the upholstery of the armrest. "No one would give me a ride this morning." She looked up at Jones. "So I walked."

"Mom, what were you thinking? Does anyone know you've left the center? Oh crap, I left my phone here when we... so how does that work?" Darcy picked up her phone and saw that six messages had come in. Most of the calls

256

were from Americus and two from Taylor. "I'll call Taylor right now. No, I'll call Americus first." Darcy scrolled her contact list and pushed call.

"Ella, how are you feeling?" Jones asked as he sat next to her. "Do you know what day it is?"

"No. But it doesn't matter because I have nowhere to be." She lay sideways on the couch.

"Did you know my husband?"

"No Ma-am. I am sure it would have been my pleasure," Jones said softly.

"Yes this is Darcy Champagne. Yes. I know, she is here now. How did she sneak out? Does my brother know?"

"I tried to call Taylor but he wasn't answering," Darcy's mother said. "I was running out of time to come home today so I just left."

Jones took her hand. "I understand. You must be exhausted after walking. Can I get you anything? Perhaps water or tea."

"Taylor, oh my god, Mom is here... No, I went out and left my phone. So the center has been frantically trying to get hold of us... I understand. She's here so don't go freaking out. It's too late for that."

"I think a nice cup of tea would help." Ella stood and staggered forward.

"Oh no, young lady, I am of the opinion that you should sit right here and I will wait on you." Jones helped her to sit back down. "I will return with your tea in a few minutes."

"Come by and pick us up. No not yet..."

"I am making tea. Would you care for a cup?" Jones asked.

Darcy covered the phone. "No, but you only need to turn on the stove, the water is already in the pot. No, I'm still here.

We haven't discussed the why, just the whens and whats."

Ella appeared next to Darcy with her hand out.

Darcy handed her the phone.

"Taylor, come pick me up. I'm done with my visit and I want to go back to the center." She handed the phone back to Darcy. "I feel like a nap." She traipsed back to the couch and lay down again.

"Okay, but hurry up. I want the doctor to take a look at Mom as soon as possible. She seems a little strange to me. Okay, I'll see you then." Darcy joined Jones in the kitchen. "He's on his way. She's acting strange. Damn it. I hope she didn't have a stroke or something."

"What amount of time will it take for Taylor to arrive?" Jones offered her a cup. "Positive?"

"No, I don't want anything, thanks. He should be here in about fifteen to twenty minutes."

"If the probability exists that your mother has had a stroke, perhaps we could go back to this morning and visit her at the center as a preventative measure."

"But can we be in two places at once? What if that undoes what we did for Roark?"

"We were here together uninterrupted this morning. I believe we could still change that part of our past and continue the day in much the same way as before. We did ostensibly, leave at 2:05 pm for Hiva Oa. Therefore, if we return at this time we will have already been to the island. Do you follow my logic?"

"Sort of?" she said sucking in air. "I'll trust your judgment, because I'm not sure I can wrap my brain around what you just said."

"I'll get the Atomotron."

"Wait. Taylor is on his way over. I'm confused. If we

travel, will my mother simply disappear? Does everything go back to the way it was this morning at the moment we arrive at the center?"

"That is the most logical explanation. We now have the ability to move, to and fro, through the veil of time. We can influence local history and all things unfold in a slightly different way from the previous blooming. This is a most exciting experience."

"We need to get dressed, *muy rapido*."

They both pulled on a pair of jeans, a t-shirt, and sneakers.

"So strap it on before Taylor gets here. Hey, does that mean… forget it." Darcy watched Jones as he hurried down the hallway to fetch the Atomotron.

"Mom." Darcy sat on the floor in front of the couch. "Look at me. What time did you leave this morning?"

"I don't know… after meds, so around nine." Ella laid her hand on her forehead.

"Okay, I love you." Darcy lightly stroked her mother's arm. "I want you to close your eyes and dream a happy dream. Okay?"

"Will you wake me when Taylor gets here, please?"

"Yes of course." Darcy rose slowly to her feet, gazing down on her mother and went to join Jones halfway down the hall. "I told her to close her eyes and dream a happy dream."

"Can you acquire the location coordinates for the center?" Jones placed the time machine on the table. "We must hurry to avoid Taylor's arrival."

"Sure. I'll get my computer." Darcy typed the location into the geocoder. "Okay here ya go. 47.925945, -122.08683 N47° 55.5567', W122° 5.2098'. And the time should be eight forty."

Jones toggled in the location as Darcy read them from the screen. "I changed the north degrees slightly to put us next to the parking lot instead of inside the building. Even that has an element of risk."

"It's 4: 53. Okay let's get outta here," Darcy said.

Jones slipped his arms through the straps, jostled the Atomotron into place, quickly pulled Darcy into his chest and flipped the switch. Nothing.

"I am *so* inclined to go back to steam. What is wrong with this switch now?" He clinched his jaws tight.

Darcy slapped the side of the time machine and smiled as it began to whirl.

"We need to fix that," she said as they disappeared.

✿✿✿✿✿

Jones looked over Darcy's shoulder to see a middle-aged couple staring. He immediately engaged her in a lavish display of affection hoping to boggle the pair. They turned away and then looked back, seeming to debate what they had witnessed as they got into their car.

"Our appearance must have been quite the shock," Jones said, still holding onto Darcy.

"Did I miss something?" Darcy turned to look behind her. "What's goin' on?"

"I believe we have been witnessed materializing before two persons. However, they also seemed to be skeptical over what they saw."

"Oh great. Let's get inside before the cops get here."

They made their way to the front desk receptionist.

"Good morning." The receptionist gave them a warm smile.

Darcy said with a smile. "Hi Sylvia. Here to see mom." She signed the visitor's form first and then slid the clipboard over to Jones.

"She is still in her room, waiting for her medication. You know where it is?"

"Yes, thank you."

"Should I wait here?" Jones asked.

"Nah, you're coming with me."

"Excuse me? You'll have to leave your backpack with me. You can pick it up on the way out."

"Eh, you're staying here then. He can just wait here. I'll only be a minute." Darcy kissed Jones and bounded off down the hall.

"Mom, how are you?" she said as she arrived at Ella's door. "I just wanted to stop by to say hello."

"Darcy," she said dragging out her name. "I'm happy to see you." She reached for her hand. "Ya know I had the strangest dream. I tell ya sometimes I don't know about this old brain of mine."

Darcy sat next to her mother. "Do you want to tell me about it?"

"Oh my, I dreamed that I left the center and walked to our house. Can you believe that?"

"That *is* a silly dream." She patted her mom's leg.

"And you and Jones were there and it seemed like the two of you were married. And the house looked very much the same as always. Ah, here are my meds."

A nurse handed her a small cup of pills.

"Could you do me a favor and check her blood pressure?" Darcy stood to one side to give the nurse room.

"Ella, I'm going to take your blood pressure, okay?" the kindly faced nurse said.

"I was right here when this discussion started," Ella said and chuckled.

"I'm sorry but we are required to let you know, okay? That's all." The nurse wrapped a monitor around Ella's wrist and waited. "Your blood pressure is too high. I'll be right back."

Darcy sat with Ella for a couple of minutes, waiting for someone to return, when a young doctor walked in.

"Good morning, Ella. Let me take your BP one more time." He wrapped the same band around her wrist. "160 over 98 is high. Have you been out jogging? I'm going to have the nurse bring you an aspirin and we'll monitor you for the rest of the day. So don't go anywhere." He nodded in Darcy's direction and left the room.

"Don't go anywhere. Where am I supposed to go?" Darcy's mother huffed.

"Are you okay today?"

"Absolutely. I'm a bit cranky that's all. The doc is kind of cute."

"Alrighty then, now I know you're safe and sound." Darcy chuckled. "I have to get going." Maybe we can do lunch together next week. Would you like that?"

"Yes. I think that would be nice. Tell Jones thank you for offering to make me tea." She looked up at Darcy. "I don't know what I'm saying. It must have been in my dream."

"Yeah, must've been. I love you." Darcy hugged her. "I'll see you soon." She approached Jones in the lobby. "All's well that ends well. She is a bit perplexed by a dream she had. She said to tell you thanks for offering to make her tea. I almost passed out. But she said it was in the dream. Holy smokes, that was tense for a second."

"When we teleport this time, we can return at 4:53 pm and pick up where we left off."

"Let's walk around to the side of the building shall we?"

262

Darcy said.

As they exited the building, Darcy saw a police car pull into the drive and park in front of the double doors. "We need to fly outta here like right now."

As soon as they rounded the corner, Darcy grabbed Jones.

"No time for any failures. Please, on the first try," Jones whispered.

The next event came as no surprise. They were home once again and back on schedule.

Darcy's phone rang.

"What now?" She pushed the phone icon. "Hi Taylor... Nope, everything is fine... Yeah don't worry about it. Love you too. Talk to you later."

Jones put his hand on her shoulder. "Pray tell?"

"Well, it seems he was on his way over here, and for some reason ended up driving to Crepe Escape instead." She laughed. "He decided he'd had brain malfunction so he bought a linner. He said he felt like something might be wrong so he was just checking in. Freaky huh?"

"I would assume, by that conversation, we are each up to present time." He stroked his chin. "I am learning still. Furthermore, I am also acutely aware that there is far more yet to be discovered."

"We've got plenty of time. No pun intended."

Friday, 29 June 2012, 2:05 pm

Snohomish, Washington

Darcy let out a big yawn. "Hey, whahoo! This is bed day, dude," she said and snuggled in close to Jones. "So whatta you wanna do first, Whitman? Well, coffee for sure, and maybe a little breakfast in bed? Scrambled eggs, turkey bacon, and toast with organic strawberry jam? Yum!"

"Do I even need to be here?" Jones chuckled.

"Just for the important parts. Don't be shy, speak right up." She jumped out of the bed, threw on her PJ top, fastening only the bottom button, and spun around. "Whatta ya think, Stink?"

"I think this is going to be a very interesting day." He beckoned her over with his pointer finger. "This is most titillating." He kissed between her breasts down to her belly button. "I like bed days methinks."

Darcy laughed and pulled away. Her laughter echoed back to the bedroom from down the hallway. "Get out here, you lazy boy."

"Sorry," he yelled back.

"If you want a mate in that bed ya better get in here," Darcy called out. A rather strange sound from behind drew her full attention.

"I am unable to control the speed with which I travel or I would have been here sooner." He bowed. "I am at your service, Madame."

"I've seen it all now. A time traveler in a bathrobe," she said as she went about gathering the assorted foods for breakfast.

"What shall we watch on the television?" Jones sidled in beside her and plucked an egg from the carton. He gently tapped it on the edge of the bowl on the counter. He tapped again harder and broke the yolk. "Perhaps I am not as proficient as I thought."

"Ya think. We're scrambling them anyway. So it's not a problem."

"Should one of us call to check on your mother?" Jones took out two pieces of bread. "How do you toast these?"

"Shocking I know, but in the toaster. We came up with these cool names for stuff, and a toaster browns bread, making it toast. See?" She took the bread, dropped them into the slots and pushed down the lever. "In just a couple of minutes they will pop up all by themselves and voila, you have toast."

"This is a remarkable invention." Jones stared down into the opening.

"Look in the pantry over there and get us a couple of trays for the food."

"Your wish..."

She plated the food and poured the coffee. "This looks yummy." She turned to Jones. "I'm really glad we are doing this together."

"As am I. I would not want to be traveling or as Master Fei-hung said 'walking great distances' with anyone else."

"Yep. I think our future together is going to be a lot of fun and full of adventure. And we're starting the fun part today. Grab your tray and let's head to the bedroom."

They carried the trays, placing them on the end of the bed.

"Let's get comfy. Do you want to see the news online or

on TV?"

"On the computer would be my preference."

Darcy pulled the laptop between them and booted up. "We can watch the highlights while we eat."

Jones picked up her tray and placed it gingerly on Darcy's lap.

She looked down at the food. "This is looking just like what the doctor ordered."

"This is interesting. Is this news? I am baffled. It seems like science fiction."

"Let me see. '*Shenzhou 9* was the first manned spacecraft to dock up with the *Tiangong* 1 space station. The *Shenzhou* 9 spacecraft returned at 10:01:16 CST on 29 June in the inner Mongolia region.' Yesterday. They got back yesterday. Cool. I didn't even know the Chinese had a space program."

Jones scratched his head. "I, on the other hand, had no idea *anyone* had a space program. When I left Boston in 1891, that was a fantasy. Jules Verne wrote a novel called *From the Earth to the Moon*. The idea was that using enough propellant to escape gravity one could be shot out of a cannon and land on the moon."

"Similar, but... really different too. We use rockets with powerful thrust engines. Lots of complicated math and very brave people." She took a big bite of her toast and jam. "Man, this is yummy."

"Perhaps..."

"Oh no. Don't go thinking you can time travel to the moon. You'd have to have a lot of special equipment or you would explode. No air to breathe. Yadda, yadda, yadda. We can read up on it tomorrow. This is a do nothing day. Like our Congress. Yeah, we can rename it Congress Day." She scrolled down to the local section. "Oh, no way, Jones." She pointed and read the first part. "Local couple report seeing aliens right here in Snohomish. They reported seeing two aliens materialize but did not see the mother ship." She laughed. "Can you imagine how many times they will tell that story?"

"I suspect as often as someone will listen." He chuckled and laid his head back on the pillows. "Whatever do you think influenced our decision to travel to see Roark at such a crucial time?"

"I don't know, but I'm super glad we went when we did. Maybe that's all part of what we'll be doing together from now on." She placed her tray to the side, leaned into his shoulder, and stroked his chest.

"Perhaps. Do you think it possible that our very existence is fated? And therefore, all of our travels have been previously calculated?" Jones glanced at Darcy and took a bite of food. He chewed slowly with his eyes closed as if he meant to take the time to savor the flavors. "This is somewhat superior to rice and vegetables and of course, coconut with mango."

"Actually, when I hear you say that, it sounds pretty darn good. Remind me and I'll pick up a couple of mangos. Fate means no choice, right? However, we're choosing and making decisions all the time. Some have bad consequences with positive outcomes, like going to jail. Not that I want to do that again."

"Yes, I am in full agreement with your assertion that being remanded over to the authorities should be a once in a lifetime event, if that." Jones sat straight up. "Forgive me, but did I tell you that while attempting to time travel in Hiva Oa I began to ricochet about time and space like a billiard ball. I physically bounced from Father Carlini, to Emily, to Master

Lee... from university to Master Fei-hung and then back to Hiva Oa?"

Darcy rolled onto her side, propped her head on her hand, and faced him.

"This is news to me. What the heck happened?"

"I can only assume that the urgency of Amura's circumstance interfered with my focus, and although I had reached harmony with the universe, I darted about to everyone that came to mind." Jones stroked his chin. "Father Carlini was none too pleased to see me, I might add. He appeared on the verge of passing out."

"Hmm. Was it good to see Emily? How long were you with her? This is getting interesting." She stroked his chest with her finger tips.

"Emily is a dear friend but she is in the past. My future is with you."

"Yeah? Prove it." She sat up straight and smiled.

"You are magnificent and a true adventurer. And to be sure, quite the handful."

"Speaking of a handful," she said as she reached under the covers. "I think it's time to show you the best part of bed day. So just lie back, relax, and let the Listener hear you call out her name."

They made love until exhaustion set in and then held each other, lingering in bliss.

"I love you," he whispered as he caressed her hair. "Thank you for sharing your life and love with me. Should we ever decide to have children, I believe you would make a wonderful mother. And with your attribute... the children could never get away with anything."

"I have no idea what the future brings, but as long as we travel together, I'm cool. We can even bring the kids along...

sorry… not a good idea," she said, raising the palm of her hand. She stopped for a moment in thought. "What if we take a *little* trip, just a tad jump forward? I wanna see what's going on in say, 2052."

"That is, my love, a far cry from a bed day."

"But we can come back to right now and finish out the day." Darcy wiggled her eyebrows. "Just for like thirty minutes or so." She tilted her head to one side and pushed out her bottom lip.

"Oh no, not the pouty lip," Jones lamented. "I am brought to complete submission by that. Whatever shall I do?" Jones stood next to the bed and offered his hand. "Shall we?"

"Shur, you betcha."

"What should we wear?"

"I'm thinkin blue jeans and tees are never goin' out of style," she said as she pulled a tee shirt over her head. "So, let's pick a place that's warm, not a lot of rain, with friendly folks and good food."

"And land-locked. Perhaps coastal regions have shifted." He pulled on his jeans. "Again, we want to appear in a safe haven."

"Hey, what could be safer than Snohomish in the summertime?" Think about it, what could possibly go wrong?"

"I suppose since we intend on a short timeframe for a visit that is a strong solution. You look wonderful by the way. We can pop in, observe the local culture, and teleport right back here."

She cupped her hands like a megaphone around her mouth. "Teleportation to Snohomish, Washington, 2052 is just a flip of the switch away. All aboard." She jumped onto the bed, bounced once and landed on the floor next to Jones.

"Wrap those arms around me, TT, and let's get outta here."

He turned the switch and they both heard the smooth whirling of gears, the speed increasing, and the building up to the perfect resonance for soaring through the universe on a quantum timeline.

They vanished. Leaving no one to hear the immense silence in the little yellow house with white trim on Cedar Avenue.

Author's Bio

Dana Bennett lived in north central Florida for the first chapter of his life. After high school, he spent the next chapter working with problem teens and their families in Pensacola, Florida and then spent time on the Colorado River Indian Reservation, in Parker, Arizona helping the Native American population. He graduated from Nova Southeastern with a degree in psychology later in life. He has had many eclectic professional experiences in the work arena, always returning to the creativity he finds in building and construction as well as crafting new stories.

He has three wonderful daughters and two adorable grandsons. He is married to his best friend and partner in life, love, and business. They have a strong supportive community of friends and neighbors who encourage them daily to keep writing.

He enjoys each day with Blakely as they work on their never finished project, life. Writing is his bliss and both he and Blakely are chasing the dream of writing full time.

You can find out more by going to:

http://danabennettblog.wordpress.com/
https://www.facebook.com/GearedToThePresent
https://www.facebook.com/fracturedfidelities

COMING SOON

The third novel

in the

Jones Whitman
Time Traveler Series

Geared to the Future

www.ingramcontent.com/pod-product-compliance
Lightning Source LLC
Chambersburg PA
CBHW022149170626
46807CB00005B/2139